# If I Could Drag You Under

Kelly Preston

eBook ISBN: 979-8-9933879-3-2

Paperback ISBN: 979-8-9933879-4-9

Hardback ISBN: 979-8-9933879-5-6

Cover by Kelly Preston

Edited by Shelley, Jessica Preston, Sheila D., Kate S. & Element Editing Services

First edition 2026

# Also by

Check out these other titles by Kelly Preston:

**The Demon To Your Right**

To all of us who weren't sure we were going to make it out alive. This is for us.

This book contains mature content meant for adult audiences. Some people may find certain themes triggering. Please proceed with caution. This book is a Horror/Thriller Sapphic Dark Romance Erotica Novel.

Trigger warnings: depression, suicidal ideation, miscarriage, psychological horror/thriller, light body horror.

# Chapter 1

Mira Hansen was suicidal. It was the only thing she took away from the hours of therapy and drugs that had done nothing to alter her brain chemistry. But knowing she wanted to die was one thing. Finding the energy to plan to end her own existence had been a fucking nightmare. She hadn't wanted to do it where some idiot might play hero and wind up intervening, so she looked for the perfect place to end it all—a remote beach house, in the middle of nowhere, during the off-season.

She unlocked her rental with more force than was needed for the *seemingly* stuck door and clung to the dark mahogany as it slammed open, narrowly preventing herself from falling flat on her face.

Briefly closing her eyes, she worked to collect herself. If she had been looking for an adrenaline rush, she would have tried skydiving. Then again, maybe that would have fixed all her problems.

Either an accident would have made everything go away or she would have been scared shitless and ready to give life another go. She sure as hell wouldn't have been out in the middle of nowhere, ready to end it all.

Mira shook her wavy brunette hair out of her face, the frizzy pieces spilling out of a day-old ponytail that she had neglected to redo because she just didn't have the energy to care how it looked. She righted herself, turning to look back over her shoulder at her bags. She had only brought a small mauve suitcase containing a few items and a large black duffel bag because she wasn't going to leave home without a decent blanket, even if she wouldn't be needing it for long.

Moving her things into the entrance hall, she released a groan when she remembered that her pillow was still in the car. She had pulled it out of the duffel bag to use it for a nap at a rest stop. Driving was far more exhausting than it used to be.

She was sure the house had plenty, but they weren't *her* pillow, the one that had taken ages to find and somehow never set off her neck pain. She wasn't about to chance using another. Guided by the path that wove through the overgrown lawn, she stomped her way back to her vehicle, angrily fisted her pillow, then found her way back inside. She didn't bother to lock her car, nor the front door. The location was remote enough, and given that it was the off season, the lack of people as she was driving in let her know that no one lived in these homes year round.

The space before her was just as sparsely decorated as it had been in the rental ad. Her eyes noted the stairs that sat unobstructed halfway through the living room on the left. That must have led to the little upstairs bedroom she had seen in the posting.

Satisfied with the fact that there would be somewhere to sleep, she moved past the stairs, leaving her things in the entrance in favor of exploring the house. The minimal furniture she found was all very basic and cheaply made, but that's what she expected. She had never needed much, and she wouldn't now.

Interestingly, the plain wooden walls were decorated with a few little trinkets, some of which she swore she had seen before due to her best friend's witchy nature. But she had never paid much attention when Wendy had rambled on about the paranormal world.

Mira approached one of the hanging items to get a closer look. It appeared to be a keychain stuck to a simple nail. The chain held a white-and-blue glass orb in the shape of an eye but a bit warped, as if crafted by hand and not some large machine.

She rubbed her arms as a draft came through the house, turning to the view of the ocean out the back and finding a window cracked open just a hair. Rolling her eyes, she moved to pull the window shut, having to throw her full weight into it to get it down when it didn't want to budge. It was starting to become obvious, even to her, that she hadn't been eating much lately. Tasks that used to take no thought or effort were suddenly requiring a lot of both.

Taking a moment to catch her breath after the exertion, she watched the large waves breaking on the shore with abandon. The ocean was a beautiful bright blue today—a perfect match for her eyes. Her shoulders began to relax as she listened to the rhythmic sounds of the water crashing and receding. Leaning her forehead against the glass, she let herself melt into the cool and steady object. Maybe a few extra days in the land of the living wouldn't kill her. She snorted at her little joke. She could at least try to enjoy the beach a bit before she ended things.

Mira wasn't sure how long she stayed at the window, but when she felt her stomach rumble, she went to search the fridge and cabinets for supplies. She had requested a few items when the owner offered a grocery run, so she was confident that the kitchen wouldn't be completely empty.

Unfortunately, some of the items were stashed behind golden wood doors that screeched with every movement. Mira squinted at the abrasive sound. Everything would need to be moved out of the cabinets onto the counters to avoid the horrid screeching, or her headaches, which she had finally gotten under control, would come back to haunt her. She was looking forward to never feeling that again, traumatized by too many emergency room visits.

At least the fridge was quiet when she opened it; it appeared to be new. She grabbed a bottle of water and the jug of milk, reluctantly going back to the cabinets for some cereal and a bowl, bracing herself against the sound. Luckily the discomfort was short-lived but the drawers weren't much better when she went looking for a spoon. Her eyes slid over the options for utensils, each one drastically different from the others and *intricate*.

Her eyebrows rose at the detail but she selected one at random. She poured her milk and bland corn flakes into a bowl before venturing out onto the deck to eat and take in the view. Her foot instantly cracked a piece of wood when she walked too far out to one side. She jumped back quickly, nearly spilling her cereal. *Rustic my ass.* This place was a death trap—probably why it was so cheap.

She had booked it for an extended stay because she wasn't sure how long she would be around and didn't want to put a timeline on things. And if the owner wanted to go after her for anything when she was dead, that was really not her problem. Leave that to whichever sorry soul would be left to clean up her mess.

Her chest tightened as she felt a wave of guilt. It would probably end up being her best friend who she had left everything to. She had long disinherited her mother and, with her wife missing, she didn't have any other next of kin. Surely they couldn't go after the only person who still cared about Mira?

She slowly inched her way toward a suntanning bed that was closer to the middle of the deck and hopefully more stable. She tested it carefully, only sitting when she was sure that the wooden bed, as well as the deck, weren't about to collapse under her weight.

Gazing down into her food, she lifted a spoonful and watched as it dribbled back into the bowl, creating little bubbles. Her mind began to wander and she found herself trapped in memories that felt ever present when she wasn't working her life away. All the events that kept her up at night, ones she had never really found a way to escape. Like the physical and emotional abuse from her mother and her two failed marriages.

Though she had escaped her mother's clutches, she had never been able to fully block her words out. And her wife repeating those same phrases only made things worse over time. At this point, she would rather cease to exist than try to wait for things to get better. For *her* to be better. Because if she would never be good enough, then what was the point in continuing to try?

Tears started to form in her eyes and she blinked rapidly as they burned, unsure if the physical or mental pain was worse. Even though her wife had treated her like shit, she still couldn't make sense of why she was just *gone*. She wasn't sure what she did that was so unforgivable that the other woman could just disappear. She missed having someone to come home to, and she refused to drag her best friend into her downward spiral again. Not when Wendy's life was moving forward and Mira's was freefalling into the bottomless abyss. Fuck, she hated feeling so alone.

She set the bowl down before rushing to wipe the offending wetness away, though there was no one around to see her cry.

Shaking her head to try to loosen her thoughts, she reached for her bowl once more. Trembling hands moved automatically to shove the food into her mouth. The sounds of her phone ringing from within the house barely registered, her body not allowing her to move from her current position to see what the fuss was about.

Eventually, her eyes lifted to survey the beach. It appeared that coming during the off season really did provide the privacy she was looking for; there wasn't a soul in sight.

The sun started to warm her shoulders around her gray tank top, a sure sign that a burn would be coming if she didn't go back inside. And yet, she stayed put. A sunburn wouldn't matter much in the end. She wouldn't be feeling it for long.

Mira remained outside until the sun started to set, finding herself confused by the passage of time and not understanding where her whole day had gone. She thought she would have grown used to the time jumps by now. Her therapist had told her that, with the severity of her depression, it really wasn't a surprise they had increased in their frequency.

When she did finally move, she found that her body had grown stiff from all the sitting on the wooden furniture. She tried to twist her back lightly and was met with some resistance. Looking down sadly at her bowl now sitting out of reach, she figured it was better to leave it. She would come back for it later. If she tried to bend down to pick it up now, she feared she wouldn't be getting back up, and a slow death by starvation was not the way she had planned to go.

She padded into the house and leaned against the kitchen island looking for some relief. A moment later, her back released with a deep pop that sent sharp pain racing down her side. She squeezed her eyes shut at the sensation, taking measured breaths in an attempt to keep herself calm as she rode out the waves of electric shocks. She remained where she was for a few moments until the pain finally subsided before going for the couch, clocking her phone on the coffee table and figuring it was close enough if she needed to call for help. Plopping herself down, she turned to face the cushions.

# Chapter 2

Her eyes fluttered open and Mira's head rose in confusion, forgetting where she was. It took her a moment to remember she had rented a beach house. As she got her bearings, she rolled over, hands searching the coffee table blindly for her phone in the dim light. Her fingers tapped at the screen, eyes instantly stinging at the contrast of the bright light with the dark room. Upon her inspection of the time, it was past midnight.

She shifted her hips around a bit to check the state of her back. A bit sore, but it seemed like it would move. She was careful to use her arms as she sat up, ready to pause at the first hint of pain, which, to her surprise, didn't come. Her fingers drifted to the area to inspect it, as if she had been mistaken. Pressing down didn't provide her with a different answer so she shrugged it off. Maybe laying down had relaxed her enough. Her attention switched back to her phone as she scrolled and took note that a few people who she hadn't heard from in a while had reached out.

Mira snorted. It must have been a cosmic joke that *now* people were worried. She locked her device and looked around the shadow-encased room. The glow from the moon outside gave her just what she needed to locate a light switch. Taking the hall, she found a bathroom, sitting down to empty her bladder and learning she had to go more than she thought. Her head hung forward in exhaustion. Everything felt like it took a monumental effort now.

She pulled up her underwear and let her sweatpants fall, kicking them off her feet at the uncomfortable heat suddenly engulfing her body. Why would she need pants tonight? If she needed them again, she knew where to find them. She wandered back toward the kitchen and found the bottle of cheap alcohol she had requested in the fridge, relieved to find that it was easy to open.

Uncapping the bottle, Mira tipped it to her lips as she drank. Her head tossed back to allow more of the liquor to flow down her throat. As she finished, she wiped at her wet lips with the back of her hand, her vision starting to sharpen with the substance working its way to her brain.

The lights flickered briefly and she jumped at the sudden appearance of voices until she realized that the large flat screen TV from across the couch had somehow turned on with the surge of electricity. Mira rubbed her chest in an attempt to calm her racing heart. Who did she think had joined her in the middle of nowhere? The boogeyman? Rolling her eyes at the faulty wiring, she hoped that wouldn't become more of an issue. She decided to leave the TV running, finding the noise to be better than the silence.

Reaching for her bag slowly, she felt her stability fading. She kneeled onto the floor and fumbled when she went to open her bag and it refused to budge. Feeling around to figure out what the zipper could be stuck on, she felt soft fabric caught in the teeth. She huffed at the nuisance as she wiggled it back and forth. When it finally released, she smiled in a fleeting moment of relief, only to find that a comfy sweater her best friend had given her now had a sizeable rip in it. "Fuck."

Her heart sank. She didn't have many sentimental things, but this, unfortunately, was one of them. A crushing feeling in her chest told her that she shouldn't have brought it, that she should have left it for Wendy to find when she cleaned out her apartment. And now it was *ruined.*

Just like her friendship with the woman.

Just like her marriage.

And she was sure that, due to her worsening mood, it was only a matter of time before she would have lost her job as well. It was hard to create art when you found it too difficult to move from your bed. The amount of sick days she had been allowed were only possible given the fact that her boss was another friend of hers.

Mira gulped as she felt a crawling sensation slide up her spine. Her mother would have taken the opportunity to remind her how clumsy she was with nice things. And how useless everyone found her efforts to try to be someone she would never be.

With the voice fresh in her head, she rushed to shift items until she found what she was looking for. Her orange bottles of pills and her metal tins of blunts and edibles. The bottles were a culmination of the drugs she had collected over the years during her failed medication trials. And though they hadn't done much for her pain, they would be useful for the reason she was here.

Experience had taught her that, though the weed would normally pacify her mind for a while, it wasn't going to cut it this time. Opting for an orange bottle, she dumped the whole thing into her hand. But as she raised the pile of pills to her lips, she stalled and had second thoughts. She had done her research on how much to take for the large white pills to be lethal, but she wasn't certain that it wouldn't have consequences that she didn't want to deal with before the end, like *more pain*.

*How does it feel when your body starts to shut down?* She shivered at the concept of the cold hard ground, and laying beneath it for all eternity.

Mira quickly placed the medicine back in the container and secured the lid. She closed her eyes and took a few deep breaths before her eyes opened to the back door. Her head tilted in thought at the prospect of escaping the confines of the room and seeing the night sky. She could always take the pills with her to the beach and decide later if tonight was the night. There was time to figure out other ways if needed. She grabbed her lighter and a blunt as well, and stumbled to the back door. When she hit the sea air, she thought she heard distant music playing.

The song reminded her of a brief moment of happiness in her childhood. There weren't many happy moments from back then, but this particular memory had been from when her mother lost her for an entire afternoon in town. Some kind lady had held on to her and fed her snacks.

The woman had taken her home and allowed her to cuddle up. Let her play with her dog until Mira's mother eventually, reluctantly, came looking for her. The woman had even offered to watch Mira sometimes, or even take her off Evangeline's hands, but Evangeline Hansen wouldn't hear of the shame. No, most of Mira's time worth living had been in her early adulthood when she had been thankful to be away from home, on her own.

The soft sounds of the music that reminded her of a simpler time called to her. Beckoned her to follow where it might lead.

The beautiful melody made her pause for a moment to enjoy it. Her eyes closed, one hand gripping the railing that led down the stairs to the sand, the beat pulsing in the wood beneath her hand. She swayed slightly, her mind drifting to remember when she had met Wendolyn Richards, the first kid to talk to her at school. Wendy was a bit stuck up, but kind, despite the fact that they had come from very different backgrounds.

Mira's mother was the Bible-thumping minister's whore, and Wendy was the only daughter of the only doctor in town, who happened to be Black. That had caused a stir when they had first moved in as the town wasn't used to diversity. But Wendy was pretty, smart, and everyone wanted to be her and her parents. Those who didn't, relied on them heavily. Luckily, there were few issues.

When a boy picked on Mira during her first recess of the year, Wendy had punched him square in the face. Then she had cried her heart out like the boy had hit *her*. That had solidified their friendship.

As they aged, the lines blurred as hormones heightened. They both figured out that, though they enjoyed a woman's body, they were definitely just friends.

Mira herself was told she was *too much*, and she found Wendy a bit too shallow for her tastes. Somehow, they found a way to remain friends over the years, despite their constant bickering. They had even moved out of their small town to the city together for school. Wendy had tutored Mira and pushed her to apply for college, assuring her that she wasn't getting left behind in that small town with her mother.

At first, Mira hadn't left with Wendy and instead ran into the arms of a man that her mother selected for her at church. A desperate attempt to appease the woman who had given birth to her and make her own life a little easier. She should have known it would never work. She couldn't stand him touching her, or the way he smelled, and it didn't take long for her to clock his mother watching her with a little too much interest. She spent more and more time at her boyfriend's home only to get closer to his mom. One day, when Ralph went off to practice, his mother pounced.

Mira had been sitting on Ralph's mother's couch reading a book when Lea had wandered in, only wearing a thin black robe and carrying two glasses of wine. She was careful to not stare at where Lea's nipples were painfully visible through her sheer clothing. Mira hadn't been sure what was going on, but she suddenly felt underdressed for the occasion with her frizzy dark waves pulled back into a low ponytail and wearing an old sweatshirt of Wendy's. Wendy had discovered that Mira's mother didn't believe in buying new or warmer clothing and found excuses to clean out her wardrobe and send Mira home with the *unwanted* items.

Mira had quickly uncrossed her legs and sat up straight when Lea set a glass down in front of her. She was not old enough to drink, but she had plenty of times, to try to let her boyfriend touch her. Reaching for the drink with a hesitant smile, she tried desperately not to look at where Lea's robe rode up her pale thighs. She took a large gulp of red wine and gasped at the strong bitter taste; it did not go down smoothly.

Lea had laughed softly as she watched Mira over the rim of her own glass. Mira remembered that, in the moment, she could barely breathe. She had been watching Lea's eyes linger on her for months with anticipation and the woman always gave her a purposeful once over every time she saw her. At first she wondered if her boyfriend's mom was trying to decide if she was good enough for her son, but that hadn't been her intent at all.

Mira set her drink down and felt a hand land on her thigh, her eyes trailing to the sensation. She felt her heart skip a beat; she was never nervous with her boyfriend, but his mother had her losing all ability to speak. Lea was *stunning*.

"Mira, have you ever been with a woman before?"

She let her mind wander back to a time at Wendy's lake house where they drank too much beer and fumbled around. She couldn't quite meet Lea's eyes as she nodded slowly. Words were elusive.

Lea smirked. "Good." Her hand reached out and cupped Mira's chin, bringing it toward her. "You're such a pretty girl, Mira."

Mira felt her stomach swirl at the praise. She licked her lips, accidentally catching Lea's thumb. Or maybe the woman had set it on her bottom lip on purpose. She finally lifted her eyes, catching Lea's amber irises. Mira gasped softly as the hand on her thigh slid upward.

"I've been trying very hard not to think about you ever since my son brought you home. My husband... he doesn't get the job done. Do you understand what I mean? Think you want to fix that for me?"

Mira's eyes stayed locked in her gaze as she nodded. Lea smirked, as if she knew that she could mold Mira into anything she wanted her to be and Mira would thank her for it. As if she knew how desperate she was to feel something, too.

"Good girl." Lea's eyes indicated the floor with an ecstatic smile. "Now, get on your knees."

Mira still remembered the first touch of Lea's hands on her. How they were so different from Ralph's, and from Wendy's. She felt her hips buck lightly at the memory. Of the first time the word pleasure had ever made sense to her.

Her eyes opened and, as her mind loosened from her memories, she instinctively searched for her wife to chase the building feeling, hoping she would be in the mood. Momentarily forgetting that her wife had not slept with her in months. Reality crashed down on her when the only thing that greeted her hands was the midnight beach air.

She reeled backward, almost falling on her ass. It had been a long time since Amani disappeared. That bitch was *gone*. She hadn't heard from her ever again. At first, she was worried sick. Then she was angry. Initially with the police, who claimed to have found nothing. Then, with Amani for disappearing. And finally, with herself for driving Amani away.

Mira took a few deep breaths to try to settle herself as she became aware of the things she was carrying with her to the beach: a bottle of alcohol, a medicine bottle, and weed. She squinted at the stairs and slowly inched her foot to the edge and down a step. She went slowly, afraid to take a tumble, until her feet met the sand. Her body was more unsteady without the handrail to keep her up, but she made it to the water.

As she gazed out at the dark sea, she felt lost, the dark water stretching on forever. The waves had calmed and now only quietly broke against the shore. And though she tried to block out her emotions, a quiet sob escaped her lips as she failed to keep her memories from drowning her. Her mother's harsh hand was only ever rivaled by her even harsher words. Those words now drifted back into her consciousness, surrounding her.

Her memories with Ralph weren't much better. They had been married briefly, and he had spit every nasty thing he could think of at her when she left to live with Wendy.

Her wife, Amani, was somehow even worse. Blaming her for the miscarriages that they had *both* endured. And refusing to hear Mira out when she told her she was struggling. That she *needed* her.

Mira didn't want to think of any of those people right now. She dropped her medicine bottle and watched it create a divot in the sand. It seemed to point back toward the house. Perhaps it was a sign to go back inside and sleep everything off. To give herself more time to think things through. She didn't need to end things tonight, did she? But she did need to find a way to make the voices stop. She couldn't hear herself think.

Her eyes turned back to the liquor bottle in her hand, and before she could drop that as well, she chugged the rest to quiet her nerves. Spluttering as she tried to consume too much this time, she covered her mouth and coughed some alcohol back up. She collapsed to her knees as she tried to breathe. Her stomach was already rolling at the burning drink mixed with the lack of food. Leaning on her hands, her head bowed forward as she groaned. She would give anything to not feel like this.

Mira tried to force a gag, but nothing came up. Her eyes lifted to the moon for a distraction, the quiet music having long faded. *If it was even real in the first place.* Sometimes her meds or the drinking would bring on hallucinations.

She rose, almost tumbling back to the ground as she started her less-than-sober march toward the water. Her mind went to darker and darker places before fixating on the dark rolling waves as a possible escape.

The promise of disappearing into its depths.

The voices finally stopping.

All the misery ending.

When the first splash of the breaking waves hit her feet, swallowing up her ankles, her whole body jolted at the chill. Her lips parted in shock. Quiet laughter nearby made her freeze before she took an unconscious step back. Her heart nearly broke out of her chest when she heard the first words spoken to her.

"I thought I was the only one crazy enough to be out here in the dead of night."

Mira frantically scanned the area, wondering if she was hearing things, then jumped when she saw what looked like a woman maybe fifteen or twenty feet off in the water, upper half above the water, illuminated by moonlight.

The stranger seemed to be entertained by Mira's unease, biting her lip as if to hold back a laugh. "Oh, please, don't mind me, there's plenty of ocean for everyone." Her tone shifted from her light humor to slight confusion when Mira didn't speak. "You… were coming in, right?" She indicated the water with a sweep of her arm.

Mira took another step back, not wanting to get too close. "I don't…" She looked for a tether to grab onto. "It's cold," she stated, as if the reason she wasn't plunging into the waves was obvious. She wasn't sure why, but she was suddenly afraid of being pulled in. Of being pulled *under*. Mira's skin now felt as if it were crawling, trying to get away from the other woman. It reminded her of when she was growing up and the men around town started watching her with too much interest, keeping their eyes on her for too long.

Words like *hunted* flooded her mind, causing her head to whip around looking for somewhere to run to.

When Mira's eyes located the woman in the water again, the stranger broke out into a smile. Her white teeth reflected in the night. Mira almost forgot which words they had exchanged when the woman spoke again. "Well, yes... the ocean does tend to be cold, especially this time of year."

Mira's hand pressed at her stomach as she felt an overwhelming urge to bolt. "I... didn't think anyone would be out here." Her breathing had grown shallow and her voice quiet. She worried that she might pass out but she fought to hold on, afraid what might happen to her if she lost consciousness.

The woman began wading out of the water, coming closer. Mira fell to the ground, causing her to smile wider. "Maybe you shouldn't be out here so late on your own. Seems you've had quite the party." Mira watched as dark eyes roamed the beach with interest. "Are there others?"

Mira's mouth opened and she regretted speaking instantly. "No.... I mean *yes*." She scooted back a little and closed her eyes, trying to get a hold of herself. She hadn't heard the woman approach, but her eyes snapped open when she heard breathing beside her.

"I'm Kah-li." She squatted and stuck her hand out, water dripping down from her dark hair. Mira's eyes traced her form and did a double take. No way she was actually naked. It was pretty dark and she had consumed a fair bit of alcohol, so she was probably hallucinating.

Mira didn't reach for her hand. "I'm not telling you my name. I don't know you." Her mind laughed at her. *As if this "Kahli" couldn't touch her if she didn't know her name.*

Kahli moved to sit beside her, unfazed. "Alright. Suit yourself." Her long fingers wrapped around her knees as she pulled them to her, eyes focused on taking in Mira beside her.

Mira wasn't sure if it was the late hour or her mind playing tricks on her, but Kahli's eyes appeared completely black. Somehow the woman didn't seem put off by Mira's intense staring. In fact, Kahli seemed to welcome it.

"So… I've never seen you around here before…"

The woman was making an attempt at conversation, but Mira was having none of it.

"That one your house right there?" Kahli tried again, turning and nodding at the house directly behind them.

Mira snorted as she shifted away an inch. "Is this how you hit on all the girls?"

Kahli tilted her head at the snarky comment. "Sometimes…"

Mira pouted, finding herself a little jealous at the prospect of this woman finding other girls attractive. She tried to console herself with thoughts about how the woman was probably horribly unfortunate to look at in the light of day, and she felt her blood run cold as she heard Kahli practically cackle.

It wasn't a comforting sound, it made the hair on her arms stand up.

"I actually am not *difficult* to look at, but thank you for trying to keep me humble."

Mira bit her lip, cursing her drunk mouth. She wasn't even sure what part of her thoughts she had said out loud.

Kahli looked up toward the beach house. "You staying here long?"

Mira shrugged and watched as Kahli's eyes located the orange bottle in the sand, her hand reaching for it.

"Don't want to leave these out here... you need them, right? What are they for anyway..." Kahli's voice was inquisitive and she sounded genuinely interested, attempting to read the bottle in the dark.

*That* set Mira off. *How dare this woman!* Mira shot her hand out, needing multiple attempts to grab the bottle from the stranger as she struggled with her coordination. "Mind your business."

Kahli raised her hands in surrender after Mira successfully snatched the bottle away. "Alright, alright." Kahli's eyes slowly slid back to the water, as if she were calculating how close they were. "I guess you don't want to go for that swim anymore. It's a shame, I could have used the company."

Mira gasped as her stomach once again made its upset known. Her hand pressed against the rolling. "You seem plenty busy now, bothering my drunk ass…"

Kahli leaned forward and laid her hand over Mira's. "You'll feel better if you just vomit."

Mira shook her head. She was not about to throw up in front of this stranger, this potentially gorgeous stranger, and not at her suggestion. She was about to argue and tell her it wasn't that bad, when she pitched herself to the side and started to puke up her guts. Somehow, the woman at her side secured her hair just in time to avoid the vomit. A firm hand was placed on her shaking arm.

"You got it. Keep going." The hand in her hair was gentle as Kahli made sure her hair continued to stay clean.

Mira coughed up a bit more as she gasped for breath. "It'll be a miracle if I don't die of dehydration…" Her stomach quivered, and Kahli's eyes looked up to the house.

"Well, considering the fact that my swim was already interrupted, I think I should get you home and make sure that doesn't happen. Up you go."

Strong hands lifted her to her feet as if she was truly weightless. The young, dark-haired woman pulled Mira's arm over her shoulders. Thoughts of how she must work out drifted aimlessly through her mind.

"We can go at your pace," Kahli offered softly.

Mira tried to take one step forward and her hand shot back to her mouth as she thought she was about to be sick with the movement, but nothing more came up. Her body sagged, completely drained. She just wanted to lie down in the sand and accept her fate, whether that be a wicked hangover on the beach in the morning or being swallowed whole by the ocean in her sleep. Why was this person trying to help her anyway?

Obviously unbothered by Mira's internal monologue, Kahli continued to lead her toward the house. Mira's brow furrowed when she wondered how Kahli knew where to go. She was also unsure how they were going to do the stairs as she wasn't sure she could even lift her foot up onto the bottom step. But when they arrived at the obstacle, Kahli scooped her up and carried her. The sudden surprise was overtaken by the way her mind grew extra fuzzy. She didn't recall the journey to her bed, but she did remember Kahli getting her there and forcing sips of water down her throat until she gave up and nodded off.

# Chapter 3

Mira blinked rapidly as morning light assaulted her sensitive eyes. Lifting a hand to try to block some of it out, she groaned at the pain it was already causing. Why was light always so bad after a night of drinking? She realized now that there were no curtains to aid her in her time of need, a detail she should have noticed when she looked at the place. Her mind must be slipping worse than she thought. Back when she and her wife took trips together, she was always the one to plan everything. One disastrous trip at the beginning of their relationship was enough to keep her on her toes so that she never messed up an important detail again.

Glancing around the room, her eyes landed on the closet and wondered if she needed to string up some sheets for her stay. It would only be temporary, and she was sure she could find some way to make it happen… once her head stopped trying to kill her.

As her mind started to function, it dawned on her that if there were no curtains, that also posed other problems. Like the fact that, if she could see out, then others could see in. But as she contemplated it, she realized that someone would need to be out in the water in order to see her from this angle. And since her arrival, she hadn't seen any boats passing by for that to happen. Nor people at all, really. Well, except swimmer girl. Maybe the lack of curtains wouldn't be much of an issue, and considering that the room didn't have much else in it, the view of the sea was at least something that wasn't plain wooden walls to stare at.

She sat up slowly, a strong pounding beginning in her skull the moment she finally made it upright. Her hand flew to the area, trying to alleviate the pain, as her vision swirled in and out of focus. The items around her devolved into shapes that refused to stay still. She abandoned her grip on her head to grasp the bed tightly when the room wouldn't stop moving. Attempting to stabilize herself only caused her brow to furrow when she found sand beneath her fingertips. It must have fallen from her body overnight after her beach adventure. A sigh escaped her lips as she accepted she would need to clean that later; the sensation of the tiny rocks prickling her skin was already causing her to shift uncomfortably.

Whispered words from the night before drifted back to her in fragments as she tried to recall the events. She slowly stalled her hand when she remembered some woman had appeared straight out of the ocean and taken her ass home, knowing Mira had no business being on her own in the state she was in.

Looking around the room, she didn't notice anything out of place. The sheets on the bed were now tucked tightly around her as if someone was worried she might grow cold in the night. Her hand drifted to her chest as she was struck with the thought that the woman from the night before might still be there. Holding her breath, she peered over the edge of the bed. When the floor was empty, she released a sigh of relief, only to tense up once more, realizing that she could still be somewhere in the house.

Mira felt uneasy, wondering for a brief moment if the woman could be hiding under the bed. She leaned over the edge to peek underneath before realizing why that was such a bad idea in the first place. Her hands reached for the ground as she lost her balance and went crashing to the floor.

"*Fuck*," she grunted as she waited for the pain to subside. Her hands lifted to massage the sore spot on her hip. She hoped that she would still be able to get up when she tried. Her back loved to lock up at the worst times.

After a few moments of lying there, she readied herself for the attempt as she pressed the dark wooden floor away from her. Slowly climbing to her feet, her hand reached out to steady herself on the bed, then the dresser, then the door, as she made her way out of the room. She was expecting her back to suddenly lock up, like it had since she had started her fertility journey, but it seemed to hold out... for now.

She inched around the corner and was as light-footed as she could be as she made it to the stairs. A creaking sound in the house below caused her to hold her breath. Her head dipped to see if the mystery woman was on her couch, breathing a sigh of relief when it was empty. She kept her movements light as she clutched the banister on her descent, waiting for the mystery woman to pop up out of nowhere. Her eyes scanned then re-scanned the room below as she made her way to the first floor.

Upon inspection, her bags were exactly how she had left them, spread out across the foyer. Except for her vibrator, which was now set out to the side. Had she moved that when she went looking for her medication? Mira shook her head, unable to recall. She continued to check for her wallet and keys and found that nothing had gone missing.

Feeling a strong breeze across her back, her eyes lifted to the back door and noticed it had been left open. Mira rolled her eyes; she figured the stranger had been bound to slip up somewhere. She supposed she should be lucky that no one else had snuck inside in the middle of the night. Swiftly, she moved to close the door before she second guessed that decision and reopened it, wondering if the younger woman could still be in the house, lurking somewhere she hadn't checked yet.

Paranoia high, her eyes widened in alarm at the thought. She took her time investigating the rest of the first floor, grabbing a knife from the kitchen to use as a weapon before checking inside closets and behind the shower curtain in the bathroom. When she deemed there to be no other signs of life, she returned to the back door and locked it, letting her forehead fall lightly against the cool glass pane as she tried to let her nerves settle. The chill caused her to wonder why she wasn't cold, and she glanced down to notice that the other woman must have found her sweats and put them on her. She blushed at the fact that some random person had helped her change in such a vulnerable state.

Slowly calming down, she looked out at the ocean through the window, right to where she had found the creepy swimmer girl lurking the night before. She half expected to see her there now, waving back, but that would have been ridiculous. No sane person would have returned to the water or would have still been waiting around.

Mira rubbed her forehead as she was forced to accept the fact that she was now exhausted and had a headache. Normally for mornings like these she would have two to three cups of coffee, but she had forgotten to request some in her groceries and would need to head into the nearest town to grab some. She scooped up her keys and her eyes were drawn momentarily to her little triquetra charm. Something that Wendy had gotten for her at an art fair the day she had left home for good, explaining that the pagan symbol would protect her through the different stages of her life. She rolled her eyes and tried to fight her smile. Wendy was always looking out for her. And annoyingly, this *was* a good reminder of that fact.

Pulling herself from her memories, Mira locked up the house, making her way to her car. The bright sun made her want to run back inside and hide forever, the stabbing pain in her head almost making her abandon the whole journey. But she pressed on, unlocking her car and settling in. Her hands blindly felt around until she found her sunglasses in the glove compartment, slipping them on with an audible sigh of relief.

As the pain dulled slightly, she brought maps up on her phone and learned that the closest town was about twenty minutes away. It could have been worse. She set her phone to route and committed to the trip, rolling down her windows and taking off, trying to take in the sights as she drove. Though to her displeasure, almost everything looked the same as the "sights" really only consisted of trees. The same type, same height, and same shape. She found herself growing bored with the view as her mind wandered back to the woman from the sea. Drifting to the timbre of her voice, her dark eyes... she became so distracted she nearly missed her exit.

Locating the town, she stopped at the first coffee shop she could find, identifiable by the image of a coffee cup and a mermaid burned into a wooden plank, along with a name she didn't read. She parked out front, sunglasses slipping down her nose a bit as she struggled to get them to stay in place. Somehow, she had missed the condensation collecting on her face during the drive, which was now causing them to sit just low enough to be annoying.

Mira squinted when the chime of the bell hanging from the door was a touch too loud for her still-recovering head. The young boy working the counter looked up and waved excitedly in greeting when he saw her making her way inside. She contemplated walking right back out and avoiding the encounter all together, not really in the mood for people this morning, but her head pulsed so intensely that she made up her mind—caffeine was an unfortunate requirement. She awkwardly tried to offer up a smile when she met the kid's eyes again, but it came out more like a grimace. Her eyes wandered his face that said he was barely old enough for all the black eyeliner he was wearing, and she wondered how in the world he came across his "look" or if he was simply the creative type.

She took her time looking over the menu hanging on the wall while the kid's bright smile grated on her. Releasing words that were far more clipped than she intended, she snapped at him. "Well, if you want to suggest something, go ahead." She lifted her hand to indicate he should start talking.

Somehow, he took it in stride. "Oh, alright. Good morning, and welcome to the SeaSide Café. I'm Benny and I'll be your barista this morning. I highly recommend the Otter Americano if you are in desperate need of a shot of caffeine this fine day, or the Ladybug Matcha if you are wanting a nice calming start to your morning with a bit of strawberry and matcha." His voice was the perfect embodiment of an upbeat salesperson.

Mira smirked as she set her hand on the counter, her nails tapping rhythmically as she pondered… Well, neither of *his* options. "I'll take a Blonde coffee."

The boy's eyes widened at her rejection, taken aback. "Oh, okay, uh, will that be the Blonde Kitten or the Golden Retriever Latte?"

Mira rolled her eyes. Who came up with these names? "I'm not saying any of that. Just make me something very caffeinated that's a little sweet." She lifted her brows as if to tell him to get a move on, and the kid quickly typed into the pad at the register.

"You got it, one Kitten—I mean Blonde coffee, a little sweet, coming right up." He twisted the pad around. "That'll be nine fifty."

Mira narrowed her eyes even as she took her card out and tapped it to the screen. Those were *city* prices. "You always rob the tourists?"

Benny's smile dropped. "We *are* a tourist destination. I'm sure that's a part of our prices..."

*Shit.* She hadn't looked into the surrounding area when she was finding a good location to... disappear. It hadn't seemed important at the time, but with the way the kid seemed surprised by her blank stare, she wondered if she should have done more research.

He continued on as if the information was pertinent. "You know, the mermaid sightings?" He pointed up at the sign indicating their mermaid logo. "That's why you came to town, right? You know legend has it that this was the first place they came ashore—"

Mira waved him off, already bored of his little fairy tales. She didn't need to hear them. "Don't care."

He shrugged and she saw his smile return as he moved to make her coffee, assuming correctly that the conversation was over. She took a look around the shop and found a corner seat to wait where hopefully no one would bother her. Well, if anyone else came in, that was. Mira pulled out a chair and sat, leaning back with her phone in her hands when the bell went off again.

Her eyes didn't lift until the patron had already moved past her, but the dark hair and its length gave her pause. She leaned forward, and before she knew what she was doing, she was speaking.

"Excuse me?"

The woman turned around to acknowledge her, but the moment she did, Mira knew it couldn't have been the woman from the ocean. This woman was much too old. The one from the sea had seemed younger—well, younger than Mira. She had surely been older than mascara boy at the counter.

"Sorry, I thought you were someone else. My mistake."

The older woman rolled her eyes as she continued to place her order. Mira shook her head and leaned back once more, settling in. She went to remove her sunglasses before she found out exactly why that was such a bad idea, setting them back down over her eyes as the throbbing in her head returned.

She refocused on her phone, and with the help of her glasses filtering the light, she became engrossed in catching up on Wendy's wedding photos. A wedding she had been invited to, begged to be in, and then had declined attending. Because how embarrassing would it be to show up at your ex's wedding, single? Even if you only dated for a couple of weeks and stayed best friends. Mira wasn't about to stoop that low. She lifted her eyes when she felt someone standing beside her table and noticed the kid holding a to-go cup.

He smiled brightly, extending it out to her with two hands. "I figured you might not want to be tied down to the shop, so I made your coffee to-go. But you're welcome to hang around if you would like. There are some games and books on the shelves if you—"

Mira's fingers stretched slowly and took the cup. The kid was a bit adorable, she had to give him that, but she really didn't want to drag this out. She tried to keep any pleasantness out of her tone, lest he take that as a sign to chat her up, when she interrupted his rant. "Thanks."

He nodded as he trailed off, offering her another kind smile before he went back to the register, pulling out his own phone when no one else came in. When he didn't bother her again, Mira drank about half of her coffee in the comfortable silence before she decided to go grab a few things from the grocery store.

At least there was plenty of parking, the mercies of a small town. If nothing else, she had to admit she missed the ease and convenience of not being in a big city. She wandered into the store and only saw two other patrons shopping as she grabbed her little basket and wandered the aisles. There were many product names she wasn't familiar with and the slim selection forced her to reluctantly choose a different brand of coffee than she was used to.

She also grabbed some sort of sushi for an easy lunch and was on her way out of the store when an old woman grabbed her arm, snatching it out of nowhere. Mira almost dropped her grocery bags.

"You've been marked by a sea devil!" The old woman exclaimed in alarm, looking at Mira's arm as if there was something grotesque on the surface. Mira's eyes followed her gaze but saw nothing. She tried to pull out of her hold.

"I'm sorry, I don't have time for this. I really need to get going..." The woman's grip tightened and Mira gasped at the pain; how could an old woman have such strong hands?

Undeterred, the woman continued. "Stay away from the sea!" Her voice was deep and strong, unbefitting of a frail old woman.

Mira nodded quickly. "Yeah… no problem. I hate the ocean, I don't plan on ever going in again. Don't you worry." She patted the woman's hand awkwardly and when she was released, she quickly ran to her car, turning back multiple times to see if the woman was following her. She wasn't, but her dark eyes followed Mira until she couldn't see her anymore.

At least she was able to find more caffeine before she headed back to the beach house.

Entering the home, Mira immediately clocked that the back door was open once more. She frowned. She could have sworn she had locked it before. Worried that someone might have broken in, she did another quick sweep of the place, only to come up empty. Maybe there was some fault with the locking system causing the latch to slip out of place that she would need to bother the owner to come fix.

She put her groceries away, closing her eyes at the squeaking hinges, mentally chastising herself for forgetting, before returning to the door to rattle the lock a few different ways to see if she could get it to unlock once engaged. It didn't budge. She chalked it up to her hangover; she must not have fully closed it earlier.

Fetching her coffee from where she left it in the kitchen, she wandered out onto the deck, once again not seeing a soul in sight. She sipped her cooling drink as she watched the waves and a group of seagulls fighting over a fish one of them had snatched from the water. She smirked. At least her life wasn't the only one that was unfair. A little bit of schadenfreude never hurt anyone.

Then she saw some movement down the beach; a woman with shoulder-length black hair in a ponytail, jogging her way. She fought the excitement that fluttered in her chest briefly before she was able to squash it. Talking to her again would only complicate things, but Mira couldn't look away. The other woman wore no shoes, black sport shorts, and a dark sleeveless cropped top, showing off all of her muscles. She slowed as she approached Mira's plot, giving away her intention to stop in for a chat. Mira forced herself to look the other way and pondered if she could still retreat inside before the woman called out to her. It appeared she was too late and *damn* if the woman didn't have a nice voice that went straight to her crotch. It had been one hell of a dry spell since her depression took over, and it seemed that her libido was waking up at the worst time.

"Hey there, feeling better?" The athletic woman had stopped to stretch, laying her hand on the bottom of the railing.

Mira's eyes widened at her overly friendly attitude. They didn't know each other.

The other woman continued on as if unbothered that her speaking partner was less than willing to participate. "You drank quite a bit last night. Almost got in the ocean with me." Her eyes sparkled with amusement, lips twitching into a smile.

The darkness of her eyes was less unnerving in the daytime. Instead of the pure black Mira had remembered, her eyes were now a golden honey. Dark until they hit the light. She bit her lip as she looked Mira up and down, still not deterred by her lack of conversation skills, and now clearly checking her out.

"You tried to get me to stay the night last night." Her eyes landed on Mira's.

Mira's words were flying out before she even decided that she *wanted* to respond. "I did not!" She took a step forward and paused at the top of the stairs as the woman crossed her arms and leaned against the banister. *Had she really made a move?* The younger woman was very pretty and she certainly had an amazing body. Maybe in her state the night before she had...

"Gotcha." The other woman winked and Mira felt her cheeks burn.

Okay, so she hadn't been that bold. It wasn't a mystery why she didn't get laid anymore, despite her friends encouraging her to get back out there. Mira's eyes narrowed as she prepared to shoo the other woman away. But before she could get her words out, the younger woman was speaking again.

"I'm Kah-li by the way, in case you forgot." She brightened even further as Mira grew more embarrassed because yes, she had indeed been too inebriated to remember her name.

Trying to distract from her discomfort and not wanting the other woman's judgment, she chose to lash out. "Are you stalking me now?"

Kahli shook her head innocently as she rocked back and forth where she was leaning. "Don't you have something nice to say to the person who got you home last night?" Her brow furrowed. "You threw quite the rager on the beach..."

Mira scoffed. "You left my back door wide open... anyone could have gotten in. What would I be thanking you for? Almost getting me *killed*?"

Kahli tilted her head, eyes wide as she stood tall once more. "Who do you think is sneaking into your home? There's no one for miles... not yet anyway. Try in a few more months. You were fine." She brushed it off as if Mira's concerns meant nothing.

Mira huffed. "You're *real* brave to be out here alone then, talking to someone you don't know."

Grinning widely, Kahli appeared completely unfazed, and Mira felt her face drop as she realized the other woman found nothing about her intimidating. "I'm sure I could take you... you look a bit..." It seemed like she was searching for a nice way to put Mira's slight body. In the end, she avoided commenting on her weight entirely, and Mira had to admit she admired the sidestep. "Well, anyways, I work out."

*Oh, she could tell, if her lean muscles were any indication.*

Kahli tilted her head toward the beach. "Wanna join me for a run? Or... a walk? I promise to feed you after." She pouted slightly and her face said she actually thought there was a possibility Mira might join her. Mira wondered why that hope made her feel so uncomfortable. As if she cared about letting her down.

"I'm not into running." She shrugged as she crossed her arms.

Kahli raised an eyebrow. "What's wrong with a walk?"

Mira shrugged petulantly again as her eyes drifted down to where her nails were peeling the paper away from her coffee cup. The truth always made more sense than any lie she could offer up. "I sunburn easily, and I'm allergic to sunscreen." Her doctors had told her after her last bout of skin cancer that it could get much worse if she wasn't careful. She prepared herself to continue her excuses, but as her eyes lifted, she saw the other woman accept the rejection.

"Alright." Dark honey eyes looked back down the beach. "Guess I'll see you later." Her eyes swept back to Mira's once more as she offered her another smile. "Hope you have a good day!" She saluted her with two fingers and continued her jog as if the rejection didn't sting.

Mira was left shaking her head at the whole interaction. So much for a quiet, isolated, getaway. This person was going to be trouble. She watched Kahli run until she disappeared behind a bend of tall rocks, and with nothing else to do, Mira wandered back inside.

# Chapter 4

Mira deemed it a little warm in the house, and though she knew that it would cool down and move the air around if she just opened a window or two, she decided to dig out the tower fan she found in the closet and drag it downstairs. She almost tripped over the cord multiple times as it unwound itself on her descent. Cursing her *bright* idea with a string of harsh words muttered under her breath, she was more careful to avoid the cord.

Once she made it safely to the ground floor, she set the fan down in the space between the back door and the kitchen, figuring that was the best spot for optimum airflow. Plugging it in and turning it on high, she set it to oscillate, then went to look through her minimal options for food. Nothing really called out to her, but she blindly grabbed some frozen, off-brand burrito she had found at the store. She supposed it would be as good as anything else at her disposal. Throwing it in the microwave, she went to take a shower, figuring it would be waiting for her when she was done.

She hoped the shower would be just the cooldown she needed, whether it was really that hot in there, or if it was her recurring hot flashes back to torture her again.

Mira flipped on the bathroom light and fan, hearing it whirl to life. She closed the door and stripped, leaving her clothes in a pile on the floor. Turning to open the closet, she found it stocked with thick, fluffy towels, and startled when above the shelves was a mask. Her heart thundered in her chest. She held her hand out in front of her, still protecting herself from the fright, as her eyes took in the mask's feminine face. Its eyes contained bright, shining crystals and multiple snakes twisted around her head.

Pinching her nose, Mira tried to calm her breathing. It was just a piece of art, nothing to get worked up over. It wasn't like it was a person.

She reached out and took a towel, scrunching it up in her hold before hanging it outside the shower. Turning on the water, her hand extended to the spray to check the temperature, and she gasped when it came out ice cold.

It took a moment, but it appeared that the water heater was working as the humidity started to warm the room. Taking in the plethora of shades of blue tiles, she watched as the water splashed across them, droplets scattering, the sound soothing enough that her shoulders released some of their tension. She pulled the curtain all the way back and stepped in, her mind calming as the water washed over her skin, the warmth settling over her and smoothing out more of the tension that perpetually lived in her body.

Belatedly, she realized that, while she had brought shampoo, she had forgotten conditioner, and now her hair was going to be a frizzy mess until she could make it back to the store. She sighed. It was going to knot so badly. She didn't want to even think about how long it was going to take to untangle.

But that was a problem for future her. She pushed the problem to the back of her mind and continued to go through the motions. One moment she was pumping some shampoo into her hand, about to wash her hair, the next, a quiet voice whispered softly into her ear.

*Get out, and go get your phone. The power's about to go out.*

She paused, snapping her head to the side, almost expecting to see a person. Of course no one was there. She snorted. Why was she having intrusive thoughts about the lights going out?

Just as she was going to get back to her shampoo, a draft brushed across her shoulders, causing a shiver to run down her spine. She looked around again and shifted the curtain aside, feeling as if another person had joined her in the bathroom. But of course there was no one else in the shower, the bathroom, or the house. It was just her and her own voice in her head. Just Mira being *paranoid*. She let the curtain fall back into place. She really needed to get better at living alone. And maybe she could start to work on her distaste for the dark.

Sure, she had never been particularly comfortable in the dark. Scratch that—she was terrified of it. And it wasn't like she blamed a world of shadows for anything. It was more her imagination and what it could conjure with the dark canvas. Her creativity was both a blessing and a curse. Maybe, if she dug deeper, it had something to do with her childhood. But *that* was something she was definitely not revisiting with the judgy woman she used to see on Tuesdays.

Mira stepped back into the spray, finally lathering the shampoo in her hands and hair, when she heard a mechanical whirring sound and the lights cut out. She instantly threw her back against the wall.

"What the *fuck...*" Her heart hammered in her chest.

*Shit*, the fucking power was out. She looked around blindly in a panic, fingers desperately digging at the tiles. Her eyes stretched open wide to try to see anything in the dark room, but the attempt was futile in the enclosed space. She closed her eyes as she tried to remember the layout of the bathroom. She needed to get out of there. She just had to make it to the door without splitting her head open on the floor first. Or the sink. Or the toilet. How embarrassing would it be if a *toilet* took her out?

Mira opened her eyes. She still couldn't see a thing. It wasn't until she focused on the shower curtain that she caught a glimpse of a thin strip of light. She shoved the plastic out of her way, letting water splash out onto the floor. The space under the door didn't cast much light, but it gave her a destination. She stuck her hands out and felt around blindly for anything that she could run into, paranoid that her hand might actually find something that wasn't there before. Her body wound even tighter at the thought.

She made her way across the floor, feet finding her discarded clothes and struggling to avoid getting wrapped up in them. When she was about halfway to the door, something behind her flashed and she instinctively looked over her shoulder. It was hard to make out, but she *thought* she saw two eyes looking back at her in the mirror. She threw herself across the room to the door, scrambling to get a hold of it and get out.

Her slippery hands failed as she tried to grasp the doorknob.

"*Shit... shit... shit.*" She tried to wipe her hands on her body, but it was still slick with water as well. Pressing herself tight to the door, she tried again, and for a moment she panicked that it appeared locked from the outside. She shook her hands wildly, hoping to dry them just enough to grip the door. She tried again and this time, they found purchase.

Mira spilled into the hall, catching herself on the opposite wall. Her breaths heaved out of her as she turned around quickly to look in the bathroom and at the mirror.

The bathroom was undisturbed.

When she looked into the mirror, at the height she thought she had seen eyes, only her reflection stared back at her.

It occurred to her a moment later that it could have been the mask in the closet, as she had left the door open. She took a second to stare at herself before her mouth twisted and she let out a manic laugh. Of course it had just been reflecting the mask in the barely lit room. She rubbed at her face. She needed more caffeine.

She dripped across the floor, hoping that the wood could handle a little water. It was a beach house after all, it would be silly if the floors weren't sealed against moisture.

Pushing her hair back out of her face, she roamed the space naked until she found her phone charging on the counter. It didn't have as much battery as she expected, but it would have to do. She texted the owners about the location of the fuse box, and wasn't exactly surprised that it was in the garage. She thought she didn't have access to that space, but found that the door was indeed unlocked. Upon opening it, she discovered what would have been an open space big enough for two cars if a whole house worth of items weren't stored out there. She rolled her eyes. So the owners were hoarders and this was where they stored their *treasures*. These people had just as much junk as her mother.

Mira found the box on the inner wall beside the garage door, and she flipped on the switch that was flipped off. The house instantly came roaring back to life. She looked around the garage, intrigued to know what the owners considered important enough to keep all the way out at the beach. There were a lot of sea-themed items, and she wondered if the owners actually put an effort into decorating for the busy season. She tilted her head at the cheesiness of some of the objects. Captain's and first-mate pillows and chairs, a ship-tilt-degree indicator, and something that had a lever with a plaque titled *Ship Engine Order Telegraph*. Whatever that was.

There were even a bunch of flags that must have all meant something. She had seen similar flags at her grandfather's house in the country growing up. She had never learned what each one meant, but knew some of them signaled that a ship was in distress. A few seemed more worn than others, as if the owners might actually display them outside sometimes, just like her grandfather would. It had seemed silly for a man who lived in a landlocked state to have so many nautical items and dress up his house as if it were a boat.

She started to look through a few things when she wondered if maybe there were cameras out there that the owners had failed to mention, and became overly aware of her less-than-clothed state.

Returning to the interior of the house, she found another message from the owners.

*Sorry the power went out, that's strange. That only seems to happen if the fan from the upstairs is plugged in when literally anything else is on. We've had the wattage checked and it shouldn't be an issue.*

Mira rolled her eyes. *Okay, no fan then.* She could live without it. She didn't need another fright in a dark shower. Unwilling to be trapped in the bathroom again so soon, she turned the shower off and left as quickly as possible. Weaving her way to the kitchen sink to rinse out her hair, she dried it with a kitchen towel before finally venturing up the stairs to put on some clothes. She opened the window just a crack to get the air flowing in the warm room and looked at her tablet sitting on the desk. She hadn't drawn for fun in a while and her mind was swirling with images from the night before. None of them were super clear, but she figured that would be better for her art exploration.

She picked up her drawing pad only to find that the battery life had drained. Rolling her eyes, she folded her hair behind her ear and bent down, sifting through her bag until she found the charger, and plugged it into the power outlet in the desk. Then she returned to her bag and rummaged around for a notebook and a pen, her mind already showing her where it wanted to go. The dark-haired woman out in the sea, her face obscured by shadows as the moon shone bright across the water. Her curves jumped to mind as Mira touched the pen to paper.

Her cheeks flushed as a slow heat started to burn in her belly. She glanced at the bed and thought about doing a different activity instead.

Unfortunately, her mind decided now was the time to dredge up the harsh memory of her mother ripping her hand away from under her own dress. She had learned at a young age that pleasure led to having the "demons" exorcised from her by whatever clergyman and means her mother deemed necessary.

Turning back to her desk, she tried to shrug off the memories of old men in stale rooms who tried to "cure" her of her wickedness. It hadn't done a damn thing. She was still gay as hell.

Her mind drifted to Wendy and how she had encouraged her to draw. Wendy had walked up to her at school and found her engrossed in a piece of paper, lost to her own world. The tall, athletic black girl had gaped in awe at her line art as if it were something to be proud of, and the first thing she had ever said to Mira was, "Can you draw *me*?"

Mira smiled. She hadn't known that her natural talent with a pen would win her a friend, but she was glad it had.

# Chapter 5

Mira had made it through another day and was ignoring the fact that the sun had gone down a while ago, but when the darkness started to become too much, she finally switched on her lamp. She was continuing to entertain herself when her stomach pains demanded that she eat. Abandoning the notebook she had been sketching in on the desk, she walked slowly downstairs.

As her feet landed on the first floor she turned, patting at the wall for the light switch, but before she could find it, her eyes traveled to the back door.

She flung her body back against the wall on instinct as her heart started to try to beat out of her chest. Though it was closed, and had remained locked this time, *swimmer girl* was standing at her back door, peering in.

Slapping her hand over her mouth to refrain from the scream that very much wanted to rip its way up her throat, she slowly lowered herself to the floor, hopeful that Kahli hadn't seen her yet. What the fuck was she doing lurking at her back door?

Her fingers wove into her hair and pulled as she tried to keep her breaths as quiet as possible, but to her ears, it sounded like she was blasting a breathing track over a speaker. She jumped when she heard a knock.

"Mira?"

She closed her eyes. She was sure she had never told the woman her name. Or had she? *There was the whole night when she was less than sober...* She started to hear singing, like the music she had thought she heard when she met the creepy swimmer girl outside.

The porch creaked and she knew the woman had taken a step back from the door. "Mira, I know you're home... your light is on in your room..."

Mira groaned quietly. She supposed that if this woman had wanted to do something to her, she would have done it the night she was completely incapacitated. And if she wasn't leaving anytime soon, she would most likely need to answer—*or play dead.*

Slowly getting to her hands and knees, she peeked her head around the table against the wall.

The dark-haired woman was visible through the glass window in the door and was staring straight up at her window, her brow furrowed in thought.

Mira had always been afraid when she gazed into windows at night. Terrified that she would see a face staring back at hers. It had started in her childhood when she swore she had seen a little blond girl with bright green eyes looking back at her and smiling through her living-room window, beckoning her to *come play* when she had gotten up in the middle of the night for a glass of water. Her mother had slapped her across the mouth for screaming and waking her and Mira's father up. She had next to no memories of that man, but apparently he had existed for a short while.

Placing her hand on the table to haul herself up, Mira reached her hand out and found the light switch, pretending she had just made it down the stairs. She lifted her eyes and caught Kahli's darting to hers through the window. An excited smile spread across her face as Mira frowned. She kept up the attitude as she made it to the door, not unlocking it at first.

"What?" She crossed her arms and lifted a brow. "Is the ocean too cold for you this evening?"

Kahli laughed and she shrugged. "Nah, but I figured you might enjoy the bonfire I made further down the beach. Care to have some fun with me? It's a little ways, and we'll have to walk, but I promise it's worth it."

Her dark eyes dipped and she held up a hand to stop Mira from responding as she dug through her pocket. Her eyes flashed as she lifted a baggie up to the window.

"I found this today when I was looking for shells!"

Mira's eyes went wide. Kahli had a sizable joint pressed up against the window. Bright eyes narrowed as she opened the door. "How do you know I smoke?"

Kahli's head tilted, her body deflating a little as her shoulders caved in. "I guess I don't... I just... thought maybe it would be fun." Her fingers played with the bag as she brought it to her chest anxiously.

Leaning against her doorframe, Mira watched the woman's expression carefully. "Why did you come to the back door? There's a perfectly good doorbell out front..." At least, she thought there was. She hadn't actually checked that it worked when she moved in.

Kahli bit her lip. "Uh, I mean, the beach is out this way... would have taken longer to walk around the front."

Mira rolled her eyes. She supposed that did make sense. "Fine. Just don't stare in my window... that was creepy."

"Will you come?" Kahli's face brightened as if Mira had already agreed to join her.

Looking behind her, Mira searched for some excuse for why she should wait, give herself time to think it through. Her eyes landed on her phone. Surely she couldn't leave the house without it. "My phone is charging."

Kahli's deep honey eyes looked over her shoulder. "Oh. Well... I... I should head back." She seemed to stall as if she was hesitant to leave without Mira. "Not that there's a huge chance of anything happening, but I should probably get back to the fire soon, you know, flames and all. I don't want to start a brush fire."

Mira snorted. "What was the fire for? Cold already?" She was going to make some crack about the idiocy of swimming in the wintertime when she noticed that Kahli didn't appear to be wet this time.

The other woman shook her head. "I don't really get cold. I do however worry that a fire could spread to the animals... it's close to the water, but... I don't know, sometimes there's wind. Don't want to burn down anyone's home." She took a step back. Her head gestured down the beach. "It's that way, if you plan to join. I'll head back." She turned toward the water but turned back when her foot hit the top of the steps. "If I don't see you... good-night, Mira." She smiled shyly as she departed.

Mira watched as she took off toward the small light in the distance. She had a choice to make... sit at home and eat a horrible frozen dinner by herself, contemplating all the demons that swirled around her head at night when she was alone... or go follow the weird woman out to her fire and probably live to tell the tale. She let her eyes drift to her fridge as her fingers drummed on her door.

*Oh, what the hell.* She was up for a little trouble.

Mira grabbed her phone and a bottle of Jack and threw them in a rough tan tote. Pulling on a thick hoodie and sweatpants, she made her way down the beach. She left her back door unlocked, figuring the danger was low. The other woman was probably right, it really was just the two of them all the way out here in the remote community. She felt the cool sand against her bare feet as she trudged along her path, looking out at the ocean every once in a while to stare at the moon high in the sky. It felt like it took her ages to reach her destination, but eventually her feet did their job.

As Kahli came into view, Mira saw the other woman get up from her seat decently far back from the fire to wade out into the water. Mira took in the scenery around her as she waited. The stars were shining brightly and the nighttime air was cool. She shook her head; it was a miracle Kahli hadn't gotten sick yet from all her late-night ocean activities.

Soon after her arrival, Kahli came jogging back out of the water a ways down the beach. When Kahli came within hearing distance, Mira indicated the water with a flick of her eyes. "Have an addiction to swimming?"

Kahli shrugged as her smile stretched wider. "Something like that. You came?"

Mira nodded. "There's nothing else to do here, an oversight on my part. Plus, you did promise me drugs, so..." Kahli's eyes drifted around in confusion until Mira pointed at the plastic bag pinned to the ground with by a rock. "The weed?"

"Oh." Kahli scrambled over to the bag. "Right. I haven't before... I was hoping you could show me how it's done?"

Mira snorted, causing Kahli to jump slightly. "You've never smoked weed before? How old are you anyway?"

Kahli bit her lip and shook her head as she passed the bag over.

Rolling her eyes at the innocence, Mira pulled out the joint and inspected it before gruffly filling the sudden silence. "I was smoking these practically in elementary school. Strict family. Made me want to rebel early. Got a lighter?"

The other woman moved to sit beside her and shook her head, remaining quiet as Mira's eyes lifted to the fire. "Get me a stick and light it."

Kahli's eyes widened as she reached for a stick from a small pile that remained nearby and inched herself toward the flames, hand outstretched as if it might bite her at any moment. Mira rolled her eyes as she set the blunt down on the bag and crawled toward Kahli, taking the stick from her hand and lighting it herself.

"The wind is calm, the flames won't get you from this side... not right now anyway." The joys of being a country kid. She learned about fires early, and not through her parents' "gentle" teachings.

Kahli sucked on her bottom lip as her eyes drifted to the water then back. As if she desperately wanted to help but had no clue what to do. But

Mira didn't need assistance, returning to the weed and easily lighting one end of the neatly wrapped paper. Her face lit up when it worked and smoke started to billow. "There."

She held the joint between her thumb and first finger and took a slow drag, eyes fluttering closed as the smoke hit her lungs. She hadn't had good flower in a long time and honestly missed the way it rapidly spread though her, calming her. She let herself hold the smoke a moment longer before breathing it out and extending her hand, expecting Kahli to take a turn, eyes cracking open when she didn't.

"You going to take a hit?"

Kahli's darker eyes watched the paper where it burned, her fingers reaching out for it slowly when Mira moved it at the last second.

"Not that end, dumbass, you'll burn your fingers." She twisted and sat up on her knees, reaching out to take the other woman's tan fingers and adjusting them to hold the correct end of the joint. "You've really never done this, have you?" Mira's lips ticked upward, her bright eyes softening as Kahli's only went wider.

The other woman shook her head slowly as she attempted to not fumble the grip Mira had helped her with.

"That's kind of cute," she teased as she watched the pink flush spread across Kahli's cheeks.

Mira's eyes trailed Kahli's hand as she reached for her wrist, shifting the blunt slowly to her lips.

"Suck." Her voice cracked as she commanded the younger woman to do her bidding, and Kahli did as she was told, causing Mira's smile to grow. "Good girl."

Kahli must have forgotten how to breathe because not only was she coughing a moment later, but she was gasping for air. The blunt dropped into the sand as she seemed to panic. Mira's sure hands gripped her shoulders as she talked her through it.

"You're okay... you're fine..."

Kahli shook her head wildly. "No... no. Can't breathe... water..."

Mira opened her alcohol and told Kahli to take a sip. The other woman chugged a bit, only to cough it back up. Her body turned toward the ocean and she moved quickly to the water before dropping to her knees as a small wave rolled in. She dipped her hands into the ocean and scooped some water into her mouth, drinking greedily until Mira's fingers took control of her actions.

"Kahli... stop. Stop." At first, her voice was full of laughter, but as Kahli made a move to try to drink more, Mira tugged on her. "Kahli, seriously, cut it out." Her amusement quickly dissipated. "You'll get sick. It's not that bad… you probably just took too big of a hit is all…" Mira cupped her face, forcing the other woman to look at her. "You okay? We can walk back to my place and get water…"

Kahli paused, fixated on Mira's calves disappearing into the gentle waves. Her eyes closed. "You came out into the water?" She sounded strained saying the words. As if conflicted.

Mira tilted her head, eyes narrowing. "Yeah, because you drank salt water, like a crazy person…" And honestly, who did that? Was it because she was high? Mira had some serious concerns about whether they should continue smoking, but after the younger woman's coughing fit, Kahli probably wasn't about to try more any time soon.

"Would you… have followed me in? If I went deeper?" Kahli's fingers were brushing her own lips as her mind seemed to wander.

Mira snorted. "You really love your late-night swims." She stood tall, her hands finding her hips as she looked out at the sea. "I mean… if you were super high, maybe…" She turned back to glare at the other woman. "Don't do that though. I'm telling you now that if you do something stupid like that, I won't be coming in after you. You've been warned."

Kahli rose slowly, gaze dipping to Mira's lips. As if she already knew what it would feel like to press against them, as if they had done so many times before and it had been far too long since she had the privilege. Kahli's hands came up, shaking slightly, to cup her cheeks. Her eyes darted back to Mira's before she leaned in.

Mira's eyes closed at the first touch of Kahli's lips, her thoughts silenced for once. As Kahli took a step back, Mira moved with her. She felt Kahli's lips split into a smile as she spoke. "You're such a liar." The younger woman pulled back, but only slightly. "You would totally follow me in."

*The audacity!* Mira scoffed. "Please... I would have stopped the moment the water got to my knees. I'm definitely not about to go for a swim over you."

Kahli reached out and grabbed her hand, lacing their fingers together, her eyes studying them as she started to hum. Mira's mind went calm... she felt warm, despite the cold water and the even colder air. She tried in vain to place the melody but came up empty.

"What song are you singing? You keep singing the same one, right?"

The humming abruptly stopped. "I'm singing?" Kahli raised her eyebrows. "I... didn't notice." She turned toward the sand and dragged Mira back up the beach. "If you don't plan on going in, you should stay away from the water."

Mira kept watching the waves as she followed, mesmerized by the way the water sparkled with the light from the moon. "Ever wonder what it would be like to disappear under the surface?"

The insistent pressure pulling her suddenly stopped and she stumbled into a solid back.

"Kahli!" Mira snorted as she grabbed onto Kahli to keep from falling. Her arms wrapped around the other woman, who was completely rigid. "You can't just stop walking."

Kahli took a large breath of air, her body relaxing minutely as she let it go. "We should head back."

Mira pressed her whole body to Kahli's back, having other ideas. "I think I want to do more weed and maybe..."

Turning slightly to look at her, Kahli muttered softly, "We can do it at your house. It's getting late and the..." Her eyes wandered over to the water and she was lost for a moment, so long that even a high Mira noticed, before finally continuing. "The tide will come in... don't want to get stuck out here." She reached out and grabbed the discarded joint and Mira's alcohol. "Come on." She started kicking sand into the fire until it appeared to snuff out.

Mira let herself be dragged down the beach, mouth running unchecked as her filter was discarded. "You know... you're not supposed to talk to strangers, or go home with strangers, or get high with strangers... some people are murderers..."

Kahli snorted. "Wow, you don't say?"

"I could be super dangerous... you don't know *anything* about me..." she continued, rambling.

Kahli turned around and faced the brunette as she walked backwards, indulging her. "I know plenty about you already... remember? I spent that whole night with you when you were shit-faced."

Mira's face dropped, her mind struggling to make sense of the words Kahli had used and uncover if they were significant. "You... stayed? But you weren't there in the morning..."

Honey eyes rolled. "I did have to go home eventually."

Mulling that over and not paying attention to where she was stepping, Mira tripped. Luckily, Kahli caught her arm before she faceplanted, grabbing onto her like a lifeline. "Thanks." She tried to settle her nerves and unintentionally leaned on her companion, causing Kahli to wrap her arm around Mira's waist and encourage her to continue walking again. The move sent a warmth spreading throughout Mira's chest, allowing her body to relax once more.

Kahli cleared her throat. "So... why did you choose to come here? Are you into the legends or..."

*Was everyone in this town crazy?* Mira dramatically rolled her eyes. "Not you too. Is that like a thing here, really?"

She had expected Kahli to laugh along with her, to agree that the idea of the supernatural was absurd, but the woman's face remained neutral. It clearly wasn't a joke to her. "So you don't believe in mermaids then?"

Mira scoffed. "I'm not a child. I've long outgrown fairy tales..." She had never really been allowed stories as a kid... unless they came from a "holy book" or were one of the ones that Wendy's parents had encouraged she share with her friend. Mira's reading level would have struggled if she hadn't practiced alongside Wendy.

Kahli was quiet for so long that Mira wondered if she had offended her and tried with her hazy mind to remember what she had said. She had actually forgotten what they had been talking about and frowned as she struggled to figure out why the cute girl had stopped speaking to her. Mira berated herself for her lack of social skills.

Eventually, Kahli began talking again, her pace slowing as she seemingly chose her words with care. "I wouldn't call them fairy tales. The legends... well, mermaids aren't *kind*. And that's putting it nicely." She sighed. "They say they're the demons of the sea. You know, they sing people to their deaths, lure them into the water before they drag them *under*."

Mira's face scrunched in thought, her mouth running away from her without her head's consent. "They've always creeped me out. Did you know, in the original fairy tale, she kills the prince? Speaking of, what do they do with the bodies though... do they... eat them? I bet they eat them." She cringed as her eyes cast out to the sea and once again pondered going under. Would it be worse if she was taken against her will or if she went freely?

Kahli's eyes widened in alarm. "Why would they eat them?"

"Why hunt something if you aren't hungry?" Mira shrugged. It made perfect sense to her. Her eyes drifted to her arm where she felt Kahli's thumb moving back and forth. The motion was hypnotizing.

"Some things are born evil, I guess. Maybe there's a long-lost reason, a vengeance. Maybe... they blame the land and those on it for leaving. Didn't all life come from the sea?"

Mira snorted. "You are such a nerd. You study myths in school? You're thinking about this *way* too hard..."

Kahli shrugged, clearly deflating at the teasing. "I just... I always thought the stories were... interesting. That's all."

Guilt surged through Mira, making her want fix the frown now plastered on Kahli's face. She hesitantly moved to even the playing field and offer something up, warring with herself on whether it was a good idea to share something so personal with someone she just met. "I had a crush on the little mermaid when I was little. There was just something about her red hair..." She stared angrily at the sand beneath her feet when she heard Kahli's light laughter, instantly regretting speaking. Of course she thought it was stupid. This was why she didn't share things with people.

"Her red hair, really? Not her tail?" Kahli's smile barely held back more of her laughter.

"It's not funny." Mira huffed. She felt her cheeks heat up at the insinuation. She wasn't attracted to a *fish*. Even if that fish were part girl.

"Ah, so I'm not your type?"

Mira tried half-heartedly to pull away, but Kahli kept her in her grasp.

"Stop, I don't need to carry you because you fell and hurt yourself. And you're right, you can love whoever you want to love... even if it's a girl who only exists in a story."

# Chapter 6

Mira had wanted Kahli to stay, but she mentioned she needed to get home, promising Mira that she would stop by the next morning. Mira had pouted, then smirked, when she noticed the effect she was having on the younger woman. It wasn't hard to draw out their time together a little longer, but eventually, Kahli did leave.

Normally Mira found sleep difficult, and this night was no different. While the weed kept her from getting up and moving around, she did remember her eyes opening many times throughout the night. Staring out at the waves, lost in time. Her eyes tracked the way sheets of rain and dark clouds moved in at the late hour, the ocean growing erratic. She was glad Kahli had insisted they go home when they did or they might have been caught out in the storm—she hoped the younger woman had gotten home in time.

She continued to drift in and out of consciousness until late into the morning. A loud knock at her back door roused her from her bed when she remembered Kahli's promise to pop by. She scrambled to untangle herself from the sheets; she hadn't even had time to brush her teeth or prepare herself for the day.

When she made it downstairs, Kahli stood at the door with two buckets and a bright smile. "Good morning!"

Mira's face scrunched up. *Why does she have to be a morning person?* She made it to the back door and unlocked it. Before Mira could come up with an excuse as to why now wasn't a great time, Kahli was already talking excitedly.

"Want to come help me search the tide pools for mussels? We can cook them on the beach tonight for dinner." She indicated the beach with a tilt of her head.

Mira's mouth dropped open. Why this woman wanted to spend time with her grouchy neighbor was beyond her. Mira couldn't have possibly been that fun either night that she was with her.

Kahli turned and grabbed a long-sleeved rash guard in white that she'd brought with her. "I found this for you. To protect you from the sun." Mira reached out and took the fabric, feeling the density of it for quality. It would surely help. The gesture settled over her as something about them spending time together set off alarm bells in her head. Did Kahli actually *like* her?

She raised an eyebrow. "Is this... a date?"

Mira hadn't been on one of those in a long time. Her mind tried to stray from thoughts about how this might mean the younger woman was interested in more than just sex. Was *she* interested in more? She felt her muscles tighten slightly at the prospect until she noticed Kahli's reaction to the question.

The younger woman blushed as she stumbled over her words. "What? I just... it's a thing to do around here and I thought... maybe you hadn't before and..."

Mira raised a hand to stop Kahli's rambling. "Too early."

Kahli looked off toward the sun, her hand blocking most of the light. "It's midday though."

Mira grabbed her arm as she pulled her inside. "If it will shut you up, I'll get ready. Just... wait here."

She took off back up the stairs and thought about grabbing her swimsuit but decided against it as she disrobed and pulled the white rash guard over her head. She snorted and raised an eyebrow when she glanced in the mirror. The white shirt was most certainly showing off exactly where her nipples were, if the dark circular outlines were anything to go by. She briefly wondered if Kahli had done this on purpose or if it was an accident. Either way, she figured it might make the day a bit more fun if she tortured the younger woman a little. She looked around and found some leggings to complete her look.

Those would at least protect her from the sun. She wondered if the black would make her too hot, but she figured she could always dip herself into the water. Grabbing a hair band, she put her long hair up into a messy bun. She caught her reflection again as she prepared to make her way back down the stairs. The ends of her hair stuck out every which way, and she rolled her eyes. Kahli had asked her to go play in the water, not out to a fancy restaurant. This would have to do. If this were a date, it seemed casual enough. Best not to overthink it.

She made her way back down the stairs and found that Kahli had wandered away from where she left her, exploring the room a bit. At the sound of Mira's throat clearing, she turned and offered Mira her attention, unbothered about being caught snooping. Kahli's mouth opened, about to speak, but nothing came out and her eyes widened. Her mouth closed and her eyes darted away, though Mira noticed the small smirk and the way her tongue darted out briefly to lick her lips.

"You look great."

Mira felt the compliment hit her, making her stomach flip. She had forgotten what a rush it was when a beautiful woman appreciated her. She chose to ignore giving attention to the feeling, not wanting to get used to it. This wasn't a long trip after all.

"Ready to go?"

Mira shrugged. "I'm not sure why you think this is such an essential life skill that I should learn, but... I didn't have much planned for today so..."

As Mira reached for the plastic tubs, Kahli scooped them both up. "I got it. We need to head north a bit, there are some solid tide pools up that way." Mira followed her out, closing up her house as they proceeded to the beach. Kahli paused before they got far, setting down the containers as she pulled a black bucket hat out of her bag and plopped it on her head. Retrieving the bins, she continued on. Mira's head tilted at the mismatch; Kahli did not appear to be a bucket hat person. She seemed more sporty than that, and Mira would have expected her to pull out a baseball cap.

Though, Mira had to admit, she looked cute in the hat nonetheless. She was personally enjoying the fact that it made it harder for Kahli to notice her checking her out. Her companion's sports bra today was black and smaller than it could have been, causing her to slightly spill out of the material. Her basketball shorts were a deep green and a little long on her. Mira wondered if that was simply how she liked them but chose not to comment.

They walked for a bit in comfortable silence, and Mira was glad she wasn't forced to come up with conversation as they headed for the tide pools. Kahli eventually grabbed her arm when it appeared they had arrived at their location and guided her toward a bunch of rocks that jutted out into the ocean with the low tide.

Kahli set the buckets down on the rocks, her honey eyes looking down into the closest pool. "Low tide is the best time to find them. We'll also check the side of those rocks poking out of the sand over there, the mussels should be against the side that points to the ocean." She crouched and pointed. "Look, here's a little cluster!"

Mira wandered over in her tennis shoes and squatted beside Kahli, trying to figure out what she was indicating. The dark, oblong shells were all clustered together. She wasn't sure what they would taste like, or if she would even like them, but she figured why not try. She let her pale fingers skim the surface of the water.

"So do we like... pry them off the rocks with a knife?" She looked back at the buckets and failed to see any tools. She was wondering if Kahli carried a pocketknife when Kahli extended her hand into the water and wrapped it around one of the shells, twisting it until it snapped.

The younger woman smirked at her companion before moving to grab a bucket. She plopped the shell into the plastic and dipped the bucket in the water. "We want to keep them fresh."

Mira looked back at the cluster, which was a bit hard to see with the rippling of the water. She almost dipped her hand into the water when she paused. "Is there... anything I don't want to be touching in there?" She tried to see for herself what might not feel so great when she heard Kahli snicker.

"Uh, well there might be a few things, but I'm keeping an eye out. If I see any crabs or..."

Mira's eyes darted to something. "Like that thing? Don't touch that, right?" Mira pointed at a little green sac that appeared puffed up and her eyes widened in alarm as Kahli reached a finger into the pool where the thing was clinging to a rock near the surf. She pressed lightly and it squirted water like a little cannon. Mira raised her hand to block the water from her face, even though it barely reached her shoe.

Kahli laughed. "That one's actually safe. Sea anemone." Pointing at another darker creature that looked spiny, her brow furrowed. "Don't touch those." She held out her hand for Mira's and waited as Mira contemplated complying. She needed a long moment of contemplation, needing to know where things were, before giving in.

Finally, Mira extended her hand and Kahli cupped it gently. Dipping their hands in the water together, Kahli encouraged Mira's fingers to anchor around a long mussel. "It just feels like a shell."

Kahli wrapped both of their hands around the shell and performed a twisting motion. Mira twitched lightly as it came loose before Kahli withdrew her hand, though her face remained trained on Mira. "Nice. Now hand me that one and do another."

Mira relinquished it and slowly slipped her hand back into the water on her own. She twisted lightly and the next one didn't budge. Her eyes glanced in Kahli's direction and grew confused at the mischief that played across her features. Mira's face scrunched as she tried to think. What could she possibly be doing wrong?

"Sometimes you have to go a *little* harder." Kahli nodded gently at the pool of water, encouraging Mira to try again.

Mira turned back to the shell as she pursed her lips and added pressure, this time the mussel snapped off into her hold and she smiled. She took it and plopped it into a bucket with a splash. Her gaze redirected to Kahli. "How many do we need?"

Mira watched as Kahli steamed the shells in a large pot she had found in the cabinet with the cooking supplies. She hoisted herself up on the counter, finding that she needed somewhere to sit, her body too tired to stay standing any longer.

"Thought we were going to do this on the beach?" While it was nice to be spending so much time in the fresh air, Mira did also find that she was enjoying how... domestic this was with them cooking in the kitchen together. She felt herself jolt at the idea. *That's not what this is.* She tucked her hair behind her shoulder quickly for something to do. Just because she missed her wife didn't mean that it was alright to play house with someone else.

Kahli rolled her eyes. "You saw the storm clouds rolling in..."

Mira had. If she were being honest, she felt excited at the prospect of them getting back to her place. Ideas swirled in her mind of how to get Kahli to stay over for a bit of fun. She tried to refocus on the task at hand and thought a little too much about what they were doing.

"This is barbaric, isn't it?" She leaned a bit closer as Kahli stopped her with a hand to her chest, dark eyes narrowing.

"Do you need to leave the kitchen?"

Mira rolled her eyes. "I'm just saying, if I was a vegan, I don't think I would be eating these."

At Kahli's blank, confused face, Mira explained.

"Vegan, like, doesn't eat animals *or* animal by-products? You know, because they are 'living beings'?"

"How would you not eat *any* animals or by-products? That seems unrealistic."

Mira shrugged. "Some people like eating plants."

Kahli pressed Mira a little further back before she continued cooking, eyeing her warily as if she might suddenly grab the pot and make a break for the beach to release the shells back into the ocean. "Go find us some butter and salt."

Easing herself off the counter to the ground, Mira gathered the butter from the fridge. Luckily, she had picked some up in case she wanted to make toast, and she was glad the house came stocked with salt, pepper, and sugar. She poured the ingredients into a bowl and placed it in the microwave, allowing it to cook for a few seconds, before taking it out and placing it on the table.

Kahli nodded her thanks as she checked everything once more more before turning off the stove. "They're done. Grab some plates and meet me at the table."

Mira prepared herself for the screech of the cabinet as she took out two plates and felt a flicker of guilt when she caught Kahli flinching in her periphery. She left it open, not wanting to chance the sounds again in case there were other things they needed, and went to set the table. Her fingers found the end of the rash-guard sleeves and played with them, wondering if this really was a date. It sure was feeling like one. They were having dinner after all, and though she had helped hunt for their food, Kahli was cooking for her.

The shells were plated in a bowl, which Kahli set between them, providing simple instructions. "You dip it."

Mira nodded as they each took a fork and Kahli showed her the most efficient way to pull them from their shells. Mira followed suit before placing one of the mussels in her mouth, her brows lifting when the flavor hit her tongue and she failed to hold back a moan. "Okay, fuck, that's good." She quickly went back for more.

Kahli seemed to brighten at the compliment as she started to eat. Her gaze, every few moments, darted up to watch Mira. As if her enjoyment was the main event.

They ate until about half of the mussels were gone, and Kahli moved the rest to the fridge when Mira stopped eating.

Mira looked around the room and wondered if there were some way she could get Kahli to stay. Although she was lonely, it sounded too desperate in her own head to actually voice her desire. She wasn't feeling confident about making a move, even though she wanted to. Maybe this was just a friend thing and she would mess it all up. Better to not risk chasing off the one person wanting to spend time with her. Her shoulders fell, accepting that Kahli was going to head out soon, when the younger woman surprised her.

"Would you... want to take a walk with me?"

Mira's eyes lifted at the offer.

"The weather appears to be letting up, and I know you don't like walks but... I don't know, it's turning into a nice night..."

Mira didn't even need to ponder what else she could possibly do instead. It wasn't like she was going to get a better offer. She stood so fast she knocked into the table. "Yes!" She cleared her throat as she stabilized the table, her face feeling as if it was burning. "I mean... yeah, fine."

Kahli moved to get the door as Mira grabbed her phone, slipping it into her yoga pants.

The night was just warm enough to not need a jacket; she couldn't believe her luck. Mira noticed the way light glistened off the sand and water. She felt a gentle breeze shift her hair into her face and she struggled to brush it aside.

Kahli's fingers grabbed the pieces and pushed them back into her bun. "There you go."

Mira floated her fingers over the hairs. Her stomach fluttered, a foreign sensation that she hadn't felt in a while, as she murmured, "Thank you." She stopped and didn't start walking again, instead tilting her head to the night sky. "You can really see the stars tonight." She indicated the faraway lights. "Know much about the stars?"

The other woman strode up beside her and let out a deep sigh, shaking her head. "No... not much."

Mira's hand fell to her side but her eyes still stared in wonder. "I used to sneak outside at night when I was little. I would watch the stars for hours, pretend I was somewhere else..." She moved to sit. "My back is getting tired, I need a minute."

Kahli followed suit and lay back in the sand as her dark eyes drifted to the sky. "Do you have a favorite?"

"I don't know much about them either. I just..." She sighed. "Thought they were nice to look at." Her eyes located a shooting star as it shot across the sky. "Oh, make a wish!" She smacked Kahli and heard her companion begin to laugh beside her.

"Okay... okay." Kahli made a show of scrunching up her face as she presumably made a silent wish.

Leaning back on her elbows, Mira twisted her back slightly, hoping some of the tension in it would fall away. When it did, she lay back in the sand. She looked for more shooting stars in the sky, because if she remained distracted, maybe she could enjoy this night without panicking about what it might or might not mean.

Her wife hadn't shared her love for the nighttime sky. Amani had hated when her childlike curiosity about the world rose to the surface. She also hated how Mira's pain issues had altered their lives... well, altered *Mira's* life. Amani didn't let Mira slow her down. If Mira needed a break, Amani would huff and go on without her while she found a bench or a patch of grass to rest on. Amani was only ever satisfied with Mira when they had sex. There was no tenderness, no checking in on how Mira was handling everything. Most of the time she was too busy staring at the ceiling. There were only so many attempts she could make to tell Amani that something didn't feel good before she gave up and just tried to get through it, hoping she would try something else. Kahli was already proving to be a very different person, and Mira felt a pang of anger at why she couldn't have met someone like Kahli sooner in life. Someone who was not only interested in her beauty, but who also *cared* about her.

Kahli reached into her pocket and produced the blunt from the day before and a lighter. Her tone was soft as she handed it over. "Want to try this again?"

# Chapter 7

Mira and Kahli stumbled back toward the house, giggling softly to each other when Kahli suddenly stopped and faced the sea. Mira ran into her back with a grunt, wondering why they had stopped and had brief thoughts about if she would get to actually put her hands on the younger woman tonight. They had already torn themselves away from a lengthy make-out session with the promise of more when they got back to Mira's.

Kahli stood frozen, muscles visibly tensing in the dim lighting.  Her voice dropped low as she disconnected their hands, causing Mira to pout. Kahli's hands had been so warm...

"Go inside, Mira."

Mira looked behind her at the house and, for a moment, thought she saw a light move inside, as if someone was in there with a flashlight. She placed her hand over her mouth to stop her scream. Someone was in the house? She reached out and grabbed Kahli's hip. Her heart hurt as it sped up. She shifted to grip Kahli's clothes, her voice barely above a whisper.

"Kahli... I think someone is in my house..." She started to wonder if Kahli could have anything to do with it. "Did you..."

Kahli turned her head slightly, but her eyes remained on the water. "What did you see?"

"Is... is someone robbing me? Because you—you could have done that the other night and I... I couldn't have stopped you... why would you send someone..."

Kahli took a step back. "Mira, I need you to stop talking. I need you to listen." The younger woman grabbed her hands and made sure she was paying attention. "Walk up the side of the house. I'll be right behind you. Don't turn around. We are going to get you into your car. And then, you will head into town while I check your house. Where are your keys?"

Mira's hands gripped Kahli's tighter. "I can't... I can't leave you here alone... what if there's someone... you can come with me, we can send the police."

Kahli sighed. "Just listen to me... okay? I'll be fine. It's just a precaution. I'll be here when you get back. Start walking, now." She pushed and Mira moved forward, her feet unsteady.

"Kahli... not so fast, I... I can't see..." Her voice was quiet as a steady hand pressed at her back. "O-okay, I'm going." She was shaking heavily and her eyes weren't taking in her surroundings well in the dark. Mira whimpered quietly. "I... I'm freaking out. What's going on?" She closed her eyes briefly. She hadn't meant to say that. A firm hand gripped her hip.

"You're okay, keep going. You're fine."

The journey to the front of the house felt like it took years in Mira's state, but they eventually made it. The front light that she always left on was somehow off. Her feet found the grass and she was about ready to run down the street on her own. The streetlamps were still working, thankfully, though they occasionally flickered as if they might forget their purpose and plunge the street into darkness.

"Kah..." Her voice cut out as Kahli turned her and cupped her face, humming softly before she started speaking. Mira's body calmed instantly as if in a trance.

"Do *not* go in the water tonight. Do you hear me?"

Mira nodded slowly. "Yes..."

Dark eyes indicated the road and a light wind started to rustle the trees. "You're going to go for a drive. Stay safe, drive slow. You are *not* going to stop your car, not until you are gone for a while, and when you come back, you will not get out of the car until I tell you to."

Mira tried to swallow but her mouth was dry. Her voice cracked as she spoke. "Come with me."

Kahli shook her head. "I'll be fine. Where are your keys?"

Mira looked past Kahli at the house as it took her a moment to remember. "They're on the side table on the left when you walk in..."

The younger woman took off, leaving Mira standing where she was. Kahli's hand went for the door and grunted when it was locked. She turned to Mira and motioned for her to stay put as she rounded the structure.

Mira's arms came up to wrap around herself, fighting off the sudden cold. She didn't like any of this. Looking around, she realized could see for at least one hundred feet in each direction. At least she would know if someone was approaching. She took an unconscious step toward the house the moment she saw Kahli again, but the woman glared and Mira stopped in her tracks. Her feet refused to move. Her mind was unsure why. She looked down at her feet and willed them to move forward. They didn't until Kahli had turned on her car and backed out of the driveway.

Kahli flung the car door open and quickly ushered Mira in. "Look. Here's your car." Wind-chilled hands cupped her cheeks. "You're fine. You're safe. Drive slow. No ocean. Stay in town a while and just drive. Listen to some music, just don't stop. After a while, come back and I'll be waiting for you, right here." She pointed at the yard. "You're okay, it's all okay."

"How long do I drive for?" She wasn't sure she would be retaining any of the instructions with the way the blood was rushing in her ears.

"Long enough. Take your time." Kahli leaned forward and buckled Mira's seatbelt. "Drive safe. I don't want anything happening to you." Kahli closed the door and took a step back.

Mira's fingers gripped the steering wheel, palming it as she tried to think through what she was doing, jumping when Kahli knocked on her window.

"Lock up." Her voice was muted by the glass.

Engaging the locks, Mira turned to make sure no one was in the car with her. Her eyes drifted back to Kahli's as the other woman pressed her palm to the window.

"I already checked. You're alone in there." She tilted her head toward town. "Get going." She took a step back, and though Mira wasn't sure if she could move... her foot pressed on the gas, and she drove off into the night.

Mira was following Kahli's orders, and she wasn't quite sure what she was doing, but she drove around aimlessly with her car's lights cutting through the darkness and only illuminating the road. As the trees all blurred together in a cloud of darkness, she figured maybe it wasn't such a bad idea to stay away until early morning. The world could look utterly terrifying at night.

There was a pang of guilt in her chest from leaving Kahli behind. She didn't know her well, and it was probably stupid to have her get in the car with her at this time of night and dictate where she drove. But on the other hand, what if someone was in the house and *Kahli* was the one in trouble? Her mind told her to turn back and at least check, but her hands just wouldn't turn the wheel.

She headed into town first, the streetlights casting a warm glow even as all the shops were closed now. Well, all except the one bar in town, but even it seemed subdued by the late hour.

Continuing on, she checked out the different storefronts she had failed to notice before. She half hoped that a cop would wonder what she was doing driving around in circles and check in on her. But she never found a single patrol car. Maybe they didn't have the funds for such things—or nothing ever happened in this sleepy town and there was no need. In a true emergency, she figured she could call 911 and head to the bar, where there were at least some people still awake.

She diverted to the highway when she grew tired of the scenery and headed north, driving along the coast and seeing nothing but fog to her left, where the road presumably dropped off into the ocean. When she looked to her right, there was only dense forest that looked like it was painted black in the night. The trees loomed over her, as if they might decide to reach out and grab her. Mira instinctively pressed the lock button to be safe.

Turning on the radio as she drove, looking for music, she stumbled across a local radio show.

*"Well, Sam, welcome to the Midnight Watchers. We hold the line against everything that goes BUMP in the*

*night. The police might tell you that it's just a typical missing person case with the girl two towns over, but all the signs were there. That someone snatched her into the water. You know what we're talking about folks. Mermaids. The devils themselves. This town was created as a barrier between the sea and the land…"*

Mira rolled her eyes. So a couple of crazies stayed up late talking about ghosts and paranormal creatures. This town was really into their legends. She was more concerned there was an actual person in her house, wanting to stab her to death. Maybe a wayward serial killer had stumbled across her and thought she made an easy mark. A single-looking woman all alone out in a secluded beach house… Okay, now that she thought about it, she seemed really fucking stupid for renting the property. Though the house had Wi-Fi for the guests, she hadn't seen a single camera. Which was both a good and a bad thing. No one potentially spying on her and making her skin itch was a perk, but on the other hand, if she did go missing, there would likely be no trace.

As she kept driving, she drifted into the far corners of her mind, lulled by the vibrations of the car. She was always the first to fall asleep on a road trip. Her eyes shifted to the side when a view of the ocean became visible and she was momentarily distracted by the white-capped waves. Some movement had her turning her attention back to where she was going. Suddenly, a black object was streaking onto the road. A pale face turned to her just as the thing made it to the middle of her lane and stopped. Her heart jolted in her chest and she swerved.

It took her tired mind a moment to catch up and realize she should have hit whatever or whoever it was—she hadn't reacted fast enough—but the car had sailed through it without an issue. Her frantic breaths echoed around the car. She whipped around and did a double take, expecting to see a crumpled body laying lifeless in the road. Remembering now with greater clarity, she had seen a *person* running across, before they paused in the middle, just waiting for her to hit them. A brief flash of a manic smile lingered in her mind's eye. Despite what she *thought* she saw, there was no person currently lying in the road.

Her head swiveled slowly to look behind her in the car, as if maybe the person had hopped in somehow. Though at her speed, and with her locked doors, that shouldn't have been possible. She was fully expecting to actually find someone looming in the backseat... but of course it was empty. She jumped anyway.

Mira really needed sleep. She was sure everything would make more sense in the light of day and she would be more practical. Logical even. The sound of ringing chimes drew her attention back to the present and the radio. The show was playing a crappy little tune to introduce the next segment and she cringed at the low production value.

"Brother..."

She continued driving for another few moments, thinking the worst was over, when a loud crack split the air. Her eyes darted around wildly looking for the source when a gigantic tree fell across the highway. She slammed on her brakes, barely stopping in time to avoid being crushed. Breathing hard, she shut off her radio and strained to listen for any other trees ready to fall. When she heard nothing, she reversed her car and rerouted.

Still on edge, she cautiously drove back to the house and waited out front, parked on the street. She didn't pull into the driveway, just in case she needed to take off at the first sight of danger.

Shivering, she grabbed a small gray blanket from the back seat and cuddled up in her chair, watching the house. Her guilt started to gnaw at her. She had left Kahli *behind*. She should have insisted that the younger woman leave with her.

What if, when she finally wandered inside, Kahli was just a body? Her mind followed the path from the car to the house. Her imagination filled in for her how the door would squeak open, only to reveal a cold, lifeless body lying there in the entryway, thick red blood spilling out and pooling around Kahli.

Mira shook her head rapidly, trying to clear away the imagery, as she muttered assurances to herself. Kahli was fine. She wouldn't have been reckless. Would she? She pulled her blanket tighter as she tried to calm down.

Time marched on and she seemed to drift, occasionally glancing around her car. At one point she must have fallen asleep, otherwise a deer had appeared in the middle of the yard out of thin air. She leaned toward her passenger window to get a better look. Its eyes bore into her, and she found that she also froze, caught in the stare down. She wondered why it didn't flee. After a few minutes, it slowly lowered its head to the ground to chew at the lawn, maintaining eye contact as it paused just before it finished its descent.

Mira's eyes noticed how the deer seemed to glow in the light, looking ethereal. Knowing Wendy would get a kick out of the sight, she looked down and located her phone in her pocket.

But when she lifted it to take a picture, the deer was gone. She furrowed her brow, surveying the yard. How could it have gotten away so quickly? She shrugged and set her phone in her lap. She didn't need more photos on her phone anyway, she was rapidly running out of memory. She began to drift again and this time she for sure fell asleep.

# Chapter 8

Mira was swimming in what appeared to be the middle of the ocean, but she didn't have a clue how she had gotten there. She looked around and saw a little boy and heard herself shout after him.

"Alex?"

The name made her pause, her breath catching. That was the name she had wanted for her son. She had always loved the name Alexandra—Alexander, if it was a boy. It reminded her of her early love for stories and Greek mythology that were readily available on Wendy's bookshelves. Amani, on the other hand, had wanted a different name. But he was never born.

The little boy with brown hair giggled as he popped in and out of the water. She had to turn around to follow his movements, worried that he might go under and not resurface.

"Alex, that's enough. Your mother wants us home…"

Somewhere in her mind she knew that she wasn't talking about Amani. Yet in the dream, she looked for her anyway, before she jolted. The little boy with Mira's bright blue eyes had appeared at her side. His hands rested on her shoulders as they treaded water.

"Momma went under. I can't find her. She's silly. How deep do you think she went this time?"

Mira's face contorted. Her eyes wide, her forehead wrinkled as her brows pushed up too hard. A cold dread slid through her veins. "She's not supposed to do that anymore…"

Alex grabbed her hand. "Come with me, it's time to find her."

Mira frantically shook her head back and forth. "Alex, I can't go down there…"

The little boy was far stronger than he appeared as he clasped both hands around her wrist and pulled. She screamed as she went under.

Mira woke up to her gasp echoing around her. "Alex, stop!"

Her eyes darted around, taking in the inside of her car. It took her a moment to connect with reality, that she wasn't in the middle of the ocean. That she was safe on land.

She hadn't had a dream about Alex in ages. Rubbing her chest, she tried to settle the deep hurt that his lack of existence always caused. She had grown so excited for him and thought that maybe things with Amani were about to turn around. But everything had slipped through her fingers.

Her eyes burned as she focused on the roof of her car, staring at the beige upholstery. That life was gone. Upset, she wiped her eyes, hoping the tears would stop soon. She didn't need Kahli seeing her crying whenever she reemerged from Mira's rental. *If she ever did...*

It took a long time, but eventually, Kahli materialized in the front window and then again when she was walking toward her across the front lawn. The sky was starting to fill with a light-peach color as day erased night.

When she made it to the car, she waved Mira out, voice muffled by the window. "It's all clear. I think smoking made me a bit paranoid." The raven-haired woman shrugged. Kahli's body looked tired, her eyes less vibrant than all the times Mira had seen them before. She had put on one of Mira's jackets and pulled at the ends of the sleeves with her hands. Despite the younger woman being alive and well, Mira didn't disengage her locks. She needed answers first.

"What the hell was all of that about?" Her voice was hard. The night had taken a turn, and she wasn't about to give up her safe location without more proof that things were taken care of... and what exactly those *things* were.

Kahli rolled her eyes. "If I wanted to kill you, or get you killed, I've already had plenty of opportunities. Your house is safe by the way. You must have seen the moon reflecting off the water or something." She shrugged, absently wiping at a small smear of blue near her lips. "It wouldn't be the first time the dark played tricks on us."

Was she calling Mira crazy? She wanted to call her out on her bullshit, tell her she knew what she saw, but kept her thoughts to herself, for now. Something wasn't adding up.

Kahli's dark eyes drifted back to the home. "I added some... protection measures for you. It's not a big deal. Just in case."

Mira raised her eyebrows. "Protection?" Had she booby trapped the house?

Avoiding eye contact, Kahli shrugged. "Like from nonhuman things. Don't read too much into it, I'm a bit superstitious. The locks are all working by the way, yes even the back door that you swear I left open. I didn't this time, in case you were wondering. The house lights work. I checked that everything is in order."

Still unsure if she wanted to open the door, Mira shakily disengaged the locks. She knew she was tired... but something felt off. "I still don't understand."

Kahli opened the door for her, placing her forearm on the frame as Mira leaned away in her seat. "You're fine. I'm sorry. I freaked out when you said you thought you saw a light moving through the house. You do live all the way out here on your own, and while it's fairly safe... things could happen once you've drawn attention to yourself. I'm only... keeping an eye out."

Her paranoia refused to subside. Mira let her fingers fiddle with her keys that still sat in the ignition, particularly her charm. "Why... is my back door constantly open?" Her eyes lifted to Kahli as if she expected a real answer. Maybe even for the woman to help her fears disappear.

Kahli's face hardened. "Because you're forgetful." She straightened and tried to shut down the topic. "I *possibly* left your door open one time, that doesn't mean that every time *you* do that it's my fault."

Mira huffed. She had experienced plenty of gaslighting in her life to know when it was being used against her. "I'm not that bad."

The other woman pinched her nose, visibly trying to keep herself in check. "Look. It was a long night. You need to eat and sleep. Just... go inside."

Gripping the steering wheel to anchor herself, Mira shook her head. "I need to text someone first. You're right, I *am* out here all alone, and I don't really know you."

Kahli's gaze held hers and she nodded. "Alright. Fine."

Still apprehensive, Mira continued watching Kahli as she blindly reached for her phone in her lap. She quickly glanced down to a text chain that had too many missed messages and she hit call, not wanting to keep her eyes off Kahli until someone knew where she was. It only rang twice.

"Mira! Where the hell are you?" Wendy's frantic voice crackled to life. The service was a bit spotty but she could hear her well enough.

Mira opened her mouth but when she realized she didn't have a good enough answer, she closed it slowly, sighing. She kept her eyes on Kahli and tried again. "I... met someone."

Sticking with some version of the truth was always easier when it came to Wendy. After all these years, she could spot practically every lie that Mira might try to fabricate.

"Fuck, Hansen. You couldn't have, maybe, let one of us know?"

Mira's hand gripped her phone harder as her gaze drifted to her lap. "I don't owe you my whereabouts, Wendolyn..." She swallowed down the bile in her throat at the guilt that appeared from causing Wendy to worry. She had always been too good to Mira, and Mira wasn't always grateful for her efforts.

A disbelieving laugh cackled down the line. "Your wife disappeared after your miscarriage... *we* are what you have left, Mir. Me, Allie, and even Lydia do give a shit about you, you know. If something happened to you, we wouldn't be okay. We care if you get kidnapped... or if you decide to unsubscribe from life..."

Mira bit her lip because of course Wendy had noticed and was finally ready to call her out on it. "Wendy, no one is going to go through the hassle of kidnapping me..." She heard Wendy's feral groan as she tried to rein in her temper. "I'm not that special!" Her eyes lifted to Kahli's when she scoffed. Mira watched as dark honey eyes turned molten for a second, the color unnaturally swirling lighter. Her brain tried to replay what she saw, momentarily distracted until Wendy spoke.

"Enough of this, where are you? I'm coming to get you."

Mira cleared her throat. "I have the beach house for another two weeks. I'm fine... you can come the last weekend I'm here. We'll... make a thing of it, I guess. Kahli checks on me plenty to make sure I am still breathing, so there's no need..."

She knew she had fucked up when it went too quiet for a moment. Wendy latched onto the new piece of information. "Kahli? That's this chick's name? Why did she need to get you all the way out to some abandoned beach house? It's fricken January!"

Mira snorted. "I went on my own, thank you very much. We met when she..." Her mind drifted to the night and she made sure to stop herself before giving too many details. "When she stopped my drunk ass from drowning in the ocean. I'm very safe here, for your information. I have a personal body guard who lives a few houses down..." She realized, in that moment, that she actually had no idea where Kahli lived, but it must have been on the beach. Why else would she be passing by Mira's day and night? Her body tingled with another warning when she was derailed by Wendy's sigh.

"Give me your location and we'll be there in two weeks. I swear to god, Mira, your ass better be breathing when we arrive."

Relaxing, her body slumped in her seat. "Yeah… I'll be here. I'm just… taking some time away. I'm… sorry I didn't tell you. I'm…" She felt a rare surge of honesty flow through her and the truth came tumbling out. "I've been struggling." She lifted her fingers to pinch her lip as she had a rush of embarrassment at being such a burden to her friend.

"Yeah, no shit. You should have come over instead of running off alone."

Mira chewed on her lip. "You have Allie now… it's not really appropriate for me to show up and stay the night…"

Wendy grumbled. "Having a wife doesn't mean I would kick my wayward *child* to the curb. You matter, you freak. And you know better, you can always come to ours." She huffed. "Can she hear me, this *Kahli*?"

Mira's eyes lifted to the raven-haired woman still watching her. "Yeah, she can hear you. She's here."

"Kahli, if she's not in one piece, I'll slit your throat."

Kahli finally cracked a smile and let out a small laugh, the tension of the night finally fading away. "Noted."

Wendy huffed. "Well... I have to go now that I know you're alright. Just... don't spend too much time alone, okay? I know how you can get."

Mira nodded though her friend couldn't see her. "I'll text you the address."

"You better. Or I'll file a missing person's report. Get your shit together, Hansen." Wendy ended the call, and Mira went back to her messages to send the address. She was finally able to breathe again knowing that someone would go looking for her if she disappeared from the face of the earth.

Kahli took a step back and extended her hand. "We got pretty trashed last night, I was a bit... overly cautious. I'm sorry I overreacted." She kept her eyes away from Mira's as she helped her from the car. "There was nothing in your house. Seriously." Mira watched how her face matched her words. She must have been telling the truth.

Mira took Kahli's hand and held it until they got to the front door, dropping it in embarrassment when she noticed the contact. She really needed to get some sleep. Before crossing the threshold into the home, her eyes noted dark blue markings that now surrounded her doorframe. She lifted her fingers to press them to her eyes, wondering how she was going to explain this "upgrade" to the owners, when she caught smudges of blue on her hands as well.

Just inside, Kahli had paused, waiting. "Mira?"

Her gaze was glued to the sticky residue on her hands, fingers testing the consistency. The dark blue looked like thick ink. "Paint?"

Kahli leaned against the wall. "Just a little. I drew protection runes... just a few, just in case. I'm... weird. It'll be easy to clean when you leave. I'll take care of it."

Mira wrinkled her nose as she crossed the threshold. "Where did you find paint?" She hadn't seen any paint cans lying around.

A moment passed before Kahli lifted a finger, pointing to the side. "There was some in the garage. It's not that bad, it's just some minor art." She placed her hands in her basketball shorts' pockets, looking a bit paler than Mira remembered her being. She swayed slightly. "It's... not a big deal."

Light hit the corner of the window and a chip in the glass she hadn't noticed before fragmented the light so that it split in different directions. One of the rays cast light onto a crystal vase with a variety of rainbow colors, creating its own rainbow. Mira watched as it cast a glow across Kahli's face, the other woman fully unaware of why she was staring. Kahli's cheeks started to grow pink.

"I should... head out." She moved toward the door as Mira felt herself moving closer, noticing her less-than-stable movements. What if Kahli passed out on the way home and hurt herself?

"Wait."

Kahli paused but didn't look at her. "Did you need something?"

Mira crossed her arms and looked around the room. "Why don't you stay? You were up all night and it... seems like it's quite the walk back to your place." Mira started toward the kitchen. "I was going to make some coffee, do you want some?"

She left Kahli standing in the middle of the foyer, staring after Mira as she brushed past. "Do you have any tea?" Her legs took her a few steps closer to Mira but she kept her distance.

"There was some in the cabinet, but it'll be a gamble." She smiled. "But I would venture to guess that you like that?"

Kahli nodded as she leaned her body heavily against the counter. "You sure you're alright with me crashing on your couch for a bit?"

Mira didn't turn to see the confusion she was sure she would find in Kahli's honey eyes. "Just sit down and relax."

Her hands busied themselves, putting the kettle on and preparing her instant coffee and a tea bag.

When the silence became uncomfortable, Mira tossed a question at Kahli. "So, where do you live anyway?" Mira pulled out the sugar and two spoons when the water finished boiling, her eyes shutting briefly as she had forgotten about the squeaking cabinets.

Kahli had moved to the couch and sat facing away from her, braiding her black hair. "Down the beach... and you're right, it is a little far, but I spend a lot of time going up and down the coast." She shrugged before her hands started to tap on her legs.

Mira watched the nervous fidgeting. So far, Kahli had seemed confident and outgoing; she wondered what was causing the change.

She wandered over to hand Kahli her mug of tea, then sat a cushion away and turned on the TV. Mira went through the app menu until she landed on a show she had been somewhat watching when she was less depressed. She smirked when she noticed Kahli instantly invested in what was on the screen, the mug she was holding paused halfway to her lips.

"The show's not *that* good. I've restarted it like five times, so I would know." Mira shook her head.

Kahli slightly turned her head, but her eyes remained on the TV.

Leaning back against the arm of the couch, Mira took a sip of her drink, getting comfortable. "I like thrillers, it gets me out of my head sometimes. This one has a decent number of plot twists to keep it interesting."

Kahli tilted her head, pointing at the girl on screen after a moment. "I think that girl is most certainly going to die. She's not even checking for the signs."

Mira turned her gaze back on her guest with renewed interest. "What signs?"

Kahli finally turned to her, her eyes practically glowing in the morning light. "For one, please, that person is so *vague*. All the information she gives the main character so far is *pointless*. And she just... smiles when she doesn't know what is going on."

Smirking, Mira pointed out Kahli's own fatal flaws. "You also like to give me vague answers to things."

Kahli looked away, her fingers tracing the mug. "It's not like you give me much information either, and I *have* been friendly." She pouted.

Mira snorted and Kahli jumped at the sound. "That was *friendly*? You've been stalking me and flirting nonstop."

"Yeah, friendly. You must like it, why else would you keep talking to me?"

Mira rolled her eyes as she scooted down a bit onto her back, the throbbing from remaining upright too long making itself known. She hissed at the pain before she continued. "Please, all that flirting is an empty promise. You haven't even made a move on me yet. So." Her eyes lifted to lock onto Kahli's, face softening slightly. "Who hurt you? Did she look like me or are you just too nervous I'll turn you down?" She raised an eyebrow, tilting her head to the side. "I can tell you like me." She heard the words leave her mouth and even she was impressed with how bold she sounded.

Kahli set her untouched drink down on a coaster, scoffing at Mira. "I could ask you the same thing." She clasped her hands in her lap and shrugged.

How classic for two women to wait for the other to make the first move. Mira contemplated not answering her, but she figured this was all temporary anyway. After this vacation, she was never going to see this person again. Maybe her friends would get her to a better therapist and she would get some real help coping with more than just the *idea* of her childhood trauma. Not that she had remotely begun to deal with that yet...

Mira pushed her feet against Kahli to encourage her to scoot back slightly. "Who hurt me? Most recently? My wife, actually."

Kahli's hand reached out for Mira's foot and at first Mira panicked that Kahli wanted to restrain her.

She quickly let out a full-bodied groan when Kahli started to massage the tight muscles in her arch, her head tipping back. "Fuck, your hands are amazing. *Shit.*"

Chuckling, Kahli continued to work out the knots. "Oh, you have no idea what these hands can do."

Mira relaxed more and more into her touch. "You would make a great serial killer, you know? Everything about you is disarming. I didn't even want to talk to you the first time I saw you and somehow..."

Kahli's voice dipped low as she emitted a huff. "You were less than coherent, you also called me ugly…"

Suddenly struggling to stay awake, Mira forced her eyes to stay open, but just barely. "You're lucky I am too tired right now or I would kick you for making fun of me. Don't be mean. That was a long night. Also… I wasn't sober, as you have reminded me. I'm not responsible for what I said." She knew that was a lie.

Kahli leaned back against the couch, seeming to accept the invitation to stay. "I thought you were beautiful when I met you." Kahli got quiet before she switched topics. "You said you have a wife? Where is she now?" It was uttered carefully, as if Mira might explode at the mention of the woman. And Mira couldn't blame her for her hesitation. She really hadn't shared anything surrounding her wife or her disappearance.

"Who knows. Who cares? She hates me. I wouldn't be surprised if she dipped just to get back at me…"

Mira's lungs constricted as she inched closer to things she didn't really want to delve into, but if she was never going to see Kahli again… what was the harm?

"We were trying to have kids… it didn't work out. I have… a hostile womb, and Amani… She had a unicorn-shaped uterus or something. Neither were working out well for us, so we went looking into what was wrong. She didn't like the answers and somehow it was all my fault. I'm better off without her, honestly." She wished she actually believed that. She knew better, but sometimes she didn't remember that it was better to be alone than with the wrong person. She had been alone a lot in her life and she had never done well with the silence.

Kahli sighed, pausing her massage. "That's stupid, it's not your fault."

Mira moved her foot a little to indicate that Kahli continue, and the massage started up again. "My mom hated that I married a woman, told me I was going to hell. Too bad I already live there…"

Kahli's fingers dug deeper and Mira whimpered. "Sorry. Why—Why would you say that?"

Mira felt her body grow limp, the adrenaline of the night wearing off. "Mental health, with like," she paused to lift a finger and twirl it in the air, "everything." Her hand dropped back to the couch. "Life's been hard. I mean… I have Wendy, but… she just feels bad for me. You probably do, too."

Her mind drifted to a time Wendy had found her in her mother's house, bleeding in her upstairs bathroom. She always wondered what divine intervention had occurred that day to have caused Wendy to come looking for her. Mira had married Ralph to stay close to his mother, but Lea had moved on to a younger woman, no longer distracting Mira from the smelly, boring, man. She had wanted to spite her own mother, so when she found that Evangeline was not home that day, Mira decided to end her existence, leaving her body for Evangeline to find.

She had filled the tub to the brim with hot water. She slit her wrists, wincing at the sharp sting. Her eyes watched the blood as it trickled down her arm and dripped into the clear water in the tub. She sat down on the floor and leaned over, shoving her wrist to the bottom of the porcelain basin, hoping she wouldn't slip to the ground when she passed out from blood loss and end the bloodletting. She briefly considered if she should just get in the tub fully clothed, if that would be the key to succeeding in her quest.

Wendy happened to be driving by on a rare weekend home and had seen Mira's car in her mother's driveway and knew something wasn't right. Mira would never choose to willingly see Evangeline. She hadn't even knocked before bursting into the home. Wendy must have remembered that Evangeline didn't believe in engaging the locks because *God was watching over her.* Her. *Not Mira.*

When Wendy found her, she had been out of it and had indeed slumped to the floor. Wendy staunched the bleeding and forwent a call to 911 as she dragged Mira's ass to the hospital herself. She had stayed with her until she was released, missing work, needing to take leave as she convinced Mira to move with her to the city.

Kahli started to run her nails up and down the top of Mira's foot as she came back to herself. "I don't... I don't feel bad for you."

That didn't feel like the whole truth.

Mira twitched as she tried to fight off sleep. "Maybe that's because you don't know me very well..."

"I may be starting to." Kahli shrugged.

For a moment, it seemed like her eyes would stayed glued to their task, but they drifted up to hold Mira's. And though it felt intense, Mira didn't look away. Kahli seemed to be conveying so much with her gaze, as if she was promising not to judge her or hurt her. And maybe Mira was starting to believe her.

# Chapter 9

When Mira woke up, the shower was running. She lifted her head to look around. It took her a while to gather her surroundings before she remembered that she had been up all night and had fallen asleep alongside Kahli.

She yawned, recalling how she had started to open up to the stranger in her home. She sighed. There was a beautiful woman nearby who was obviously interested in her and kept coming back. She should take advantage of that while it lasted, even if the thought of making the first move seemed like it might give her a heart attack. It had been a while since she had been with a woman, or had any sort of feelings stirring inside of her, and she was finding that the more time she spent around *crazy swimmer girl*, the more she started to feel... *things*. Like missing the feeling of a woman's hands on her body.

Mira stood carefully as she rubbed her eyes and wandered over to the bathroom. She poked her head in and found Kahli humming to herself. While she wanted to listen to the singing, Mira decided it would be a better idea to announce herself. "C-Can I join you?" She gripped the door, waiting to see if she was going to be told to get out, cursing the fact that she stumbled over her words. The humming stopped but Kahli's voice floated to her gently.

"Come on in, the water is much warmer in here. I think you'll like it." Her voice was light and teasing, poking fun at the fact that Mira had yet to join her in the cold ocean.

Mira smiled as she closed the door behind her softly and forced her fingers to find the end of her top. Her fingers scrunched into the fabric as she took a breath, starting to overthink her actions. Would Kahli like what she saw? Would she be able to distract her long enough from things she didn't want her to see? She started to panic that maybe she was taking too long, which made her rip off her shirt and throw it over her head before pushing her pants and underwear from her hips. She hurried to move the curtain aside as she stepped one foot into the shower. Her mind buffered as she took in the parts of her she hadn't had a glimpse of before, eyes sweeping over Kahli's body as the other woman stood with her back against the far wall. Toned and tanned and glistening under the spray. Her breasts were proudly on display as she arched her back slightly. Mira wasn't sure what she had expected. But it was as if Kahli had been waiting for her, not showering at all. There was no scent of soap in the air, nor hint of it on her body.

Kahli's eyes flashed as she smirked at Mira checking her out, her tone full of mock innocence. "Did you need something?"

Her smile told Mira all she needed to know, that this was exactly what Kahli had planned when she left for the bathroom. Mira took no time at all to fall for her trap. She felt her body heat up as Kahli's eyes started their slow sweep over her. Before her gaze could linger too long, Mira stepped into her and tilted her head up for a kiss. Kahli let their bodies connect without protest, moving her hands to lightly rest on Mira's hips as she drew her in. Mira's mind went fuzzy, as if she was high. Thoughts flew from her head as her only intention was to feel her companion all over her. She kissed Kahli slowly, biting her lip before tugging. The responding groan had her smirking before she leaned in and swept over the other woman's bottom lip with her tongue. Kahli's mouth parted just enough for Mira to get in as a soft whimper escaped.

Mira's hands drifted from Kahli's face to her breasts, squeezing lightly before Kahli's head thudded back against the shower wall. Hard enough that Mira nearly paused to ask if she were okay, but the grip tightening on her hips spurred her on. She dipped her head to suck on Kahli's throat, just making contact with her tan skin when the doorbell rang, interrupting the spell between them. She froze. The sounds of the shower, of Kahli's breathing, started to drift back in. Mira leaned back and turned her head toward the bathroom door.

"What the hell?" No one knew her here, and Wendy was the only person she gave her location to. She was sure she had been convincing enough on the phone not to warrant an emergency visit. At least... she thought she had been.

Kahli's hand threaded into her hair on the side of her head. "Ignore it." She pulled Mira back to her and used her other hand to bring Mira's hips flush against her own. The kiss resumed until the doorbell sounded again, and kept going.

Mira took a step back out of Kahli's hold, her voice breathless. "I should at least see who it is."

She squeezed Kahli's side as she turned to exit the shower.

Kahli looked back at her with wide eyes, as if Mira choosing to leave her alone was unfathomable.

Mira lifted a hand to indicate she should stay. "Stay warm. And don't pout—I'll be right back." She smiled as she quickly toweled herself off and threw on her robe, heading for the door. She hoped she could deal with this quickly and get back before her nerves, or Kahli's, got the better of them. She really could use the endorphins.

As she padded through the hall, she saw a Wendy-colored outline through the distorted glass in the door, complete with the shaved head look she had rocked since their early twenties. She rolled her eyes and yanked it open, no greeting, just a wide-eyed stare. At first Wendy jumped, which made Mira's enjoyment of the situation improve, but then the woman pushed past her and entered her temporary home. Mira's mouth dropped open.

"Okay. Rude."

"You didn't think I was going to not check up on you for two weeks, did you?" She eyed the space, noting that Mira's suitcase still lay spread open on the living room floor. Her eyes took in the pile of medicine bottles as well as the large vibrator. "Good to know you've created your own wellness retreat…"

Mira closed the door and grabbed her friend's arm in frustration. "Wendolyn, you've gotta go. I have a friend over…"

Wendy didn't budge as she narrowed her gaze. "I'm your only friend… you still call Allie and Lydia *acquaintances*." She used her fingers to aggressively air quote the last word.

Mira's gaze shot toward the bathroom door anxiously. "Okay, since when did I ever cave that *we* are actually friends?"

Wendy snatched her arm away. "I'm going to ignore that comment." Her eyes drifted back over to the medicine bottles, eyeing them suspiciously. "Are you supposed to have that many medications?"

Mira crossed her arms and bounced on her feet, shrugging. "Who knows." She walked over and used her foot to close the suitcase. "Wendy, seriously, I have someone over and—" Just as she was about to finish her sentence, Kahli appeared, wrapped in a towel.

Entering the living room, she paused, her eyes going back and forth between Mira and Wendy before breaking the oppressive silence. "Is this your wife?"

Wendy's eyes widened in alarm. "Excuse me?" Two sets of brown eyes looked expectantly at Mira.

Mira turned to Wendy and started to push her toward the door. "No, this is Wendy, and she was just leaving. Out you go, Wendolyn..." She pushed with all her might, but Wendy didn't have to try very hard to thwart her efforts, digging her heels in and addressing Kahli.

"How long have you known Mira? She didn't tell us that she was seeing someone... until this morning." Her gaze fell back on her friend. "What *was* with that call? You never wake up that early..."

Kahli shrugged as she looked away. "We met on her first night here. Down on the beach."

Wendy turned and tilted her head at Mira. "Interesting." Wendy grabbed Mira and dragged her off to the kitchen, throwing a fake smile at the dark-haired woman in the hall. "Could you excuse us for just a moment?"

Mira grunted as she was moved.

Wendy's voice dropped to a hushed whisper, speaking quickly. "Okay, psycho, are you trying to get murdered? You brought home a hookup to your remote-beach depression getaway?"

Pouting, Mira's eyes darted toward Kahli and then back. "What's so wrong with a little fun?"

Immediately, Wendy started to number things off on her fingers. "One, have you seen her eyes? I've never seen an eye color like that before. It's... eerie. It's dark one moment and then it's like catching light the next. How is it doing that? Two, where the hell did you find her? The woods? She is creepy... and she's way too still."

Mira rolled her eyes as if to mock the stupid suggestion before offering up the even more unreasonable truth. "I found her in the ocean."

Wendy opened her mouth to laugh but shut it quickly when Mira didn't look like she was joking. "You're serious?"

Mira nodded. "I was drunk off my ass, and she stopped me from going in the water. She was... already out there."

Wendy raised an eyebrow. "Why was she swimming in the water at this time of year?"

Tilting her head, Mira smiled at Kahli, who was still hovering in the hall. "I don't know, Wendy, why don't you go ask her yourself. She is *right there*."

Wendy closed her eyes before looking back at her friend. "Answer me this: were you or were you not out here to do something stupid?"

Mira snorted. "Does it matter? I'm fine, and she's distracting me. I told you I would be good. Can I get back to my fun now? People who have fun don't kill themselves." She went to walk by Wendy, who grabbed her arm.

"Mira, that's not even remotely funny." Wendy stepped in front of her friend and walked over to Kahli, extending her hand. "Wendolyn Richards. I work with serums. I have an apothecary. Witchy stuff."

Kahli's hands gripped her towel tighter, avoiding the touch. "I'm Kahli... Delmar. I, uhm, work with the ocean. Marine studies." She took a step back. "I should go get dressed." She quickly turned to escape.

Wendy stomped back over to Mira, pointing a finger in her face. "I want you to check in every day. You hear me? I don't care when, but I need a call, or I come back *here*." She threw her pointing finger forcefully toward the ground, indicating exactly where they stood.

Mira grunted as she responded. "Fine, will you leave me alone now, *Mom*? I'll make sure to use protection."

Wendy huffed as she threw her hands in the air. "For now. Do you realize how far I had to drive to get here? I used almost a whole tank of gas."

Mira followed her to the door. "I didn't ask you to come." Wendy turned and stopped her in her tracks with a look that went straight to her gut.

"You didn't have to. I..." She took a breath and cleared her throat. "I promised you the day you ran away from Evangeline's that you weren't alone. I meant *ever*. Just... be careful with that girl. Also... give her my number. I don't trust you."

Mira saluted as her face scrunched into mock seriousness. "Yes, Officer." Her eyes went wide when Wendy surprised her and pulled her into a firm hug. She could count on one hand the number of times they had ever hugged. Wendy wasn't a big hugger. Allie was changing her.

"I love you, you absolute psychopath."

Mira felt her throat close with emotion and all she could think of to get Wendy off her was to pat her back quickly, which seemed to do the job.

"And if the condom breaks—name it after me." Wendy turned and headed out.

Mira rolled her eyes fondly as she moved to lock up. When she turned around, she jumped at Kahli standing right beside her. "Shit. How long were you standing there?"

Kahli shrugged. "Are you getting back in or..." She angled her body as if she were about to return to the bathroom.

Mira chewed at her lip. Wendy had the unfortunate ability to always make her at least think through her impulses. As she gazed at Kahli, she felt the pull to drag her back into the shower and finish what they had started. But with Wendy putting thoughts in her head, she wondered if that was such a good idea anymore. She wanted to kick herself.

"I should... probably lay back down. Headache." She bit her lip as she waited to see how Kahli handled rejection. Maybe she would light her car on fire on her way out... good thing there was an ocean behind the house.

Kahli's shoulders tightened. "Right." She disappeared and returned with her raven hair combed flat back against her head. "I should head out."

"You... have plans for the rest of the day?"

Kahli shook her head, mildly irritated. "No, not really."

Mira's tired eyes trailed back to the couch, pausing there. As if she had gotten ensnared by the object and it was doing something far more interesting than just being a couch. She had slept so well with Kahli beside her.

The other woman called out a few times, and when Mira didn't respond, Kahli tapped her fingertips to Mira's elbow. "Hey."

Mira shook her head as if she were waking up from a dream. "Sorry." She lifted her hand and rubbed the back of her neck. She felt Kahli's eyes as they roamed all over her face.

"Did you want me to stay for a bit?"

Mira shifted uncomfortably. "I won't be much fun if I'm asleep."

Kahli wrapped her fingers around her arm. "You were fine before. I don't mind... the couch was a little small, and you like to spread out... if you want me to stay, perhaps the bed?"

Mira felt her blood rush. "That's..." She chewed on her lip while she indicated the stairs. *So much for slowing things down.*

Kahli nodded and walked by Mira to head upstairs. Mira was left staring long after she had disappeared from sight. She hadn't wanted her to leave, but she wasn't about to ask her to stay. Asking for things was how she got labeled things like clingy, needy, even *desperate*, by her wife. She wondered if she fell asleep on the couch if Kahli would leave on her own. But she was a bit curious about sharing a bed, if more might happen once they were that close again. Her logical brain was at war with her crotch as she blew out a breath. Then, her mind provided some very enticing images of what Kahli might be capable of doing in bed. She tried to shove her anxiety down as she took the stairs. Reminding herself that none of this was that serious, and she could just go home at any time.

When she entered the bedroom, she saw Kahli's reflection across the space in the mirror. Cursing out loud, she stumbled back into the nightstand, hip harshly colliding with the wood. Her eyes darted to the actual woman, who had been turning the covers down and was now looking up at her with concern.

"You good?"

Mira wasn't sure what she thought she saw, but she knew her heart had felt like it was about to burst a moment ago, as if she had seen something terrifying. Clearly, she needed sleep. She shook her head and waved the other woman off as she climbed in, her heart still racing. Scooting down, she tried to settle in for the weirdest interaction she had had in a long time: soberly, platonically, sharing a bed.

She turned away from Kahli, facing the wall, and gripped her pillow between her hands, palming at it slightly until Kahli slotted in behind her. They were both quiet for a moment when Kahli shifted a bit, the bed creaking beneath her movement.

"Did you want me to..." Kahli placed her hand lightly on top of her hip and she found herself leaning back into her, her body deciding for her that she desired the comfort of a warm body. A moment later, Kahli's body pressed softly against her.

Mira closed her eyes as her mind drifted to when things had been... well, not good with Amani, but *better*. Had there ever been a time she had felt this safe?

Kahli's voice released a puff of air against the side of her neck as she spoke. "Get some rest."

With the way their bodies were intertwined, Mira was sure that was not about to happen. But when the room began blurring out of focus and her thoughts quieted down, she drifted off to sleep.

# Chapter 10

Mira was back at the stupid coffee shop with the upbeat emo kid, and she tried to ignore his little happy wave the moment she walked in. She rolled her eyes as she looked at the menu, debating what Kahli might like. Not that she was going to get her anything. She didn't even know if she would be by today.

When she had woken up from her nap the day before, Kahli was gone and had left a note, with a single purple wildflower. Mira hated how her stupid heart had done somersaults. She didn't need to get attached.

Looking over the menu, Mira could feel the excited energy radiating off the kid when her eyes slowly drifted to his.

"I love your whole look today! You're like... my style icon!"

Mira tensed as she looked down and saw she was wearing a pair of black leggings, with a black racerback tank over a dark purple sports bra. She had let her brunette hair dry naturally after her shower and knew that it had fallen into nice waves, instead of the rats' nest she had come in with last time. Despite attempting to ignore him, she felt her face twitch at the compliment. Her finger pointed up at the board.

"Can I get a…" She shook her head. "I still can't with these names. Just get me a normal coffee and make it sweet. Two, actually." Well, apparently she *was* getting something for Kahli.

The boy nodded. "You got it, two…" He seemed to catch himself before uttering the silly names for the drinks. "Coming right up." He turned the tablet around for her to pay. "That'll be ten fifty."

Mira looked up at him, sure she had heard him wrong. "I said *two* coffees…" She emphasized the number with two fingers to be sure he got it this time.

He shrugged. "I get a friends and family discount. No one else is coming by today, might as well share it with you."

Mira bit her cheek as she tried not to let the kindness affect her—the kid was just overly nice. She tapped her card and tried to offer him a smile. "Thanks." She turned to walk away then closed her eyes, feeling the pull to do something kind in return. She turned back and grabbed her wallet from her pocket and took out a five, handing it over silently to the kid.

The boy looked at her with confusion, his head tilted. "You already paid." He tapped the side of the tablet. "We're all good."

She rolled her eyes. "It's a tip, just pocket it so they don't make you pay some of it to the government."

His little eyes went large. "That's too much. That's nearly a fifty-percent tip."

Mira shook it at him, indicating he should just take it. When he didn't, she grunted and pulled out her wallet once more and slapped three dollars on the table and the kid looked around before he knocked two of the dollars to the floor. Mira watched him as he stooped down and placed them in his pocket.

While he was on the floor, she pushed the last dollar over the edge so it floated down and his curious eyes lifted.

She indicated the bill with a tip of her head. "You forgot one."

He smirked and quickly pocketed it before standing. "Thanks...?" At Mira's blank stare, he tried again. "I'm Benny, and you are?"

Ignoring the obvious attempt to acquire her name, she ignored the kid and walked away.

"Oh, come on! It's clear you're going to be coming by sometimes..."

Mira sat at a table and leaned back against her chair. "I'll let you guess." She smirked.

"Well, my mom's name starts with an M, so I guess that's as good of place as any to start." His eyes flashed as he saw her face tense. "Oh my god, it starts with an M? Yes!"

She swept her hair over her shoulder. "It'll take you a while."

He beamed as he moved to start on the coffees. "Ah, ha! Another clue."

Mira sighed dramatically as she waited, pulling out her phone but feeling more at ease... maybe she was making friends in this weird little town.

She found a text from Wendy demanding a response and she sent a photo of her crotch and hit send.

*Mira: thanks for the block yesterday.*

She smiled ear to ear as she saw Wendy have to start typing multiple times.

*Wendy: I don't want that, I'm a married woman. And please, that girl is so into you. I'm sure you'll get another opportunity.*

Mira looked up when Benny appeared and handed her two to-go cups in a tray, a slight blush covering his face. "I'll see you soon! And uh... good luck!" He winked as he had obviously gotten the wrong idea about her sending a photo to her friend. Though a tad bit embarrassing, she didn't feel the need to correct him as she left the building and walked to her car. The abnormally warm weather seemed to keep her in good spirits on her journey and maybe little Benny had something to do with her good mood continuing.

As she arrived at her vehicle, she dropped her keys and stared at them sadly as she prepared herself to bend down and retrieve them. Her back did not like the couch, and less so the bed, but there wasn't much she could do at this point.

Right as she bent down, a man passing by swiped her keys, dangling them above her with a wide grin. His eyes were strange, almost yellow. A color Mira had never seen before and wasn't even aware a person could possess. It reminded her of Kahli's in direct sunlight, but even more unnatural. On instinct, she shifted back.

"Your keys." He smirked as he extended them out to her.

She reached for them and tried to shrug him off. "Thanks." Mira couldn't avoid the thoughts that slipped across her mind. About how this man looked like exactly the type of man Mira's mother would have wanted her to marry. Tall, cocky... white. She felt her jaw tighten. Her mother was the reason she had wasted so much time with Ralph. Thank gods his mother noticed her eyes lingering, or she might have been trapped with him forever and never gotten the courage to leave.

The stranger tilted his head, taking her in. She hated the feeling of being appraised by a man. No doubt he was sizing her up to see if she was still of childbearing age. Why did so much of their attraction boil down to mating? Mira much preferred being worshiped by a woman.

"No problem, gorgeous. I'm Theo." He added a wink. "I think I've been seeing you around town. You're new, right? I was wondering..."

Mira turned back, pissed. It was clear where this was heading and she wasn't interested. "Your gaydar is shit."

She unlocked her car and got in, slamming the door before he could find a response. As she drove off, she made sure not to look back, to not give him anything. Her mood plummeted. Why couldn't men just be friendly without trying to get into her pants? She had enough of that her whole life and missed wearing her wedding ring, as that would at least deter *some* men. Maybe she needed to start wearing it again...

Pulling up to her place, she took her coffees to the back, deciding to go sit on the beach this morning as there was still some shade from the house. She wasn't out there long when Kahli came jogging by. She wondered how the other woman always had perfect timing.

Kahli plopped down beside her, throwing herself to the ground. She heaved out a few breaths before she sat up. "I started the other way down the beach to make my run longer. Damn, I think I pushed too hard." She smiled, looking up at Mira. "Morning, beautiful."

Mira blushed, noting how different the feeling was when a beautiful woman offered up the compliment. She set the extra cup in the sand beside Kahli's head.

The other woman's smile fell as she pushed up on her elbows to look at the offering. "What's that?"

Mira shrugged. "Coffee."

Kahli tilted her head. "Is it for me?"

Mira nodded but kept her eyes on the water. "Don't make it a thing. I was already in town for some errands and figured you were probably going to stop by and bother me anyway." She caught herself smiling, and instead of kicking herself for the display of emotion, she let it sit.

Kahli sat up all the way, picking up the cup. "Oh... thank... thank you." She held it between her hands as if Mira had given her something special. Her hands lifted the drink after a moment to press it to her lips. She seemed to attempt to fight the cringe that came over her face, not doing a great job of hiding it, and Mira smirked.

"Too bitter for you?"

Kahli bit her lip. "I'm... not much of a coffee person." Mira opened her mouth to apologize, but Kahli quickly took another sip. "But I can make an exception." She grimaced again at the flavor, completely failing at hiding her distaste. "How's your morning so far?"

Mira took a sip of her drink as she contemplated the question. "Well, there's an annoyingly upbeat kid who works at the coffee shop. Have you met him? Apparently, I'm his idol now and he pays for part of my order. Maybe I can get him to give me free coffees before I leave. He... isn't a bad kid, I guess." She picked at the paper wrapper. "Had some guy hit on me on the way back to my car. It just... gets me that some of them think they are gifts to this earth. I swear, he just had to make it weird when he could have just..."

At the mention of the man, Kahli's eyes narrowed. "You're into women, right?"

Mira snorted, looking away for a moment. "Yes, Sherlock. I'm into women." Her eyes swept over Kahli in her outfit, a dark green sports bra and black basketball shorts, which seemed to be a variation of her usual running uniform.

Kahli tried to chug a bit of her coffee and started to cough it up

Mira's hand went to her back instantly. "Woah! You good?"

The woman continued to cough for a moment, her eyes watering until she got it under control. She shook her head. "I might... not handle coffee well..." She offered up a sad smile. "How do you drink this stuff?"

Mira grabbed the cup and moved it away, mentally chastising herself for the poor choice. "I'll get you something else next time. I didn't know."

Kahli's spirits seemed to lift at the idea. "Next time?"

"I mean, if I'm already there. What would you like?"

Kahli shrugged. "Maybe a light tea is more my speed."

Mira scooted a bit closer, needing to know she was alright. "I could go make you some, if you want? It won't take long."

Kahli glanced over at Mira's lips and shook her head, looking away. "I'm alright. I'll run in and grab water if I need something, no need to get up."

Leaning toward her, Mira winced at the sharp pain in her back. She tried to recover from it quickly, but Kahli took note of her quiet gasp.

"You okay?"

Mira tried to wave her off. "It's just some dumb hormonal thing. My body doesn't stretch like it's supposed to. It fucked up my lower back during pregnancy, and I'm told it's just something I have to live with from now on."

She went to crack a joke, but before she could come up with something, Kahli's fingers were digging into her muscles and her eyes closed, breath catching in her throat.

"Oh my god."

Kahli's fingers seemed to home in on exactly where she was feeling the worst of the tension. "This the right spot?"

Mira whimpered as Kahli found a particularly sore knot, but she nodded her head. The younger woman continued to work on it. Mira set her coffee down and pulled her knees to her chest as she lay her head down, trying to relax into the feeling. Amani had never done anything like this for her. Wendy had, on a few occasions after she had bitched and complained for so long that Wendy practically had to wrestle her into submission to work on her knots. She'd claimed that Mira needed to go to a professional as she wasn't going to fight her every time her back hurt. And that she should just have a standing appointment to keep it under control.

"You have kids?" Kahli's voice was labored as she continued her task.

Mira shook her head as she focused on the feeling. "Nah, none of them ever took."

After a while, Kahli spoke softly. "Try and move around a bit. Is that better?"

Sitting up, Mira shifted her hips and twisted her back. Her body had released some of its tension and the pain was far more tolerable. She blushed as she tried to look back into Kahli's eyes and failed. "Thanks."

Mira's eyes widened when Kahli stood.

"Where... Where are you going?" For a moment, Mira worried that she had done something wrong.

Kahli turned, tilted her head in confusion. "For a swim? I'm sweating."

Mira frowned. Kahli was going to swim in her clothing? What had she been wearing when they met? She tried to remember but really couldn't recall.

"I'll be back..."

Mira grumbled as she crossed her arms, defensively pouting. "Fine. I don't care, do whatever."

"Did you not... want me to go?"

Mira moved to stand, her back feeling fully functional. "I should... check some emails. See if work wants me back sooner."

Kahli took a step toward her in a panic. "You're leaving?"

Mira tilted her head at the frantic look on the younger woman's face. "I'm just going inside. The sun is coming out, and you have your swim to get to. You can come find me after, if you want. And no, I'm not going *home*. Not today."

Kahli dug her toes in the sand. "But you will eventually."

The finality of those words caused a tightness to spread across Mira's chest. She *would* go home eventually. She would leave Kahli behind, back at the beach, and probably never see her again. "I mean... this was just a small trip to unwind."

Kahli mumbled her next words, but Mira made them all out. "That's not what you were here to do."

Feeling a bit exposed, Mira narrowed her gaze and attempted to push back. "Look... I don't know what you're implying—"

Kahli took a step away, cutting her off. "It's fine. I should get to my swim, I'll see you later. Thanks for the drink." She turned and didn't wait for Mira's response as she waded out into the water. Disappearing quickly, she stayed under for far longer than Mira was comfortable with before finally reappearing a ways down and continuing along the surface.

Mira hated to admit it, but maybe she was having second thoughts about leaving and never seeing the other woman again. But Kahli didn't need to know that yet. Not while Mira was still making up her mind.

# Chapter 11

Mira had waited for Kahli that night. She had made tea in the evening for both of them and wandered outside to wait on the cold beach as she listened to the waves and looked up at the stars. But for the first time, Kahli didn't show. She looked to the water every time she thought she heard something, but it was never more than a fish jumping or a bird diving to catch its prey.

She tried again the next morning, even sat out in the sun for a bit so she wouldn't miss Kahli when she ran by, but she never came. Mira felt her mood fall. Kahli must have realized there was a time limit on whatever they were doing and decided to end things.

Tapping at her phone, she paced the living room before she called Wendy, feeling the need for someone to guide her. Wendy picked up on the first ring.

"She eat your soul yet?"

Mira snorted as she wandered around. "Very funny. No, she... might have dumped me, actually." Her fingers pressed at her forehead which had started to throb.

"Did you forget to go down on her?"

Snorting louder, Mira wished Wendy was there in person so she could shove her. "*What*? No... well *yes*... but I thought I had more time." She heard her friend hum.

"So, she was only in it for the sex. I'm sorry, but maybe she wasn't right for you right now."

Mira twirled a lock of her brunette hair with a single finger, needing to do something with her hands. "I brought up going home soon and she... withdrew." She ran her hand through her hair. "I think she likes me? I don't know." She shrugged. "Doesn't matter." She flicked her hand at the window. "Now she's gone."

"Mira... if you like her, just tell her. Invite her over and actually bang her brains out. Show her what she's missing. From the reviews in college, you give pretty good head."

Mira smirked. "It's a gift. And I would, but... she's now disappeared, so..."

"What do you mean *disappeared*? Like actually, like Amani? Or you haven't seen her in five minutes?"

"I'm not *that* desperate... I haven't seen her since yesterday morning." She played with her lip as she waited for Wendy to either tease her or help her down off the ledge she was teetering toward.

"Honestly, I'm glad to hear you're worried, it's been a moment since you even wanted to look at another woman. Amani did a number on you... How is the missing woman? Any word?"

Mira's stomach soured at the mention of the redhead that haunted her nightmares. "No... she's still..." She made a *woosh* sound, like the woman had disappeared without a trace. She practically had.

"You don't need her. Plus, if she never shows up, that's an easy divorce. Just have her pronounced dead. Get a little revenge. And maybe... continue to date the creepy swimmer chick. I assume she has a car if she lives all the way out by the beach."

Mira sat down on the back of the couch. "I mean... it's not like it would go anywhere..."

Wendy was quick to jump in. "Oh my god, Mira! Just ask her. All she can do is turn you down, and then you come home anyway."

Mira's eyes lifted to the front door and she dropped her phone. Someone was trying to peer inside. Someone who was most certainly *not* Kahli.

She scrambled down to pick up the phone. Keeping Wendy tight to her ear, her voice went quiet. "Someone's at my door."

"Well, is it *her*?"

Mira gripped the couch, hiding behind it, keeping her voice low. "Definitely not her. What the fuck. Kahli told me no one lives out here year round but her..." She stared over the edge of the furniture and heard the fucker start *whistling*. She heard Wendy sigh.

"Mir, it's probably just a neighbor wanting to be too friendly or maybe like the mail person. Just go tell them to go away, be your charming self, and I'm sure they'll never speak to you again."

"You're staying on the phone... I am not getting murdered today..." As she stood, she heard Wendy mock her over the phone.

"Unless it's by a hot swimmer girl..."

Mira rolled her eyes. She ripped open the door, recognizing the man from town, Theo. Her eyes narrowed as she stared him down. "What?" she snapped.

"Oh, hey there. Funny running into you. I live down the street. What a coincidence! Just wanted to introduce myself in case you ever need anything. I'm the second house after the bend. I was just taking a walk and saw your car. Figured you had just moved in. I know we got off to a bit of a rough start in town, but I just wanted to say, *Welcome to the neighborhood!*" He smiled, his creepy golden eyes maintaining eye contact. Mira still wasn't having it.

"Great." She went to close the door, and he jumped in once more.

"If you ever want to go for a coffee..."

Mira turned and deadpanned. "I'm married."

Theo rolled his eyes good-naturedly. "You could just say no if you're not interested..."

Mira glared. "I am legally married. To a woman. Have a nice day." She turned and shut the door with a bit of force this time.

She heard him scoff as he started to walk away, muttering to himself, "Bitch."

Wendy snorted down the line. "Nice job. I bet he moves on after that."

Mira walked over to the back door and stepped outside. "I hope so." Her eyes subconsciously looked for Kahli. "I should have asked where exactly she lives..."

Wendy snorted. "Oh, Mir, it's good to keep you humble. She'll be back, give her time. I can't imagine why, but she likes you."

≈ ≈ ≈

Mira opened her emails on her phone in the bedroom and started to work through them. She was lucky that her boss was her friend or she would have been fired a long time ago. Mira smiled as she read the incoming text message.

*Lydia C: Wendy tells me you've run away with a new woman. Good for you, it's about time.*

Mira shook her head. Lydia had been the first to make things casual in their relationship, no matter how hard Mira fought to keep things professional. Wendy had helped her get the job in the first place, since Lydia was her godmother.

*Mira: It's not like that. Wendy exaggerates.*

The older woman was typing again, but Mira's eyes lifted as she heard her porch creak. She moved to look out the window, and there stood Kahli, hovering by her back door. Mira moved quickly, not wanting Kahli to decide to leave before she even knocked. By the time she got to the back door, Kahli was wandering away. She struggled with the lock for a moment but made it out, shouting after her.

"Wait!"

Kahli spun around so quickly that it was a miracle she didn't stumble down the steps. She looked at Mira then back at the house. "Were you... waiting for me?"

"Do you want to come in?" Mira crossed her arms. There was an extra chill in the air, and though she would stay outside if Kahli refused, she really hoped she wanted to step inside to talk.

Kahli glanced back at the sea. "I should probably..."

Mira advanced and placed her hand lightly on Kahli's arm. Her thumb brushed back and forth, hoping to entice her to stay. "Please?"

Dark eyes shifted in the dim light. Mira saw the moment of contemplation before she gave in. "Okay." Kahli watched as Mira's hand reached for hers and led her inside.

"Thank god, it's freezing outside tonight. So strange, it's been so warm." Once they were safely in the kitchen, Mira turned to her guest. "Where... where did you go?"

Kahli bit her lip as she pondered the question. "I just... needed a moment to myself." She reached in her pocket and pulled out a small, intact, conch shell, with many twists and little horns around the widest part. "I... found this and thought of you." She set it on the counter, and Mira couldn't help her smile. So Kahli wasn't done with her then. That was good.

"It's pretty."

Kahli seemed to like that answer and she opened her mouth to speak. Mira beat her to it.

"It would be fair if I knew where you lived or at least got your number. You know... in case there's an emergency. You're the only person I know here and..."

Kahli stilled. "I... don't have a phone. I live with... family. I can just be good about checking in while you're here."

Mira felt her nerves increase. If she didn't have a phone, did she at least have a computer? Did people out here still communicate via mail? Because there was no way she would be able to settle for once-a-month letters. "What if I wanted to still talk to you, after I go home?" She tried to keep her voice from rising at the end.

Kahli seemed to take the idea into consideration before she nodded slowly. "I... would need to work on figuring that out." She let her finger skim the flecks in the granite countertop. "When do you go home?"

"In two weeks. Well, a little under that now. We still have time to see if you still want to talk to me after."

Kahli nodded. "I'm sure I would want to. I don't often find people that interest me."

Mira leaned back against the counter, feeling at least a bit special. "Is that so?" She raised an eyebrow playfully and watched as Kahli drew closer, hands landing on either side of her hips, trapping her. Nodding, her gaze roamed all over Mira's face.

Kahli's eyes darkened, consumed with mostly black as her pupils dilated, but she waited.

Mira then lifted her hands to thread into her black hair. "Your hair is really soft," she whispered, as if the room was full of people and she only wanted Kahli to hear her being so gentle. Her own eyes focused on Kahli's lips before they lifted slowly. She wanted this, she wanted to kiss her, yet a voice whispered to her to be careful. She wished Kahli could read her thoughts because she needed the younger woman to put them both out of their misery.

Not a moment later, her prayers were answered. Kahli leaned forward, pressing a soft kiss to Mira's lips. Mira's pale fingers anchored in her hair, afraid she was imagining the whole thing. The younger woman's tongue darted out to hesitantly explore her mouth, drawing out a low groan with the way she seemed to know where to press. Mira had never been kissed this carefully before. It was as if Kahli was worried that she might do something she wouldn't like. As if she could shatter her with a kiss. Mira tugged her closer and took control, deepening the kiss and keeping it slow, but she hinted that Kahli could go harder.

Kahli's hips rolled into Mira's on the next swipe of her tongue, boosting her confidence. Mira let her hands take their time as they trailed down Kahli's throat and over her chest, stopping briefly to circle her nipples which were now standing up through her sports bra. She smirked as Kahli's breath hitched audibly. The kiss was momentarily forgotten as Mira inched back, watching her own hands as they trailed lower.

"It's been a while for me..." Mira offered, as some sort of apology. Not that she had ever gotten a complaint in her life, but there was always a first time for everything. Her mouth, at least in the bedroom, was the one thing Amani hadn't complained about.

Kahli's eyes watched Mira's hands, entranced. As if Mira were casting spells across her skin and she was powerless to stop her. Kahli's stomach twitched as pale fingers dipped under the hem of her bra, and she closed her eyes. "Upstairs. Now."

Mira smirked as she let her hands fall away, turning to very slowly approach the stairs.

Growling, Kahli swooped in and wrapped her arms around Mira's torso from behind. She pressed her lips right to the space below Mira's ear, causing her legs to buckle. Mira released a quiet mewling sound at Kahli's voice rough in her ear. "That's not what *now* means, Mira."

Mira gasped as Kahli withdrew her face and supported her to the stairs, throwing a glare over her shoulder. "You're terrible for making me wait."

With Kahli's hand on her back to keep her steady, Mira moved carefully up the stairs. The moment they reached the bedroom, Kahli knocked her back onto the bed. Mira's eyes went wide as she yelped.

Kahli was hovering over her in an instant, kissing at her neck and hooking her fingers in the waistband of her pants. "Can I take these off?"

Mira groaned, her hand scraping at Kahli's scalp. "Do it."

Inch by inch, Kahli slowly eased her pants and underwear down. Once they were off, Kahli's hands grabbed her waist and scooted her down the bed toward the edge. Mira was about to ask what she was doing when she watched Kahli kneel, and the sight almost made her come on the spot. Amani never gave her head, and it was something she missed.

"*Fuck.*"

Kahli laughed as she ran her tongue up Mira's inner thigh, biting firmly just below her sex. Mira whimpered as her hips shifted.

"Kahli..." She was close to begging with the way her crotch began to throb at the sight.

Tan hands spread her legs wider, and Mira sat up on her arms to watch. The first touch of Kahli's tongue had her crying out. Her hand flew to the back of Kahli's head, encouraging her to draw closer. The woman licked her as if ice cream had melted all over her and Mira had told her not to get it on the bed. Which might have been an accurate visual with the way she was already dripping. She rolled her hips and felt as Kahli's fingers joined her tongue, outlining the shape of her, locating her entrance but not going inside yet. As if she first needed to memorize the shape of it.

Mira tried to push her inside, but Kahli caught on and shifted her fingers away. "Not yet." Mira was about to complain when Kahli's tongue flattened and started the agonizing path up her slit. Mira dropped onto her back with a thud, her mouth frozen open before a long, drawn-out groan made it past her lips.

Her eyes scrunched shut as she focused on the feeling, and the obscene sounds of Kahli sucking on her. There were no coherent thoughts in Mira's mind as she tried to ride Kahli's face. The other woman snickered as she sat back, two fingers trailing up and down Mira's wetness.

Mira fought hard to open her eyes, looking for Kahli, who seemed to sense her request that she look at her while she leaned back in and ate her out. Mira whimpered as she took one of Kahli's hands and pressed it to her entrance. "Please… Inside, baby."

Kahli nodded as she moved and used her knee to press harder into Mira, shifting her up the bed. The pressure rocked through Mira as she cried out. Kahli lay her clothed body on top of her as her fingers played with Mira, judging the amount of wetness. "I think you're ready."

Mira pressed her fingers on top of Kahli's and they slid in, her gasp echoing around the room. Her body stretched to accommodate the intrusion.

The rhythm Kahli chose was perfect, pumping in and out of her at a good pace. Not too slow, but not too quickly either, taking her time to stretch her out. Kahli's lips touched Mira's ear as she started to hum, Mira's senses heightening. She felt like her nerves were pulsing, but not in the same way they did when it was caused by her chronic pain. This felt amazing.

Kahli kissed the side of her head as she continued her pace. "You feel so good. Fuck, Mira, you're so beautiful."

Mira felt her hips twitch. *Good?* She wasn't good. She had always wanted to be. She wished it were true as Kahli tipped her face to her. Nothing about her was good. Her mother's voice ringing in her head never let her forget that fact. She was *wicked.*

"Can you come for me? I promise next time I'll stay down there till you come... I just... wanted to see you at least once."

Mira's eyes closed, a groan vibrating in her chest. "Please... please."

She wasn't even sure what she was asking for anymore, but she trusted that Kahli would give it to her anyway. Kahli's weight on her disappeared the next second, and she felt the loss as the cold air swept in. She was about to call her back when she felt Kahli's mouth back on her sex. Mira screamed as Kahli's tongue darted inside of her, thumb circling her clit. Her body arched off the bed, strung out as a high-pitched scream tore through the air, before crashing to the bed, boneless. She tried to push Kahli's head away, but the other woman seemed dedicated to licking up her wetness before it got all over the bed.

Mira's lips twitched up into a smile as she shifted away. "Enough... I'm too sensitive."

Kahli looked up as if she wasn't aware of the concept. Her face was tense. "Did I hurt you? Are you..."

"No... you didn't hurt me... I just... need a moment is all." She took a deep breath and let it out slowly before grabbing Kahli's hair and pulling. "Get up here."

Kahli crawled up her body as Mira's fingers cupped her cheeks and brought her down into a brief kiss.

Mira tasted herself on her lips, before she dropped back to look at her. "Fuck, you're good at that. And I thought I was the queen of the head game."

Kahli's smile grew wide. "I mean... you're welcome to try. After you rest, of course."

"I'm going to have you begging me to come. When I can move."

Tangling her fingers in Kahli's hair, Mira delighted in the little whimpers she pulled out of the younger woman with every tug. As Kahli's eyes started to droop, Mira decided that wouldn't do. She pushed herself to sit up and Kahli's eyes flew open, her body shifting off Mira's. Mira turned and leaned over her, bracketing Kahli's arms beneath her.

"You sure you can handle me?"

Kahli gulped as she nodded hesitantly, her bravado momentarily nowhere to be found. "I... think so."

Mira snorted as she mounted one of Kahli's legs, bending at her elbows to lean in and press her lips beneath Kahli's jaw. Her tongue darted out to trail down her throat. She slid her center against Kahli's leg as she shifted down further, her own strangled groan escaping due to the pressure on her overly sensitive clit. It took her a moment to realize her voice was not alone. So, she liked *that*. Mira leaned in and swirled her tongue around one nipple until it stood tall, her teeth biting down firmly as one of her hands scratched down Kahli's body.

Kahli rolled her hips. "Lower."

Mira slipped two fingers inside her without pretense, parting her fingers into a wide V and feeling her pride surge when Kahli gasped. "You like that, baby?"

She felt Kahli move, and she looked up to see her biting down on her lower lip and nodding. Mira let her two fingers come back together as she slowly traced Kahli on the inside, focusing on which spots made her twitch. She started to slowly rub Kahli's clit with her thumb.

"You know... I'm also good with my mouth." She sighed. "I don't generally jump straight to that though... you must be special. I am a bit curious to see what *you* taste like." She felt the slight vibrations rippling across Kahli's body. Mira's head bowed and she let her tongue replace her thumb, pressing firmly. Kahli's head tipped back as she let out a deep groan. Mira slowly extracted her fingers, making sure Kahli felt every inch of the slow movement. She looked up to see if Kahli was still enjoying herself, a brief moment of anxiety causing her to wonder if maybe she was faking it.

At the lack of stimulus, Kahli started begging. "Please... please don't stop. I... I want to come... you feel so good—"

Her voice cut out as Mira lowered her head and flattened her tongue to her entrance. Kahli screamed.

"Fuck!" Kahli started panting and dripping onto Mira's tongue. Her taste was salty like the ocean and she almost paused to make a joke, but the adrenaline rush from driving Kahli wild was too good to pass up. Mira moved her head at a glacial pace, savoring the moment, loving how Kahli whimpered. But as she continued, she noticed a twinge in her neck. So, despite wanting to draw things out, she moved her fingers back to Kahli's entrance, pushing in, then out, slowly.

She turned her head to the side and bit Kahli's inner thigh and the other woman gasped.

"Please, Mira... harder... please..."

Mira shifted to insert a third finger, hitting Kahli's G-spot. The sound that erupted from the other woman was inhuman. She fell limp a moment later, eyes closed as she tried to breathe.

Satisfied with the way Kahli seemed unable to move for a moment, Mira leaned her head on Kahli's thigh as she also tried to catch her breath. She was beyond tired now. She wished it had been longer, but she figured she could up her game next time. If there was a next time...

A few moments later, Kahli was up again. Mira's face fell as her energy dwindled. She wondered if she would even be able to keep up with her younger lover. She hadn't been too worried about the age gap, but with the way Kahli bounced back, maybe she should be.

Kahli encouraged her to shift to her stomach, and when she did, Kahli's fingers returned to her body, working on her back. "Don't want this to tighten up after all of that. Gotta keep you ready to go again later."

Mira nuzzled down into her pillow, surprised, but not complaining. Kahli's massages were almost as good as sex... almost.

# Chapter 12

Mira thought she would see Kahli when she woke up, but the other woman was once again gone, off to do... whatever it was that she did all day. She had left a note, telling her she had a good time and would see her later. Mira's fingers played with the paper for a long time, pondering if maybe she should ask Kahli to go out with her to the coffee shop next time. Sure, there would be annoying looks from the child who excitedly bounced around every time she entered the establishment. But it could be worth it if Kahli enjoyed it enough to come back and show Mira how much she appreciated her efforts. Preferably in the bedroom.

It had been a while since Mira had sex, but Kahli had been *good*. At *everything*. Mira frowned as the thought brought back her raging libido. Her mind cursed her for not bringing her vibrator up to the bedroom. She slipped her hand down her front and found the wetness that had started pooling, but grunted when it just wasn't as good as the memories of the night before. Annoyed, she threw off her covers and picked up her clothing strewn around the room before moving downstairs. Spotting her vibrator sitting out in the middle of the floor, she blushed, realizing she had never cleaned up her things. Her head tilted; it appeared shifted from where Mira remembered it. Maybe one of them had kicked it as they maneuvered the space. She picked it up, as well as the bags, and moved them up to the bedroom. It seemed like it was finally time to settle in. Her reason for coming on the trip may have been thwarted—she was still alive after all—but maybe there was a little more pleasure meant for her in this lifetime. Maybe it wasn't all so bad.

Opening the small dresser, she put her items away neatly. When she was done, she grabbed her sparkly purple vibrator, plopped back on the bed, and scooted up to sit against the large wooden headboard. She clicked through the settings until she found the strength that would bring tears to her eyes, wanting to hurry things along. The way her clit was throbbing was too distracting for her to do anything else.

She pressed the vibrator to the apex of her thighs, gasping quietly as she shifted her hips forward to try and gain more pressure. Her face scrunched when it wasn't enough. Luckily, her sweatpants were stretchy enough that it wasn't a hassle to get them shifted off her hips and over her ass. Leaving them where they were, she again pressed the wand to herself. This time, her hips jerked as the strong vibrations traveled further though her, her head tilting back as she let out a low groan.

*Fuck, why had she ever stopped this pastime?* It was amazing. Maybe if she had been taking care of her orgasms more often, she wouldn't have been contemplating if life was worth living. Amani hadn't been about sex, but Kahli could be. It could be that simple.

Letting her mind wander, she imagined Kahli there with her, using the device to make her body move to the rhythm. She gasped as words tumbled out of her into the quiet room. "Kahli... please, baby..."

She slouched a bit to give the toy more contact, biting her lip. Kahli hadn't cared about how her body had changed post failed baby-making attempts. She either hadn't noticed, or didn't mind, the white stretch marks. Or the way she hadn't been able to pull her body back into the tight shape it had been when she and Amani were frequenting the gym three times a week.

Rubbing herself across the toy she wondered what else Kahli liked in the bedroom. What got her hot? Did she have any kinks? Would they match up well? Was she into anything that would be too much for Mira?

Her mind went blank as her orgasm started to build, her eyes slipping shut before she gasped for air. "Yes…"

She was so close when the sounds of the previously buzzing device went silent.

Mira's eyes snapped open in shock. "What the…" Her hand clicked at the power button a few times before she accepted the fact that the thing had died on her, and at the worst possible time. Chucking it to the side, she placed her hands over her face, letting out her frustration with a groan. She didn't have time for the stupid thing to charge, not with how turned on she was.

Flopping her hands to the side, she closed her eyes and felt how strongly she was pulsing below her panty line. Frustrated tears gathered in her eyes and they started to fall as her hand reached back to her sex. The sensation was just not as good as the vibrations. She tried to speed up her movements, but the feeling she was chasing was waning.

Her hands slowed to a stop. She lay there a while before she was able to move. When she finally sat up, her clit jolted as it came in contact with the bed, still sensitive. Getting up, she went to look for her charger, digging through both bags twice before it dawned on her: she had left the charger plugged in, in the wall outlet next to her bed, at home. She facepalmed. She was not driving all the way home to go get it.

Groaning again, she looked around the room in defeat before she made her way downstairs, desperate to distract herself from her unintentional edging. She padded her way to the bathroom and emptied her bladder, conscious of the fact that she did not need to get a UTI from not peeing after. As she went to wash her hands, her eyes drifted to some smudges along the top of the mirror. She kept glancing back, as if possessed by the small detail. They appeared to be letters. She went to find her phone to shine a light on it. There were definitely words drawn on the mirror. Had she missed them before? She turned off her phone light and set it on the closed white toilet lid before turning on the shower and closing the bathroom door. When the words appeared, they showed up much sharper than she expected.

"I am capable of achieving my dreams... and living my best life."

Her eyes strained as she tried to read the rest of that sentence.

"I will create *something*. I want the best for me and my loved ones..."

It seemed like someone who had stayed here before had been an optimist or heavily into affirmations. While it was a nice sentiment, Mira didn't see herself taking up the practice. Her eyes swept over the next line, and the handwriting changed. It appeared to be a response.

"May the *bodies* of your loved ones be... found at the bottom of the sea..." She couldn't make out the rest.

She leaned away at the abrupt shift in tone. "What the fuck? Well, someone's an ass."

Creeped out, she wiped at the mirror, erasing all of it from sight. She wondered if Kahli had been trying to be funny by responding when she had been in here. It was probably harmless.

She was moving to turn off the shower when she heard something shatter. Her head perked up at the sound. She opened the door and wandered back into the main area, searching for what might have caused the sound. The glass eye that had been hanging on the wall in the sparsely decorated kitchen, now lay shattered on the floor. She figured the little chain it had been hanging on had probably snapped.

But when she picked it up and inspected the chain, it was perfectly intact.

She grabbed a wet paper towel and scooped up the pieces of the dumb hippy protection charm. Wendy had plenty of those glass eyes hanging around her home. She said that they warded off negative energy and people with bad intentions. Mira didn't really get all of that. She looked around to see if there were any further clues that the place had spiritual connections. It would be just her luck that she had rented a haunted house.

Nothing else seemed to be out of place, but when her eyes lifted to the front of the house, she saw a shadow pass over the front door. She quickly moved across the open floor plan to look out the window to see who it was, but there was no one there. What she did see was an empty, slightly overgrown, lawn leading out to her car. No animals, and certainly no people.

She figured she should let the owners know the keychain broke before they tried to blame her for it. They probably would anyway. She grabbed her phone and sent a photo.

*Just wanted to let you know that the chain that held this little thing up broke while I was in the other room.*

Almost immediately, she saw that the owner had read the message and started to respond.

*No worries. We had a "witch" stay there before who told us that we needed to add protections to the house against "supernatural" things. We weren't quite sure what that meant, but we bought a few items. Every once in a while they seem to break. We have a bucket of things like that in the garage in the back right corner, under some blankets if you want.*

Mira relaxed, glad it wasn't special.

*Totally fine. I don't need anything, but I appreciate the offer.*

Locking her phone, she looked around the room. No longer plagued by her raging libido, she now found herself more than bored. She contemplated watching TV but couldn't manage to get herself to move to the couch. Instead, she went upstairs and put her swimsuit on. It was a dark purple thing that shimmered in the sun. She had bought it to try and re-spark things with Amani, but didn't get the chance to show it to her before she disappeared. Maybe Kahli would appreciate the aesthetic.

She grabbed a towel, her bag, some sunscreen—which would definitely give her a rash and require a lot of antihistamine later—and a bottle of water, then headed out into the afternoon sun.

# Chapter 13

Mira had been walking down the beach in the direction Kahli always came from when her back decided she had walked far enough. Plopping her things down in the sand, she spread out her towel and got comfortable. The beach was in full sun, and she knew she would need to actually put on sunscreen. Her pale skin was already slightly itching in anticipation of the rash that would appear randomly across her body. She opened the bottle and squeezed some onto her hands anyway, when she heard commotion down the way.

Lifting her eyes to the water, Mira tried to fight her smile as she saw Kahli swimming along the shoreline. She raised her voice to shout, hopeful to capture her attention, though she wasn't sure if Kahli would be able to hear her. "Kahli!" She waved, and at first the swimmer kept going. She tried once more, and that seemed to get the other woman's attention as she abruptly stopped, turned around, and missed the wave that crashed over her, sending her tumbling.

Mira's eyes widened, but she couldn't help the way she snorted at her peril. Surely she could handle the waves. If she didn't surface soon, Mira would go out there and try to find her. But before she could really start to worry, Kahli broke the surface, gasping and waving excitedly. She turned and let the waves push her toward the sand.

Leaning back on her arms and pushing her chest up a bit, she awaited Kahli's arrival. Her lips stretched wide when she saw the exact moment Kahli opened her mouth to speak but her eyes landed on Mira's body and she tripped—stumbling as if she was just learning to walk—before she caught herself. Her hair fell to cover her face and she didn't move to right it.

She quickly sat down next to Mira, beside her towel.

Mira quirked her head. *That* was a decision. "Well, I would have allowed you to join me up here, but now you're covered in sand."

Kahli looked down at where she was sitting, her face falling. "Oh. Damn." She pushed her hair back out of her face. "It's cool, I'm good like this."

"If it gets hot you can sit at the bottom of my towel." She watched as Kahli looked at the area, then back hopefully. Mira rolled her eyes. "Fine. Sit there." She pointed. Kahli jumped up, brushed herself off—which didn't do much—and settled on the end. She turned away from the water and faced Mira fully, crossing her legs under her.

"So... sunscreen? Thought you were allergic?"

Mira bit her lip as she nodded slowly, her eyes dragging to the bottle. "I am." She realized then that she had smeared the glob in her hand on her towel in her haste. "I'm not doing a great job of putting it on." She lifted her eyes to Kahli's before she grabbed the bottle and shoved it into her hands. "Help me."

Smiling, Kahli immediately took to the task, squeezing way too much lotion into her hands before she started with Mira's legs.

Mira gasped at the freezing lotion. "Cold!"

Kahli licked her lips as she turned her hands up to the sun for a moment to gather warmth. "Sorry, the water's not as warm today." She turned them back over after a minute before wrapping them around Mira's legs, massaging the muscles as she went. A particularly tight tendon had Mira wincing.

"That's connected to my lower back." She tried to breathe as she felt Kahli continue to work on it, but she was more gentle this time.

Dark eyes focused on her task as she spoke. "You really need to stretch this out more. Moving would really help." She lifted her face with a shit-eating grin. "You know, like swimming, or *walking*."

Mira narrowed her gaze as she lay down all the way. "Sounds like a lot of effort."

"It doesn't have to be that bad, it helps if there's good company."

Mira used a hand to shield her eyes from the sun so she could see Kahli better. "And you're *good company*?"

"Yeah." Then, as if needing to defend herself from Mira's unimpressed look, she tacked on, "I'm fun!"

Mira shifted as Kahli's hands made it to the bottom piece of her swimsuit, reminding her of what those hands had been capable of in the area. "Shame we're out in public... cause I wouldn't be opposed to some *fun*."

Kahli's self-satisfied smile fell flat. "Oh, did you want to go? We can..."

Mira waved her off. "As much as I would love to drag you into my house and have my way with you, I have already committed to the rash this lotion will cause, and I might as well get some vitamin D for my efforts. Maybe you can come over and take care of *that* itch later." She heaved out a sigh. "If the meds catch the rash before it's too crazy." Her body tingled uncomfortably at the idea that Kahli might see her skin's reaction and decide that their play needed to end. Mira busied her hands with smoothing out the towel, trying to not panic.

Kahli floundered at Mira's suggestion, trying to lean over her without getting more sand on her towel. She moved back to the sand and kneeled at Mira's hip, her hands squeezing out the lotion directly on Mira's stomach this time.

The coolness momentarily jarred her once more, causing her body to twitch. Mira's mind unhelpfully shifted to focus on the fact that if Kahli hadn't been looking at her body before, she surely was now. Her stomach had a slight curve to it, and she shivered as Kahli's hands started to massage the lotion in wide circles, unintentionally turning her on. Mira tried to hold herself back from any kind of physical reaction, but her hips involuntarily rolled. She didn't have to look up at Kahli to know she was brightening at the response.

"Don't say a word. I'm just a bit touch-starved. It's noth-ing." Her voice hitched as Kahli's hands circled her lower abdomen.

"Your skin is so soft." The younger woman sounded as if she were hypnotized by the body before her.

Mira closed her eyes as she let the touch continue, trying not to overthink things. "I don't do much but stay out of the sun. That's why I'm so pale." She took a deep breath, and almost stopped herself before giving a bit more information. "Amani hated how *sickly* I looked in the winter. She claimed I looked like a ghost. I figured I could make an effort, but after hours in tanning beds, I had to have more skin cancer removed. I also had to stop laying on a towel in the yard during the summer, which sucked. My skin's super sensitive." Her mind drifted to other imperfections in her skin. She ran her own hand along her stretch marks to see if they were still as bumpy as she remembered. Kahli's hand shoved hers aside.

"I've got it." It was as if she sensed that Mira didn't need to be fixated on the area.

"Are they super visible in the sun?" She meant the lines that raced up her stomach. At first, Amani had helped her put lotion on her skin as it stretched. But she became busy, and Mira had grown forgetful with all the hormones and couldn't keep it up. It was a wonder the marks weren't deeper.

Kahli's thumbs added pressure to the massage. "The tissue can be broken up more. If you keep working on it, it'll smooth out, given time."

The tension Mira was holding slowly bled out as Kahli's fingers worked on it. Mira looked up again. "I thought you worked with the sea. How do you know so much about this? Were you a pre-med or something? Physical therapist?"

Kahli shook her head. "It's just tissue. If it's tense, you work on it till it's not."

Mira sighed as she felt Kahli's hands slide up to just under her swimsuit top, the feeling not even close to where Mira wanted her. She swallowed. "If no one is around... you could..."

Kahli giggled. "Damn, didn't know you were into *that*." She tossed her a wink.

Mira watched as Kahli carefully spread lotion only slightly below the cups of her top, before moving to her sides and her chest. "I could be open to it. Maybe not with your hands covered in that though." She indicated the white lotion.

Kahli hummed. "Good to know." She continued on to Mira's arms and neck, then her fingers lightly spread white across Mira's nose, cheeks, and forehead in stripes.

Mira's face scrunched when she didn't rub it in.

"Aw, you look so cute." Smiling, Kahli leaned down to press a kiss to her lips as Mira pursed hers, not amused.

"Finish what you started. That's going to leave horrible tan lines."

Kahli leaned her elbows on either side of Mira's head as her hair dripped water onto her. Her hands came up to spread the lotion. "Fine. Can't have that now, you might burn."

Mira wasn't sure where to look with Kahli this close. She felt her heart speed up an unnatural amount and struggled to slow her breathing, her body thrumming with energy. In an effort to escape the tension, she chose to look out at the sand.

Kahli finished up and leaned her body against Mira's briefly to sit back up. "Done with the front. Did you want me to do the back?"

Mira contemplated the thought before reaching her hands out for Kahli, who helped to pull her up to sit. She turned over onto her hands and knees and blushed when she heard Kahli fight back a small whimper.

Popping her ass more than necessary, Mira smirked. "You can finish the job." She lowered herself slowly, crossing her arms and resting her head on them with her ass in the air before extending her legs out, one by one. She wondered if she was about to be fucked into oblivion with the way she was torturing Kahli.

But her good girl didn't go for it. Mira did, however, feel lotion start at her thighs and trace down the back of her legs. Kahli worked out all the kinks before she moved up to her back, really digging in and focusing on the tightness she found there.

Mira groaned. "Shit, that feels amazing."

Kahli's hands dug deeper and she felt her back pop in a few places that had been stuck. She gasped at the sharp pain of the release, but it quickly subsided.

"Don't let me fall asleep out here, cause I could," Mira mumbled as the sounds of the waves and the occasional seagull started to put her in a trance, the sun's warm rays on her back aiding her body's attempt to go offline. She felt Kahli's hands slide up to teasingly tug at her top.

"I mean… I don't know that I could wait till you wake up. I'm not the most patient person."

"Well, I told you I wouldn't be opposed to a little public indecency." Mira felt Kahli's hands leave and wondered if she had pushed too hard, if Kahli really wasn't okay with potentially getting caught. After a moment, she heard what sounded like Kahli washing her hands.

Mira pressed her hands to the towel to push herself up and apologize when she felt her swimsuit bottoms slipped to the side and two fingers slide up her slit. Dropping her face back down, she pressed into the blanket, hands trying to curl into the fabric beneath her.

"Oh, my, god." She pressed her hips back to chase the feeling of Kahli's retreating fingers. "More... please..." Her voice hitched as Kahli spread her, and she whimpered at the way her body was begging Kahli to enter her.

She tried to shift closer, but Kahli's other hand pressed at her back, keeping her down. Mira huffed as she tried to grind into Kahli's hand. The laughter she heard made her want to sass back even harder.

"Here I was about to ask you out on a date... but you're... so rude." She gasped as Kahli circled her entrance but didn't go in.

Kahli's voice dipped lower. "Oh? Where are we going?"

Mira closed her eyes as the feeling continued to build, much better than the vibrator that had left her hanging. "I don't move fast..." Her mind was struggling to formulate a coherent sentence. "Drinks. Daytime. To start."

"Ah... that sounds respectable. What is it that you do anyway? I've been wondering."

Mira didn't have a fucking clue right now. "I'll show you later. Just... fucking *rail* me already."

Kahli's fingers dipped inside, but only barely. "You really want that? Out here?"

Mira felt like she would die if she didn't get it. She could think of nothing else right now. Her voice was rough. "If you don't *fuck* me, I am not taking you out. You leave me hanging, and I will lock myself away and not see you again."

She had somehow missed Kahli's movement because she was now whispering in her ear. Her breath hitched as the words hummed through her, the tingling sensation crashing over her. "Oh, Mira... that's not fair. I've already fucked you so good, baby. Don't be mean to me."

Mira panted as Kahli's fingers slowly entered her. Mira's mouth dropped open as she struggled to breathe.

"We should head back," Kahli whispered.

Mira's hand reached behind her and tried to stop Kahli's retreat as she felt her pulling out. "Don't. I... I need... you."

The building sensation halted when Kahli's hand stilled. "I will fuck you much better than this back at your house." She gently withdrew her fingers despite Mira's protests.

Mira's heart raced as Kahli collected her things, wondering if the woman was going to finish the job.

"Grab the towel and I'll come back with you." She reached out her free hand when Mira moved to her knees. "Come on."

The apex of her thighs pounded with need. She struggled to stand, relying on Kahli's grip to get up. When she didn't reach for the towel, Kahli leaned back down and retrieved it, throwing it over her shoulder as she wrapped an arm around Mira's waist.

"I promise it'll be worth the wait."

Mira huffed and refused to speak to Kahli the rest of the walk back.

By the time they closed the back door, Mira was livid. She turned to tell Kahli off when the woman dropped her things and grabbed her face, backing her into the wall. Mira's back hit the solid wood with an audible thud, breath and thoughts gone as Kahli's tongue darted out to lick at her lips before her teeth bit down.

Mira moaned as she wrapped her hands around Kahli's neck and pulled her closer, hoping she would devour her.

Kahli's tongue explored her mouth for a moment before she moved to Mira's neck, leaving a wet trail from her clavicle to just under her chin. Mira's pulse beat so heavily, she wondered if Kahli could feel it on her tongue.

Mira puffed out short little breaths as her hands moved to Kahli's shoulders. "That feels *so* good." She leaned back fully against the wall and watched as Kahli's eyes lifted to hers, her heart stopping for a moment as she saw Kahli move to her knees, taking Mira's swim bottoms with her.

"Can you stand long enough?"

Unable to find a retort, Mira simply nodded.

Kahli's hands gripped her hips before she maneuvered one leg over her shoulder. "Tell me if this hurts, I'll readjust." She waited for Mira, and when she nodded, Kahli kept eye contact, opened her mouth, stuck out her tongue, and flattened it against her, sliding over Mira's slick folds so slowly it was torture.

Mira's head slammed back against the wall, her neck straining as she cried out. Kahli's tongue swiped through her faster on the second pass, as if she was more focused on tasting her than driving her wild. Mira started to rock against Kahli's mouth, her lower back loosening up, when Kahli's tongue plunged into her, causing her to cough at the intensity.

"Shit!" She gasped. "More."

A low groan vibrated through her as Kahli's fingers joined her tongue and Mira bit down on her lip so hard she wondered if it wasn't just going to be swollen later when she checked in the mirror.

Kahli's fingers continued to map inside of Mira, exploring her walls, as her mouth changed direction and found her clit, sucking softly at first. Mira screamed.

Mira's hips bucked and she dug her nails into Kahli's shoulders. "Kahli!"

She felt Kahli circle her clit with her tongue before she tried the suction again. Her body tensed as her mouth dropped open soundlessly at first. She went lightheaded just before her scream finally burst into the room, ricocheting off the wooden walls. Her body collapsed, completely limp against the wall, her eyes lidded as she looked down at Kahli, and her mind blank as she focused on simply breathing.

The younger woman was careful as she extracted herself from the position, shifting Mira's leg off her shoulder with care, making sure her foot was planted properly on the ground even if she couldn't use it. Mira's knees buckled the moment she tried to stand, and Kahli's arms wrapped around her waist.

"I got you." Kahli smiled up at her softly, looking about as she held her. "Couch? Bed?"

Mira huffed. "There's no way you are getting me up those stairs..." Kahli raised an eyebrow and Mira shook her head. "No! Don't you dare."

Kahli's lips split into a grin before Mira was tipped over her shoulder and lifted into the air, yelping.

"Kahli!" She wrapped her arms around Kahli's back, just in case Kahli decided to let go of her legs—she did not want another concussion. She'd had one in middle school, and it had been a nightmare. Luckily Wendy's mom kept her for observation, or she surely would have died in her sleep with the way her mother complained that she was fine.

She felt each step as Kahli climbed the stairs. Even when she was consistently working out with Amani, neither of them had ever gotten strong enough to carry the other. Strength had never been either of their goals. It was much shallower than that, the quest for physical beauty that did nothing but lure others to you... or keep your spouse's eyes from wandering. She felt Kahli try to set her down on the bed, but she sent them tumbling when she refused to let go. Kahli gasped in surprise as she was pulled off her feet.

Mira burst out laughing at the shock on her face as they remained in a tangled heap on the bed. Her eyes took in Kahli's body as her gaze narrowed, having forgotten all about how things had started before they escalated. "You got sand in the bed."

Kahli rolled her eyes as she moved Mira off her. "I'll change the bed later. I think I deserve some rest after all that." She raised a brow in challenge, and Mira tried to fight back her smile as she contemplated the request.

"Fine. I guess your head *was* good. You can stay." She turned over, facing away from Kahli and got comfortable, waiting anxiously to see what her swimmer girl would do. Amani would frequently disregard her immediately after if she got Mira off, but that was a big *if* that Amani was actually willing to put in the time and effort to make sure Mira finished.

Mira's body practically hummed when Kahli wrapped herself around her, their bodies slotting together perfectly. Kahli's arm held firm at her waist as her leg intertwined with Mira's. Her warm body already had Mira starting to drift. Mira bit her lip as she grabbed Kahli's arm and hugged it to her chest, flushing as she heard Kahli's quiet laughter. She didn't let go though. She figured they would both be asleep soon and she would be able to explain away her instinct to cuddle as post-coital insanity.

She hummed as her lips formed words she wasn't aware she was thinking until they were released.

"I like this." Mira felt her stomach drop at the admission. A moment later, she settled as Kahli kissed her shoulder.

"I like this too."

# Chapter 14

Mira heard her phone ring but refused to open her eyes as she slapped her hand around the nightstand to locate the device, which was still on its charger. She blindly unlocked her phone and pressed it to her tired face. Her voice was rough from all the screaming she had been doing before she fell asleep in Kahli's arms.

"What?" She felt Kahli stir, the arms wrapped around her tightening.

"Well, I know what you've been doing…" Mira's eyes shot open as if she had heard a disembodied voice, and she might as well have.

"Ama-ni?" Her voice cracked from overuse. She sat up, pushing Kahli's hands away from her so she could breathe. "Where the fuck are you?" She heard a heavy sigh waft down the line, as if her wife didn't know why she was being so dramatic. She *always* thought Mira was being dramatic.

"We need to talk. Is this a good time?"

Mira's heart raced. Amani was *alive*. Her breath caught in her chest. Was she ready to come home? Had she just cheated on her wife? She pondered that a bit longer and wondered if Amani hadn't been off doing the same. She rubbed her face in an effort to get more blood to flow to her brain. "It's..." She looked down at her phone at the time. "Afternoon. Of course I have time to talk..."

She drew her knees up to her chest as she wrapped one arm around them, closing her eyes to focus on the call and not be distracted with the conversation she was going to have with Kahli after. Her chest constricted at the thought of telling her that things were over before they began. Did she want to end things with Kahli when she made her feel lighter than she had in years? She felt tears prickle her eyes when she felt Kahli's nails start to lightly scratch up and down her back. She hated herself for scooting back into the touch.

Amani huffed. "You would *think* you would be happy to finally hear from me. Or have you forgotten me already?"

Mira's eyes flew open, her throat trying to close in anger. "I called you for months! I was worried sick when you didn't come home. I filed a missing person... I thought you had *died, Amani!*" She lashed out and just about started to sob before she felt a hand press at her back. It was warm and steady, and she didn't even try not to lean into it.

"Well, I needed some time to process... everything. And a missing person report was a bit over the top."

Mira cleared her throat. "Not when I called your friends, your work, and no one had heard from you..."

At least, that's what they all told her.

Taking a moment to try to stay calm, she took a deep breath, then let it out slowly. "You could have at least told me *something*..."

She heard Amani's hushed voice as she spoke with someone. Mira held her legs tighter.

"Who... who's there with you?" Her voice grew quiet, like how most of their fights ended. Because she was scared that if she didn't quiet down, Amani would leave.

"I met someone. It's getting serious, so we need to sort our shit out."

Mira's stomach rolled. She tensed her back so tightly that it popped, and her eyes squinted at the pain. "Alright." She felt like if she said more, she might plead for Amani to come home. Or maybe threaten to kill herself. She wasn't sure which would hurt more when Amani didn't care.

"Let's be honest, the legal definition is half. Let's avoid lawyers, it can get so messy."

Mira curled herself over her knees. "Okay, seems fair." Before she could say more, Amani continued.

"Great. I want half the embryos."

Mira's spine went rigid. "No."

Amani practically growled. "Mira. We made them together, I paid for them. They're practically children..."

"Not children."

Amani screamed. "Hansen! Just because you don't agree about when life starts doesn't mean you can talk about them like that."

Mira released her legs and they fell crossed as she leaned forward. Her hand came up to pinch her nose. "They're *my* eggs. *My* genetic material. We used up all of yours..."

"And whose fault is that? We put most of them in *your* body."

Mira scoffed. "Your body sucked too, remember?"

"Mira."

"I'm not giving you *my* children to raise with someone else. I don't know this woman..." When her wife remained silent, she felt her face harden. "They are... a woman... right?"

She felt the silence before Amani answered in every beat of her heart.

"The person I'm seeing now is, so don't be like that. The man was a dalliance—she's what's real, what *we* never had."

Mira felt the double insult and chose to leave that where it was for now, knowing she would surely have some harsh words for her "lesbian" wife later.

"Nat doesn't have eggs," Amani continued. "She had her ovaries removed years ago due to a medical issue."

Mira snorted. "How sad for her. I think you can go ahead and go through the process. I seem to remember you telling me they were *just shots, Mira, stop crying.*"

"You think I can't do the shots? Please, I did one of them to show you, it wasn't that bad, remember?"

That was true, but Amani had only done one. The sensitivity in the area only intensified as the scar tissue from all the injections built up over weeks and months.

"You're not getting them. Any of them..." Mira's voice trailed off as she gasped. "Oh my god... you've already tried, haven't you!"

There was an awkward pause, and then a grumbled, "They need your signature."

Mira let a humorless laugh escape her. "You can go to hell."

"I'll see you in court!"

The phone went eerily silent. Her hands started to shake as she dropped it into her lap, her chest forgetting how to expand. It was then she registered that Kahli's hand was still at her back, her voice entering her ear.

"Breathe."

Mira closed her eyes and felt the tears she fought during the call start to stream down her face.

"She's a bitch. I can't believe... I was so worried about her..." She choked on a sob, and Kahli's arms encircled her.

"Keep breathing."

Mira didn't want to. She wanted to stop breathing, to die right here on this bed and make Amani come to collect her body and feel horrible for driving her over the edge. But she knew the reality of the situation was that Wendy would be more likely to come clean up her mess, like she always did. Amani might have a fleeting moment of regret at her ceasing to exist, but she knew she would move on quickly. Mira had never mattered that much to her anyway.

They had been fun and wild together, but as she begged Amani for more, the redhead kept her at arm's length, never giving her what she truly needed. And yet, Mira clung to her, refusing to let go. She had proposed, exactly the way Amani had always dreamed of. She had offered to do the injections when the sperm they bought from the clinic failed in both of them.

Mira was the one who endured the pain and sickness quietly, while Amani rarely gave her attention. She had craved being away from her mother, away from Wendy, who reminded her of her past and who she really was, but that escape had come crashing down all around her.

The night Amani hadn't come home, she broke her no contact with Wendy. A no contact that Amani had encouraged since Mira and Wendy had dated once when they were thirteen.

She had crumbled on her floor, and at first Wendy hadn't answered. Why would she? Mira had been the one to cut her off, Wendy didn't owe her anything anymore. As she fell apart, her phone eventually rang. She had hoped at first it was Amani with some sort of explanation about why she wasn't home. But Wendy's concerned greeting completely broke her.

"She's gone. I don't know what to do… I…" She heard Wendy's voice with all the authority she had always commanded.

"Mira. Slow down. Where did she go?"

She had gasped as she struggled to find oxygen. "I don't… I don't know. She's not here. Didn't come home. She's not responding…"

Wendy had figured out Mira's fear of abandonment long before she had. That Mira was terrified that if she cared for someone, they would cast her aside. Like her mother had. Like her biological father had, wherever he had fucked off to, while leaving her with the harpy that was Evangeline Hansen.

"Come home, Mira. Even if it's just for a little while. Your bed is still here…"

She wiped at her face, lips quivering. "You… still have my things?"

When Mira met Amani, things had been hot and heavy and she U-hauled quickly, leaving most of her belongings behind. Her things were meaningless to her as her life was *finally* moving on from her past.

As the relationship with Amani cooled, she realized there were things that she wanted to collect from Wendy but never got around to it. Especially since Amani had... encouraged her to cut contact.

"I have all of it actually. I just... wasn't ready to move on. Allie told me to take all the time I needed..."

Mira stiffened. Right, Allie, Wendy's girlfriend. Things must be getting serious between them. She had missed a lot.

"I can't... I can't come home. You have Allie now—" she was promptly cut off.

"I've told you. She understands our relationship. We're family, Mira. You're coming home. You're not staying in that empty house all alone so that I can find your body one day."

# Chapter 15

Mira came back to the present, wishing desperately that Wendy were there with her when she noticed Kahli was now sitting in front of her. Cool fingers held her face as Kahli's thumbs cleared away her tears.

"You're going to be okay."

Mira shook her head slightly with a huff. "No... I'm not."

The grip on Mira's face firmed up. "Yes. You are. We are going to get you showered, dressed, and out of the house. You wanted to take me to coffee. Let's do that."

Mira grimaced. "There's no way you want to go out with me when I'm like this. I'm a mess..."

Kahli's eyes held her gaze. "I think going out is just what you need. I want to spend time with you. Even if you're like this."

Mira bit her lip. She felt guilty. Kahli made her feel safe, just like Wendy. She wanted to curl up in her arms and hide away from the world, not go out and face it. Inching closer, she hesitantly pressed her face to Kahli's neck, inhaling deeply and smelling the ocean scent that lingered from the woman's swim. She felt gentle fingers tangle in her hair and start to lightly scrape at her scalp.

"It'll help. I promise."

Mira stayed where she was until Kahli encouraged her to move. Her legs were a bit weak and sore, but functional. She made it down the stairs with Kahli spotting her. Somehow, she got herself to shower, finding clothes Kahli had laid out for her when she moved the curtain.

Dark gray sweats, blue cotton underwear, blue sports bra, and a worn-out white cotton shirt were neatly folded on the toilet lid. Mira smiled; she hadn't folded any of them like that before putting them in the drawers. Dressing slowly, she looked at her hair as it took on the humidity. Her brunette curls were limp and frizzing so badly because she had only shampooed and didn't have it in her to style it. She rubbed her red-rimmed eyes, feeling completely wrung out. Unable to leave the bathroom, she sat on the toilet, waiting for Kahli to find her.

Who did eventually come in, without question. She simply took her hand, grabbed Mira's purse and keys, and led them out.

As they left the house, Mira noticed that the other woman had borrowed some clothes. Kahli must have washed up in the kitchen sink because she only lightly smelled of sex and ocean now. Mira had started to find that scent calming.

Mira stayed quiet about Kahli taking the driver's seat. She had only ever let two people drive her car. Wendy and Amani. With Wendy, it was always a fight after Mira had been drinking. With Amani, she had always caved to the other woman's whims, hoping that if she allowed it, she would get some warmth in return.

Kahli's driving was slow and careful. That normally would have grated on her nerves, but they weren't in a rush, so she spent her time watching the trees pass as they made their way to town. Her head lifted a bit when they arrived and she noticed there were booths lining the streets. Though there weren't a lot of people, there were more than she had ever seen in town. Her gaze turned to Kahli and the other woman nodded.

"Art festival. Happens every year. I... might have known it was today. Thought you would enjoy it."

Mira sat forward as she tried to catch a glimpse of what was on display as they drove by.

"Figured you would want your coffee first, then we can browse." Kahli's cheeks went red. "I... may have left my wallet at home... I can pay you back later."

Mira relaxed into her seat. "Don't worry about it. I have money." Her eyes continued to take in the scene. She hadn't even told Kahli that she did illustrative work. That she was indeed into art. That if Kahli had known her better, this would have been the perfect first date. Or third. Or anniversary event.

She felt the car slow as Kahli pulled into the parking lot. Undoing her seat belt, she exited the car before she opened Mira's door, extending her hand. "My lady."

Mira snorted but took Kahli's offered hand and extracted herself from the car. She released it before they entered the establishment, her eyes watching how Benny's lit up the moment he saw her. He stood up straight, his mouth dropping as he looked from Mira to Kahli then back.

His smile was way too wide for his excited little face.

"Hiya!" He waved eagerly.

Kahli tilted her head to whisper, "Oh, I see I have competition."

Mira rolled her eyes as she looked at the menu, already knowing it by now. She cleared her throat as she crossed her arms, tossing her question at Kahli. "What do you want, since I'm apparently buying?"

Kahli's voice was quiet. "Oh... uhm, let's see..."

Mira turned to watch her as Kahli's arms crossed, her fingers nervously tapping. Mira's own grip on herself loosened as she took in Kahli's nerves. Was this really a date? Had Kahli been planning on bringing her here all along?

Her companion pointed at the menu, momentarily disrupting her spiral. "I'll try the Ladybug Matcha." Kahli turned to Mira, waiting.

She looked at the board and shrugged. "Coffee." She glanced at Benny. "You know what I like."

The boy nodded enthusiastically. "You bet! That'll be..." He struggled for a moment and Mira sighed.

"You don't have to give me the discount, kid. I'm a big girl. I can afford it."

Benny shook his head. "Maybe I can borrow from my code for tomorrow? Sorry, with the festival, someone I know already came in... but I think if I just..."

Mira slapped her card on the table. "You can make it up to me later."

Pursing his lips, Benny nodded, noticing the line that was starting to form.

Mira's voice was low and just loud enough for him and Kahli. "I'll tip you when you come to the table. Be discreet."

She turned and headed for the most secluded spot, which was luckily still available, and Kahli followed. Sitting across from her at the small table, Kahli's dark eyes took in the decorations, which were mostly paintings of cute sea animals and mermaids. Mira had never taken the time to really dwell on them before, but now looked over the place with a new appreciation, due to Kahli's interest.

"This place is cute."

"They have coffee." Mira shrugged, watching Kahli's eyes continue to wander. "How did you wind up here anyway? It's a small town."

There was another moment that passed before Kahli's eyes returned to Mira. "I study..." She licked her lips and Mira noticed the hesitation. "Marine life." She looked away, seemingly embarrassed. "I like the ocean, so sue me."

Mira tapped her fingers on the table. "Why are you so ashamed of it? Seems like a good career."

Kahli distractedly nodded. "Yeah. Sure."

Inwardly, Mira wanted to groan at the lack of pride. She also had a family—well, mother—who was never satisfied with anything she did, and she couldn't understand why someone as beautiful and smart as Kahli could feel the way she did about her accomplishments. Mira rolled her eyes. Kahli had taken the time and care to make sure she didn't wallow in everything going on with her ex, so maybe she could give a little.

"So... I actually like art." When Kahli's eyes refocused on her with renewed interest, Mira rubbed her neck. "Love it... actually." She fought her smile. "I'm an illustrator."

Kahli's mouth opened and Mira raised a hand.

"Not yet, I'm... not ready to show you. Not the personal stuff, anyway." She felt herself cave a little at the sad look Kahli cast her way. "Maybe some of my work stuff."

Eagerly, Kahli leaned forward, crossing her arms on the table. "What do you draw?"

Mira lowered her arm as well as her eyes to the table. "Lots of things. But my favorite pieces... they actually have to do with the ocean, as well as women. Nude," she coughed, "women." She looked up and shared a secret smile with her new lover.

Kahli flipped her hair out of her face. "Well, I definitely have to work my way up in the ranks to see *that*."

Subconsciously, Mira bit her cheek, remembering what exactly her personal drawing entailed. "It's inspiring, to say the least. Though... so was earlier." She felt herself flush at the memory and phantom touches tingling across her skin.

Kahli beamed. "I enjoy the process. Getting creative on the go."

"I was ready to kill you when you didn't let me finish on the beach." Mira's hand went into her hair, tugging lightly to keep a hold of herself. She did not need to be thinking about all of that right now, in a public place, where they could do nothing about it. Bathroom stalls were disgusting.

Dark eyes slid away momentarily before confidently reconnecting with Mira's. "Wasn't it worth the wait though?"

Mira started to tap her foot. "Don't turn me on... the closest beach is twenty minutes away... and I did want to look at some art acquisitions while we're here." Her mind drifted to the tents they had seen on their way in.

Kahli snickered. "You started it."

Mouth dropping open in mock shock, Mira pointed an accusatory finger at Kahli. "You asked what I did for a living. This is *your* fault."

Kahli rolled her eyes. Their gazes both lifted when the scrawny, emo kid arrived with their drinks. He set them down, and Mira stalled him with her hand in the air. "Hold on."

She reached in her bag and dug out a five. The boy started his protest when she cut him off.

"There wasn't a discount today, it's not fifty percent. Just take it."

"Thank you." He bounced excitedly like he was about to explode with his question, eyes darting repeatedly to Mira's companion. "This your girlfriend?"

Mira's brow furrowed. "Do you want me to take that back?" She extended her hand for the cash.

Kahli snorted as Benny twisted his body slightly away. "I'm just *asking*. I don't get to see a lot of other gay people out in the wild. It... means a lot when I see someone like me."

And damn if she couldn't relate. Mira grumbled. "Not my girlfriend..." Kahli's shoulders tensed and Benny's face screwed up, looking like he was searching for an apology when Mira conceded. "I *am* gay though."

Benny brightened right up. "I knew it! I have a boyfriend!"

Trying to act disinterested, Mira snorted. "Good for you."

Benny set their drinks in front of Mira, who slid Kahli's in front of her. Kahli's eyes lifted. "Thanks, Mira."

Mira's eyes widened as she looked over and caught Benny's shit-eating grin. He had indeed heard her. She shooed him away with the flick of her wrist and Kahli raised an eyebrow, silently asking her what that was about.

"Kid was trying to guess my name. I like to keep an air of mystery about myself. Seems that's ruined now."

Kahli took her drink in her hands but didn't try it yet. "You're a bit stingy on details..." She laughed. "Perhaps you're ensnaring me into a trap of your own. There are stories, you know. About beautiful women like you. All the way out here by the sea."

Mira's eyes narrowed. "You're so weird." She took a sip of her drink, glancing out the window before speaking again. "The phone call wasn't fake. That... I wasn't expecting any of that. What... what would *you* do?" Her fingers played anxiously with her cup.

Kahli remained quiet.

Unsure what to do with the silence, Mira rambled on. "I mean the eggs are mine, but let's face it... I'm probably never going to find someone to use them with, so... maybe I just let her have them. I mean, Amani would be a good mom and... I'm sure she wouldn't pick someone completely terrible to raise them with. Sure, it would be weird when they do one of those DNA tests and come to find out the full story one day..."

Lifting the drink to her lips, Kahli waded in carefully, clearly trying not to set Mira off. "I would tell her no. If they are yours, maybe... you do want them. You're not that old, you could find someone. Who knows if you want them yet."

Mira placed her chin in her palm. "It's expensive to store them. Do I really need to be spending the money on something that is only a possibility?"

Kahli shrugged. "You're spending money on *me*."

Mira smiled. "That's because the sex was amazing."

Kahli blushed as she took another sip of her drink.

Blowing out a breath, Mira hesitantly continued. "I come with a lot of baggage. It's probably fair that you know up front. Religious upbringing, horrible mother, internalized homophobia... and," she let her voice trail off, quietly finishing with, "suicidal ideation."

Kahli hummed. "Got it. That paints a picture. Though, if I'm being honest, I had guessed as much. I don't have a lot of family either...." She seemed to catch herself. "Aside from who I live with, of course." A beat passed while Kahli tapped her nails on her teacup. "I wouldn't disappear on you."

It was the first promise Kahli had made to her, and Mira felt herself wanting to both reel back from and cling on to it for dear life.

Mira chose emotional stuntedness. "I'll get the kid to give us to-go cups. I was serious about looking at the art."

She stood and made for the counter, Benny's eyes already alight with questions.

Mira felt Kahli's hand brush at her side as they walked around the festival, guiding her gently. They had already stopped at a booth with beautiful paintings of ocean waves, and Mira had caved, buying one with a mermaid prominently in the foreground. Although only her back was visible, she knew she must be beautiful. Maybe it would remind her that there were other fish in the sea after Amani. Like Kahli.

Thankfully, the vendor agreed to hold the canvas so they could continue to shop. As they wandered, Kahli's eyes were drawn to a stall with little horse statues, and Mira grabbed her hand to guide her over when she couldn't stop staring. Kahli's tan fingers glided over the different stone carvings. The horses looked ridiculously lifelike. She stopped on one that was dark purple but shifted between gold and rainbow in the sunlight.

Before Mira could ask, Kahli was giving her an explanation. "Purple labradorite." She lifted and held the little horse in her palm. "Protection, grounding, heightens supernatural abilities." She bit her lip.

As soon as she paused, Mira was removing the statue from Kahli's hand and purchasing it from the merchant. Returning with a teal plastic bag that she handed to Kahli, Mira smirked. "Didn't think purple was your favorite color, though you *did* seem to appreciate my swimsuit."

Kahli's fingers played with the bag as she followed Mira out of the stall. "Figured it might be *your* favorite color."

Mira slowed, casting a confused look at her.

"It'll help me remember you, when you leave." Before Mira could say anything, Kahli pointed at a stall up ahead. "We should get you something green! That's my favorite color." She grabbed Mira and pulled her along. Kahli's eyes excitedly took in the stall that appeared to be all black and green gemstones shimmering as the afternoon light cast its rays across the display.

Mira took her time browsing the color variations as Kahli pointed enthusiastically at a specific one.

"Oh, that's a really good one!"

"What's so special about that one?" Mira compared it to the others around it, and though they all looked different, she wasn't sure why this one stuck out to the thrilled black-haired woman beside her.

Placing it in Mira's hand, Kahli was practically vibrating as she explained. "Can't you feel it? That one's buzzing with energy."

Mira let her gaze fall to the rock and turned it every which way before offering her assessment. Her face remained flat. "It's a... pretty rock."

Kahli rolled her eyes before shaking her head. "Trust me, that's the one. If you buy it now, I'll find the money to pay you back for it. I want to get it for you." She looked so eager Mira could hardly tell her no. Maybe it would turn out to be good luck.

After purchasing the gemstone, Mira looked at it more closely. She could see the delicate black veins running throughout the crystal. "She need a name?"

Kahli looked at her weirdly. "Why would she need a name? That's silly."

That was a surprise. Mira had asked because naming a rock seemed exactly like something Kahli would do.

Shrugging, Mira led them out of the booth, and Kahli began to ramble. "So that's nephrite jade. They're super powerful. Protection, emotional healing, compassion, fosters healthy relationships and self-love…"

Mira grumbled, taking in the pointed meanings. "Ah, so it was a targeted gift."

"It's great for *healing*. It'll help you. Don't be so negative."

Mira lifted the stone up to her face again as Kahli guided them to the next area. While she was distracted, someone bumped into her shoulder and she nearly dropped her rock, clinging on to it for dear life. Kahli turned to steady her.

"You alright?" Kahli's eyes searched warily around them, as if expecting something to happen again, when Mira brushed it off.

"It's fine. I didn't even see who it was. Just some asshole. Can I put my rock in your bag for now? I don't want to lose it."

Kahli wrapped her arm around Mira's shoulders, protectively drawing her in close. "I guess I gotta keep a better eye on you." She took the rock gently and settled it beside her horse which was at least wrapped in paper, then pulled Mira toward the food booths. "Let's grab something to eat, I'm starving."

Mira had to admit, she felt much better after getting some air and being dragged around by a pretty girl. One who was a nerd for rocks and the ocean, apparently.

"Sure, spend all my money..." she joked lightly.

Kahli turned her head as they continued, her shoulders falling slightly. "I thought you said you had plenty?"

Mira nodded. "Luckily for you, I do. You can thank Wendy for all the years she forced me to continue living with her and not paying rent.

Rent's a killer. I mean, you know, you live with your family."

The woman beside her grew quiet and Mira wanted to smack herself.

"It's not a bad thing, Kahli. I don't think less of you." It was her turn to pull Kahli along. "Look, they have sushi, you must like that, right?"

Kahli's eyes widened in alarm and Mira felt like an idiot for assuming.

"Oh. You don't, do you." Mira's shoulders tightened. She thought she had been doing a good job of figuring Kahli out when reality came crashing back. They had only known each other for about a week; she didn't know her well at all.

Kahli continued staring at Mira strangely. "No, I... do. I'm just..." She looked away. "Surprised you do, is all."

"Well, I do. And fish is always fresh by the coast, right? Let's have that." Mira maneuvered them into a line and started to pester Kahli for her preferences. "So what are we talking about here? Are you like a California Roll Girl, or super adventurous and about to make me re-try fish eggs?"

"How adventurous are *you*?" Kahli smiled, the previous playfulness returning to her tone.

Mira lifted her chin a bit, proud that she wasn't inexperienced when it came to seafood. "I've tried most of it. With Wendy, actually. She was the first person to get me to try it, on a dare. Her thirteenth birthday party was at a sushi restaurant."

Kahli pondered the choices with a false innocence that wafted off her, clearly up to something. "Even... jellyfish?"

Well *shit*. She hadn't actually expected Kahli to find something new. Cringing at being forced out of her comfort zone, Mira reluctantly responded. "Okay... maybe not that." She looked ahead. "But if you get some... I'll try it."

Kahli nodded excitedly. "Noted."

Mira waited until they got to the counter to reveal her order. Unagi rolls. She let Kahli order the rest, which might have been a mistake. Kahli seemed ready to test what Mira was willing to try.

They found an empty table beneath some trees in a picnic area that overlooked the water, and Mira grumbled as they sat down. "Didn't even know they made jellyfish sushi..."

Snorting, Kahli laid out their food.

Mira got an impressed look from Kahli when she reached for chopsticks instead of a fork. "What? I'm cultured." She had learned after getting disapproving looks from the staff at a Japanese restaurant during college. Public shame really did work for some things.

Kahli pushed the plastic tray with her selections over to Mira, using her own chopsticks to point out the first trial. "That's the jellyfish. It's actually my favorite." When Mira hesitated, Kahli rolled her eyes, took one, dipped it in sauce, and held it out to Mira.

"You're making a mess on the table." Mira's eyes were locked on the food before her, and she contemplated if she was too old to try new things just to impress a cute girl.

Who was she kidding? She absolutely wasn't.

Kahli held steady, not inching the piece of fish closer or pulling it away. "Just try it. I won't even bother you if you have to spit it out."

Mira started to part her lips and Kahli waited as Mira wrapped her lips around the bite. Her eyes scrunched as she took in the texture and shivered.

Kahli laughed. "Mira, it's not that bad, it's just chewy."

Keeping her mouth closed, Mira opened her eyes to glare, chewing aggressively as if *that* was her response. When she swallowed, she pouted. "It was... crunchy in the middle. That was gross."

Kahli took the next one and plopped it into her mouth, flashing her eyes at Mira in challenge.

Not taking the bait, Mira took a piece of unagi and settled in, happily chewing now with the flavors bursting across her tongue. Sweet and warm, just like she remembered.

Mira continued to chew as she pondered something. She should have a large rash covering at least a third of her body by now; it never took this long to appear. "I don't have a rash. Do you see one?" She twisted herself around looking for the pink, bumpy, raised patches of skin that always accompanied her use of sunscreen.

Kahli just stared. "Maybe you found a sunscreen you're not allergic to?"

Mira shook her head. "Nah, I've had that one a while, totally broke out before. That's so strange. Better take some antihistamine when I get home just in case. Maybe a delayed reaction."

Apparently unbothered by Mira's missing rash, Kahli shoved more fish in her mouth as she shrugged. Mira took into account the way her eyes avoided her now, wondering if the younger woman would decide she wasn't fuckable anymore once she did see her rash.

Kahli was strange, but with the way she was making Mira feel, it didn't seem like a bad thing.

# Chapter 16

Mira tossed her keys onto the hall table as she kicked off her shoes. Kahli followed behind her, setting Mira's new painting and their bag of keepsakes on the floor. Mira turned to watch, taking note that Kahli's shoes appeared slightly too big for her feet, and she wondered if Kahli's family had money problems. She didn't want to pry, but she figured she could at least snoop at some point and get the other woman better-fitting shoes before she left. She turned to go for the stairs, but when she placed her hand on the railing, she paused. Her eyes turned to Kahli, who was standing awkwardly, looking around the living room. Mira's eyes drifted up the stairs, before landing back on the younger woman.

"So, I did some thinking on the drive back. You can see one piece of art." She took a deep breath as she tried to steady her nerves. "Be nice, I'm… sensitive about my hobby art." She didn't wait for a reply as she led them upstairs. Going to the desk, she tried to turn on her drawing tablet, but had to plug it in to charge when she found that the battery had drained despite not using it. She redirected her attention to her computer, finding a certain folder with her secret hobby art.

Behind her, the bed creaked as Kahli took a seat, waiting for her to offer up whatever she was ready to show her.

Clicking on the first file, she felt her heart race a little as an intimate image of two nude women appeared. The woman in the back had her arms wrapped around the woman in front, eyes looking down at her with admiration. The woman being held seemed unaware of the attention as her eyes were closed, enjoying the quiet moment.

Mira unplugged her computer as she moved to sit beside Kahli, tucking her loose hair behind her ear. She shifted the laptop to face Kahli at an angle.

"This one is one of my favorites. I never was able to decide if they were lovers or if this was some play on self-love or something equally cliché. So..." She felt her stomach cramp with the anxiety that came from sharing her personal art. She didn't do it often. She had shown Wendy in middle school, and Wendy had encouraged her to hone her talent. Hell, even Wendy's mother had been supportive when she had accidentally walked in on Mira drawing. Mira's face had flushed bright red when it was a nude drawing of a fairy in a forest.

Wendy's parents had always been kind to her, but she never allowed herself to bask in their attention for long. They were meant for Wendy, not her. She wasn't supposed to have parents who hugged her, who told her she was beautiful, or that they were proud of her... or that she was a good person, even if she didn't feel like it.

Because she was so closed off to them, Wendy pushed harder to parent Mira herself; she was the only one who was able to get that close. Mira, at one point, had mistaken that for romantic love. Hell, Wendy had too, in their youth. They just couldn't figure out why they didn't fit in that way. They tried but it always felt... wrong, somehow.

Mira refocused on the screen in front of her, before drifting to Kahli's honey brown eyes, watching as she took in every stroke of the figures. Mira felt the back of her neck tingle anxiously. Maybe she shouldn't have shown Kahli her work.

A hum broke Mira out of her panic. "This feels so real, look at her face. Like, I can imagine exactly what it would be like to reach out and hold her if she were here in this room right now." Kahli's eyes continued to trace the image. "How did you do that?"

Mira pursed her lips and shrugged. "Lots of practice." She tilted her head. "Lots of time spent staring at photos of beautiful women. Some... life-drawing classes."

Kahli turned to her, intrigued. "Life drawing?"

Mira shifted uncomfortably. "Nude models. They would sit on a chair, placed on top of a desk, in the middle of a room and we would just 'draw what we see.'"

"Show me." Kahli's voice was resolute. "Show me how you do it."

Mira snorted. "It's not a quick process. This image took hours."

Kahli shrugged, looking far too excited. "I have time."

Grasping for an excuse, Mira looked around. "I don't have an extra chair up here..."

Kahli was already standing and going for the door. "I'll grab one from downstairs! Don't worry, I'll put it back when I'm done." As Mira started to protest, Kahli waved off her concerns. "I need somewhere to sit to watch you draw anyways."

Mira went back to her seat. She heard the other woman bound down the stairs, a scraping sound in the kitchen, then the creaking of the steps as

Kahli lugged the thing up with her. She appeared at the door, triumphant. "Got it!"

"You realize I didn't say yes, right?"

Kahli wasn't deterred as she set the chair next to her, giving her plenty of space. "You didn't say no either."

Mira sighed and opened a new document, grabbing the digital pen and placing it over the pad. She started to trace eyes and a face.

"Doing the beginning lines is the most important, then I'll refine them before adding dimension with other lines and shading. I'm not doing all of that today though."

When she glanced at Kahli, she saw that she was leaning forward on her elbows, mesmerized. Mira turned back to the screen and continued drawing the rest of the outline.

"It's always better when I have a reference to look at, if I'm drawing a specific face or body. My mind just kinda… sees it in 3D on the page and I just… outline what my mind sees here." She indicated the tablet.

Kahli's chair creaked as she shifted. "Okay, so draw me. Come on."

Mira's hand twitched and the line she had been drawing dragged off the page.

"You said it's better with a reference." Kahli stood and looked around, picking up the wooden chair before she placed it in the middle of the room. "Is here good?"

Mira's mouth dropped open in shock at the fact that the opportunity to draw—and unabashedly stare at—this beautiful woman completely naked, was happening. Trying to search for a reason why she shouldn't draw Kahli seemed futile. "That's fine."

Kahli turned the chair around and sat with her legs spread over the set, leaning forward onto the back of the chair. "Like this?"

Mira snorted. "It's not very helpful if I can't see the shape of your body."

Nodding, Kahli she took off her shirt, revealing that she was braless beneath it. Mira's eyes widened. Kahli hooked her thumbs in her shorts as she pulled them down. The underwear she had borrowed were all that remained. "Do these come off too?" She looked at Mira seriously, waiting for direction.

Mira swallowed, but her throat felt dry as she tried to get her response out. "Ye-Yeah." She cleared her throat. "That would be good."

Kahli took them off and stood there, completely naked. "Can you show me how you want me?"

Mira was struck with the realization that she had touched this body, brought it to climax, but she hadn't been allowed to just *stare* at Kahli before. She found herself almost shy as she tried to push her feelings aside from the technicality of the process. Kahli was *just* a body. She nodded as she stood, forgoing the chair and tilting her head toward the bed. "Help me push this against the wall."

Kahli's strength came in handy as Mira barely had to exert any effort. The bed slipped into place easily, and Mira tested that it wouldn't budge.

"Climb up and put your back against the wall. Put a pillow behind your lower back, we'll be here a while. Feel free to tell me when you need breaks."

Obediently, Kahli climbed up on the bed. Mira rolled her eyes when the other woman just sat there, so she joined her on the bed to position her. She made sure Kahli was leaning back so her breasts were resting against her body rather than hanging down. Bending one of Kahli's legs, she let it fall to the side and tucked that ankle under the other knee. One of Kahli's arms was left lying across the bed, the other placed on her stomach, before Mira felt Kahli move it to her own neck. Mira's eyes went wide as she took in how close they were and felt her body heat up. When she pulled back, Kahli smirked.

"I mean... we could skip the drawing lesson..."

Mira huffed. "No. I... haven't had someone to practice with in a while. This will... be good for me. Just... lay there."

Kahli maintained her pose as she inclined her head, eyes flashing in challenge. "Okay, Mira."

Mira turned and retreated to her chair, turning it to face Kahli. She picked up the stylus and stared at Kahli's face, sketching the shape on her tablet screen before mapping the dimensions of her body. Taking into account the unique way her outline sloped in the physical space. Her mind could already see it on the page.

On her next glance up, she noticed Kahli's face had scrunched and she was about to ask what was wrong when she sneezed, trying adorably not to move a muscle. "Sorry!"

Mira smiled softly. "You're fine. Did you want to take a break and stretch? I think I have the outline solid enough for now." She didn't *have* to have Kahli lay naked anymore. She could come up with the rest on her own. But if she wanted to capture the *exact* way the sun came through the window, and the way the shadows around the room draped across her skin, she *could* use her for a bit longer.

"I'm good. Comfortable." After a moment, Kahli hesitantly added, "Am I doing okay?"

Mira had never seen a model be so still before, be so patient while she sketched her features onto the page. Her voice was soft as she spoke. "You're doing amazing. Very still."

Kahli's chest puffed up a bit at the praise.

Shaking her head with a smile, Mira kept drawing before she looked back up to take in the slope of Kahli's breasts. She remembered the weight of them in her hands and it helped her add depth, knowing when she had gotten them just right. Knowing that if she were to reach out and cup the Kahli in the drawing, gently, it would almost be hard to tell the difference between the art and living versions. She smirked. This was coming together nicely.

Kahli's voice wafted into her consciousness. "I don't have any pictures of me."

Mira continued to work on her chest. "Drawings?"

"No. Like... any."

Mira's hand slowed as she looked up into Kahli's intense gaze, deciding that her eyes were the next feature she wanted to add more detail to. "What do you mean? Your parents never took photos of you?"

Kahli nodded dejectedly. "Maybe I was an ugly child…"

If Kahli's parents actually thought that of her, then they had more in common than Mira thought. Mira frowned and tried to reassure the other woman. "Kahli, I'm sure that's not true." She wanted to punch whoever had made her think that in the face. Kahli was absolutely gorgeous, quite possibly the most beautiful woman she had ever seen.

The younger woman took a deep breath, causing her breasts to shift slightly with the motion. "It's just nice to be immortalized. Like there might be something that remains of me after I'm gone." Her eyes trailed over Mira. "Do you have drawings of you?"

Mira tried to avoid the melancholy in her voice as she instead focused on what she assumed was the reason for her request. "Why? Are you asking for one? You know, if you had a *phone*, I might be inclined to send you actual pictures."

Kahli's brows pulled together. "I don't…" Her hips shifted unintentionally and she sighed. "I'll work on finding one…"

Contemplating the fun she could get up to with Kahli over a phone, Mira licked her lips. "It would be nice to be able to find you when I need you."

Kahli's eyes lifted, mouth parting as if she wanted to say something, but she seemed to change her mind and let it fall closed. Her eyes wandered away before returning a moment later. "Can I see?"

Mira glanced down and added darker shadows around the eyes, nose, and mouth, starting on her neck and adding initial lines for her hair. "One sec." She finished up what she was working on then stood to show Kahli, her fingers pinching the image to zoom out. "Here." She turned it and held it up before Kahli's eyes. "It's not nearly done yet."

Kahli's mouth dropped and her eyes sparkled. She was almost giddy. "That's amazing, I didn't know my body looks like that. My eyes look really pretty."

Mira let her shoulders fall slightly. Why did Kahli not see herself the way she did? It was one thing when she criticized her own body, it was another when someone else did it to themselves. Kahli was stunning and she couldn't imagine what she might see, or what might have clouded her vision. She made an attempt to try to alter her perception.

"This is exactly what I see when I look at you." Her eyes darted back down to the screen. "You should take a break from your family. You're welcome to stay here with me until I leave…" She felt her skin prickle at the suggestion. Afraid of the rejection that might follow such an offer.

Sitting up, Kahli crossed her legs, her fingers playing with the sheets. "You want me to?"

Mira nodded. "Why not? It'll be easier to plan my days if I'm not being randomly interrupted by your appearances. We could… plan them together, I guess." This felt a lot like she was jumping headfirst into another relationship. Mira tried to reason with herself that it wasn't that serious, it was just a vacation romance, and who knew how serious Kahli was about it. Or what she would want in the end.

Kahli grabbed a pillow and pulled it to her chest. "Maybe for a couple days. I don't want to take up all of your time."

# Chapter 17

It was almost too comfortable living with Kahli. The other woman was clean, if a little forgetful. She was constantly half-finishing what she was doing before wandering away, but Mira found she couldn't be too annoyed as she did the exact same things. Except now, when she left things half completed, Kahli would usually find them and finish them up, and Mira would do the same for her.

Kahli loved to stay up late either talking or watching Mira as she drew. She seemed to prefer that to watching TV, though when Mira turned on the TV, it almost felt like Kahli was a toddler, getting lost in the moving pictures for hours.

However, every night when things would wind down and she would head to bed, Kahli would get comfy on the couch and tell her goodnight. Mira tried not to take the disappointment to heart. Maybe she wasn't aware that Mira wished for Kahli to join her, and Mira didn't want to pressure her, too afraid that Kahli would go home if she suggested it.

So like she had every night for the past five nights, Mira stood suddenly from her seat on the couch after agonizing over leaving her companion's side for at least an hour. She tucked her hair behind her ear to stall as she looked around for her phone. Locating it on the corner of the table and tapping her fingers against it lightly, she rounded the couch and departed quietly, getting halfway up the stairs before she heard Kahli.

"Goodnight, Mira!"

She paused and smiled to herself. At least Kahli didn't ever make her feel like she was invisible. Unlike Amani, who never seemed to notice her presence or how she was quietly screaming for physical affection. She turned her head, tossing a goodnight over her shoulder, before continuing her ascent.

Entering her room and closing the door softly, she plugged her phone in beside the bed and climbed in, getting cozy. Things seemed much less stifling with another person around, and that somehow that was improving her sleep at night. She looked toward the door and sighed. She should just go ask Kahli to join her. Did she really think she was going to storm out at the mere suggestion?

She pushed up on her arm, contemplating asking from the top of the stairs, when she heard the TV turn off. Kahli must be ready for sleep. Shaking her head, she leaned over and turned her lamp off as well so that the only light in the room now came from outside. She nuzzled down into her sheets, pulling them up around her chin, and started to drift.

≈ ≈ ≈

The dream started as they always did, with her mother.

Mira was standing in her childhood backyard, the familiar wildly overgrown lawn surrounded by a forest of trees looming above her. She looked around her as her mother screamed, red in the face. The actual words weren't important, Mira had heard them all. She tried to take in the clearing surrounding her with a critical eye, but it was hard to focus on any one thing. Gazing skyward, the trees were so tall she couldn't see their tops, as if they went on forever. When she looked back, her mother's eyes were completely black. She jolted, stumbling backward as her mother tried to grab her, but she was faster. She turned and ran for the tree line.

As she tore through the woods and the tree trunks started to blur, Wendy cut into her path out of nowhere.

"This way!" Wendy shouted as she took a hard right, and Mira followed her without question. Wendy had never led her toward danger, she always led her away from it. She heard her mother's thundering footsteps, as if there were a loud, malfunctioning sound system amplifying them. She covered her ears, attempting to drown it out, and continued sprinting. Wendy darted to the left and Mira felt herself slowing.

"Wendy! Wendy, I can't... I can't keep up! Slow down! Please..."

She pushed herself, but the more she pushed, the slower she got, allowing Wendy to briefly disappear from sight. She kept going, feeling like she was pushing through water, until she burst into a round dirt clearing, where a Black girl with Wendy's brown skin and shaved head was laying face down.

"Wendy? Wendy, are you okay?" She inched forward and crouched, still looking out for her mother. Her hand connected with Wendy's shoulder, eyes going wide when she didn't feel her breathing. A loud ringing in her ears momentarily distracted her from her racing heart as she hurried to flip the girl, revealing a face covered in blood. There was so much of the thick crimson liquid that she couldn't tell it was Wendy anymore. She screamed, reeling backwards. Who had done this?

Her hand shot up in an attempt to cover her mouth, but it was too late. She pitched to the side, vomiting.

Mira gasped. Though she couldn't smell it, or feel it, the sight of the fluid on her fingers drove her over the edge as she frantically tried to wipe it off.

When she finally calmed down enough to survey the area, her eyes landed on a bloody rock that lay beside her. She reached out to pick it up with a shaky hand. If someone joined them in the clearing, they would think she did this to her friend. What was she going to tell Wendy's parents? *"Fuck. Fuck. Fuck..."* She panicked, trying to figure out which way to go for help. Maybe she was mistaken. Maybe Wendy's heart was still beating, even if it was faint.

Suddenly, music started to play, shaking the world with the deep, reverberating tones. She figured there must be someone with a car nearby and bolted toward the sound, everything blurring as she ran. Maybe it wasn't too late if she could find help *now*. Maybe she missed that Wendy was still breathing. Maybe she could be resuscitated.

Mira was almost to the edge of the trees when someone grabbed her.

"No!" She tried to shake them off violently.

Another voice crossed the barrier into her mind. "Mira! Stop! What are you doing?"

Mira's eyes flew open. The sound of the ocean was far too close and she felt her body sway as water shifted around her waist. She tried to see through her tears. Wendy couldn't be gone, what would she do without her?

As she started to focus more on her surroundings, she moved from panic to dread. Why was she in the water? Where the fuck was she? Her lips trembled from the cold, her breaths coming quickly as the music she had heard in the dream continued in her waking life. Her hands went to the familiar arms wrapped around her waist.

"Wendy... Wendy's hurt." She tried to take a step deeper, as if that's where Wendy was, and Kahli pulled back so hard her feet slipped out from under her. The younger woman's arms kept her above the surface.

"No, she's not. She's not even here!" Kahli huffed as she pulled her back further. "You can't just dive into the ocean like that! *You* don't even know what's out there."

Kahli held Mira's body tight to her chest, as if she might slip through her fingers and plunge under the surface if she didn't, and Mira felt her mind slowly absorb everything. She was outside. In the ocean. With Kahli. Well, Kahli appeared to be trying to drag her out of the water.

Mira shook her head. "How... How did I get out here?"

Kahli continued to walk her backward. "You were... asleep. You never told me you sleepwalk. Could have used the heads-up..."

Mira's breathing was uneven until they hit the sand. Kahli's arms didn't loosen.

"I don't... sleepwalk."

Pressing her face into Mira's shoulder, Kahli tried to speak. "You scared me. You were so quiet, if I didn't hear the deck creak I wouldn't have... I wouldn't have grabbed you in time."

As reality washed over her, Mira gripped Kahli's arm. Her skin felt the way her wet clothing clung to her. "I... tried to go under the water?"

Kahli nodded as she focused on turning Mira and checking her over. "Does anything hurt?"

Mira shook her head. "No... I'm... just cold."

Kahli wrapped one arm around Mira and led her toward the stairs and into the house. "I'm blocking the doors tonight. Maybe I should stay in your room with you."

Mira felt her body warm a little at the thought. This wasn't how she had planned to get Kahli into her bed, but she was happy with the result nonetheless.

After carefully locking up, Kahli steered her toward the bathroom. "Get warm, I'll make some tea."

With Kahli gone, she found that she was actually very freaking cold. Mira quickly stripped off her clothing, hearing it slap against the tiled floor. She turned on the water and waited for it to warm up. Climbing in, she turned, resting her forehead on the wall. She had never been plagued by sleep-walking. Not even in her youth when her stress had been at its peak. The idea that she could get from her bed all the way outside, down the stairs and into the ocean, was terrifying. If Kahli wasn't there, would she have drowned, or simply have just gone for a swim?

She pressed her palm flat against the wall, drumming her fingers to distract her from the numb terror she felt crawling through her veins at the thought of drowning. How her vision would blur while she gasped for breath. How she wouldn't have been able to see which way was up in the dark, if she was already too deep. She shook her head. The darkness was too overwhelming, so she opened her eyes, only to be greeted with *more* darkness.

Mira screeched.

She slapped her hand against the wall to make sure it was real, afraid she was still caught in her nightmare. The sound of the shower spray continued to beat down, letting her know she really was in her bathroom. She fucking shrieked when the curtain moved and hands grabbed her.

"Mira!"

Her body dropped against the wall. Kahli. Kahli had come to find her in the dark.

Mira felt around frantically for Kahli's shoulders, wrapping her arms around Kahli's neck. She started to sob. Kahli's hands stroked up and down her back reassuringly.

Kahli didn't tell her to stop, or that she was being ridiculous, that it was just the dark. She let her cry. Mira heaved in air a few times before she was able to start to settle. The dark was still suffocating, but it felt like she was protected from the worst of it in Kahli's arms.

The younger woman started humming and Mira felt herself relax even more.

Focusing on her breathing, Mira blocked everything else out, leaning heavily against Kahli as she gathered herself. "I could have drowned…" She groaned. "That is not a way I want to go."

Kahli placed a kiss to her thick head of hair. "You're not going to drown. You didn't. We just… need to figure out what caused it." She felt Kahli's fingers slide through her wet hair. "I'm going to go reset the circuit breaker. You know where it is, right?"

Mira nodded. "I'll come with you. I… can't be in here alone."

She couldn't see, but she heard Kahli turn off the water and move the curtain all the way to one side. Kahli wrapped a towel around Mira, who glanced at the mirror as they made their way to the door, drawn in by something shimmering in the moonlight. Stuck in her stress response, she didn't linger on the visual disturbance, her mind too unstable to remember what she might have seen for long. It was *very* dark, and she couldn't focus on much besides that fact.

Kahli had no trouble opening the door, and the dimly lit house spilled some light from outside across them. Mira took Kahli's hand as she led them to the garage. Her hand reached around the corner and felt for the circuit breaker, resetting the tripped switch. "There."

She felt a deep sigh of relief release pass her lips.

"I swear, every time I fucking shower…"

Kahli snorted. "You could leave the door open."

Mira rolled her eyes. She extracted her hand from Kahli's, noticing she was still holding on. "I should get dressed." She turned to go, needing a moment to finish collecting herself.

"I'll grab your tea."

Mira turned and shook her head. "I don't want it. But thank you." She chewed on her lip. "Are you going to stay with me tonight?" She wanted to kick herself with how whiny her voice sounded, but the urge quickly dissipated when Kahli nodded and placed a hand to her back, following her up the stairs. She pulled out her clothes and dressed while Kahli turned down the bed. When she was in her tank top and some fuzzy lavender shorts, she climbed in. Snuggling into Kahli before she could overthink it, she wrapped her body around her. The woman in turn looped her arms around her waist.

"Rest. I'll make sure you don't go anywhere."

# Chapter 18

Mira found that planning meals happened now because she didn't want Kahli to starve, despite her own lack of appetite. Her house guest seemed to pick up on the routine, timing her twice-daily swims to when Mira was preparing breakfast and dinner, always checking first to see if she wanted help. Invariably, Mira responded by shooing the younger woman outside with assurances that she wasn't going to burn the place down.

She was more relaxed now that her mind wasn't crushing her. Though the fight over the embryos loomed, she felt confident that she could stand up to Amani and put her foot down. And with Kahli eagle-eyed about her sudden sleepwalking, she wasn't worried that she would end up back in the water.

Kahli had taken their art from the fair and mounted Mira's painting up on the wall in the living room, assuring Mira the owners wouldn't notice the minor damage when she left. She placed her horse figure and Mira's rock near the back window, claiming that the moonlight charged the gemstones.

The other woman was also helpful whenever Mira had any aches or pain, massaging her tight muscles and tendons unprompted. The moment Mira's hands subtly drifted to an area, Kahli would move to replace Mira's hands with her own.

Mira started to dread her own departure and the necessary conversation about their future. Would the other woman be willing to commute to see her sometimes? She didn't want to spend all her time driving to Kahli. She had done *that* relationship before, and it always ended up being one-sided. Plus, she wasn't sure where she would stay if she did come back to visit. Kahli didn't have her own place like she did.

As they sat on the couch in comfortable silence, she looked up and watched Kahli, who was watching TV. Kahli lay on her side, her head nuzzled into a throw pillow, with Mira's blanket draped over both of them. Although Kahli swore she didn't get cold, she seemed to love the idea of sharing with Mira. She rolled her eyes as she got up from the couch.

Kahli's eyes lifted to her, abandoning her show. "Where..." her voice trailed off as Mira stood before her.

"Scoot back."

Without asking for a reason, Kahli shifted until she was up against the back of the couch. Mira settled herself in front, about to ask for some of the blanket when Kahli draped it over her, her arm resting around her waist as they continued to watch.

Little comments from Kahli occasionally drifted into the room, making Mira snort. "Kahli. Just watch." She didn't really mind the little asides, but she did find that they often kept her awake when she wanted to nap. She leaned back further, into the solid body that made sure she knew she wasn't alone. Amani hadn't liked to cuddle.

But Mira had craved it. She tried not to want all the gentleness that she felt wasn't meant for her, but she couldn't help it. At times she was willing to do anything for that comfort, willing to cave to any of Amani's demands so that she could have her touch.

Mira was quiet as her mind tried to settle into the sense of safety that she felt around Kahli. Yet she found that the show no longer held her attention, not when her thoughts were swirling like a storm.

Taking a deep breath and letting it out, Mira resigned herself to a conversation she needed but didn't want to have. "So... I have been thinking." She waited for Kahli to focus on her, but at the other woman's silence, she thought she had lost the battle for it. Turning back to look over her shoulder, she was pleasantly surprised to find the other woman looking back at her.

Kahli's honey irises looked darker at night. Sometimes it was hard to tell what color they actually were. Bright when light reflected in them, dark when it didn't. Those eyes were currently trained on her, watching carefully as if Mira's body language would give away her thoughts before her mouth did. Her mind was buzzing as she finally spit it out.

"How do you feel about kids?" She felt her heart throb with pain from how hard it started beating. Although, if she passed out, she wouldn't have to deal with the answer, or that she had ever asked in the first place.

Kahli remained still as her eyes shifted across Mira's pale features. "Why?"

Not, "*Do you want them,*" not, "*With the right person,*" not "*No,*" but, "*Why?*" Mira's brows pinched together as she huffed. The younger woman wasn't going to make this easy.

"Don't know, maybe because you told me to keep the embryos I had in case I find a partner I wanted to use them with." She knew she was being immature, but she couldn't help the bite that entered her tone. Kahli had told her to fight to keep them. Had she really not considered that maybe Mira might actually want to use them? With *her*? Assuming things went well.

She felt as Kahli shifted further away. "I don't really know much about the subject. Perhaps... we could start smaller? A pet maybe?"

Mira scooted further toward the edge and Kahli's hand reaching out to grab her as she almost toppled from the couch. "If there's no point in me storing them, I'll have them destroyed... or just give them to Amani. Hell, I know it'll make my divorce go a lot smoother if I just let her have them. There... will be a divorce I have to deal with soon."

She wasn't under any delusion that Amani was going to change her mind and come back home. She knew that once Amani made a decision, it was always final. Mira had respected that about her, but that respect faded when she was on the receiving end of her decision-making.

Mira felt Kahli lean forward and kiss her shoulder as Mira went to wiggle away. "I shouldn't be jumping into something else. I still have a wife to deal with. Now that she's back from the grave there's too much I need to sort through." She felt her heart constrict but didn't move from the couch. She felt like she was going to be sick as she forced the question past her lips. "This was all just some fun, right?"

She was terrified to hear Kahli's response, because this *wasn't* just a little fun. Not to her. She was beginning to feel like she had maybe found someone that actually fit her in ways that Amani never had. That maybe Kahli could handle her having friends in her life, friends like Wendy and Allie, and even her boss and mentor Lydia. She covered her mouth with her hand. Kahli was taking her time responding. Or maybe was planning her escape.

Kahli shifted, scooting out from behind her. "Did you want me to go?"

Mira shook her head before she could make up her mind about her response. She turned when Kahli remained silent, watching tan fingers pick at the pilling on the couch cushions.

"You... said you couldn't have children, that you couldn't carry them. I... I can't either. Well, I'm pretty sure I can't, and it's not fair to you to not know and think that maybe I could be the way you have a child. It's just... not in the cards. Not with me."

Her voice was so small. Mira's heart felt like someone had grabbed both sides and was slowly tearing it apart. She remembered when the doctors had told her that her womb was *hostile*, that it would attack anything that tried to implant. She remembered the day that she had sat in the exam chair staring at Amani's bright green eyes as they grew even greener with the loss of their future. They already knew Amani couldn't carry a baby, but they had never thought that Mira's body would fail them as well.

Had Kahli also been to a doctor and sat on a table and been told that her body simply didn't function right? Had anyone been there to hold *her* hand? Had Kahli even wanted kids at the time? And had there been a partner who felt betrayed at their potential to have biological children stripped away?

Mira didn't say a word, she just reached out and took Kahli's hand. Amani hadn't even held her hand on the way home. She had been completely invisible, as if she didn't matter. She didn't want Kahli to feel that way.

"Did you ever try and..." She watched as Kahli's face tensed.

Kahli shook her head but didn't pull away. "No... I just... I don't really want to get into it, but I can't. And... that's something you want. You deserve to find someone who can have that with you." Dark eyes started to sparkle with tears.

"I mean... there are always surrogates, right?" Mira hadn't been super opposed to the idea, aside from the high price tag, as well as the moral implications of finding someone who really wanted to do the job and not someone that felt they had no other choice.

Kahli took her hand back to wipe at her face. "I'm not sure what you mean."

"We can pay another woman to carry the baby for us if... if that's something we want... one day."

Growing up, Mira had always thought that she wouldn't be a mom. Not with the way she was raised and the issues she had. But when she met Amani, it was something *she* had wanted. Mira had pushed herself on the tough things to see if she could be capable of what would be needed of her. She cared for Amani, she had been able to care for Wendy, she figured that she had enough love for one more person in her life. She had been terrified of messing up a kid, but felt that if Amani was there, she couldn't fail.

Looking over at Kahli, she saw the same safety net. That if she ever did take that journey, Kahli wouldn't let her fail, wouldn't leave her alone to raise a child by herself. She squeezed Kahli's hand as she scooted a little closer. "I bet we would make some pretty cute babies."

At Kahli's snort, she felt her own heart flutter.

"Want to go to bed and practice?" Mira heard how rough her voice was as it came out and rolled her eyes internally at herself for how desperate she thought she sounded. The embarrassment faded as some of the tension fell from Kahli's shoulders.

Kahli smiled wide as she smirked. "We can try."

# Chapter 19

Their night of passion had been long. Kahli had really taken to putting her all into Mira's multiple orgasms. Somewhere in the night she had passed out from the intensity. Her mind vaguely remembered hearing Kahli get up and take the stairs. At first, she had assumed she would return to bed, but when Mira dozed for a while and she wasn't there when she woke up, she started to wonder if Kahli had left. Mira extracted herself from the bed, hoping that there wasn't a goodbye note. That she hadn't asked for too much too quickly and scared Kahli off.

When she arrived downstairs and rounded the kitchen island, she saw a note scribbled on paper.

"Mira, I went for a swim, I'll see you later." There was a heart and a *Kahli* in swoopy handwriting, and Mira tried to relax despite the way her brain tried to warn her that there was more behind the simple words. That Kahli hadn't just gone for a swim but had left her.

She shoved the demons in her head aside as she continued on with her day.

Mira grabbed her phone and checked her calendar. Her vacation would be coming to a close soon, and given that she was still alive, and potentially with someone new in her life, it appeared that she needed to make some plans for the future. Like returning to work.

She went upstairs and opened her laptop, starting an email to Lydia. She suggested that she needed a day or two when she got back to the city but that she was refreshed and ready to go, and that she had more than a few ideas for the campaigns that were coming up. Taking out her tablet, she did some preliminary line drawings and sent them off. Hopefully, Lydia would be satisfied and would not fire her for taking such an extended holiday.

Her shoulders sagged in relief when she received a response not even five minutes later that Lydia couldn't wait for her to return, and that two more days would be fine. Lydia had always been overly generous compared to all the other work experiences she had survived. She was glad she hadn't done something stupid, like quit when she was sure she hadn't wanted to be around after her trip.

Mira started to think about her apartment and how, while it was more than enough space for her, she would need to rethink her living arrangements if she and Kahli were to become a long-term thing. How long would it be until Kahli would be ready to move in with her? She was already having some kind of issue living with her family, and so far they got on well enough when they were around each other all day and all night. Was it crazy to ask her already?

She pondered where they would place her new painting, because while there was room for it in the entry hall, that wasn't exactly the heart of her home. Maybe she could rearrange some of the wall space in the living room. She was sure Amani was going to want some of the art now that she was taking half of everything.

There was a large windowsill in the living room, and she figured that would be as good a space as any for Kahli to charge their rocks. She wondered what the woman would want to bring with her to Mira's when she moved in... She caught herself and closed her eyes. *If* she moved in.

She looked out the window at the water and pondered if she wanted to try to go for a swim.

Picking up her phone to check the water temperature, she blanched at the sub-fifty degrees. For sure not in her plans for the day then, no matter how bored she was.

Standing and moving to the dresser, she looked through the subpar options she had brought to clothe herself in. Never in her wildest dreams did she think she was going to find a girl she wanted to impress, in the middle of winter, at a remote beach house. She smiled; it was always at the strangest times when her life would take a turn for the better, usually just when she had given up hope.

Closing the drawer, she decided a trip into town was in order. She grabbed her keys and her hand had just wrapped around the front door when she paused, worried about when Kahli might return. Briefly, she considered leaving the door unlocked, but something inside of her told her not to. She wouldn't be gone that long, and Kahli wouldn't mind relaxing in the sun while she waited for Mira to return.

Backtracking through the house, Mira grabbed a pad of paper and scribbled a quick note that she she left on the back door. Satisfied that Kahli wouldn't be worried, she hopped in her car and connected her phone, opting to play some music from her playlist as she took the short drive to town.

There was a spot in front of the cafe that she swung into before she went inside. It was quiet as usual, but there had been at least some people on the street. She watched as Benny leaned over the counter, flirting with a boy with dark tan skin and curly black hair with buzzed sides. She raised an eyebrow when Benny's eyes lifted at the sound of the bell; he blushed.

The boy he had been talking to turned around and smirked. "That *her*?"

Mira squinted at both of them as she slowed her approach. "Are we gossiping about patrons on the clock?"

Benny smiled and shook his head. "This is Eddie, my boyfriend. The one I told you about?"

Mira raised her chin and eyed him up and down, noticing how quickly her gaze made the boy nervous.

"Uh, h-hi, Miss Mira..." He stuck out his hand, and she stared at it for a moment to let the kid think she *wasn't* about to shake it, before she let her hand dart out at the last possible second to snatch his. She smiled when he gripped her hand back.

"Firm handshake." She looked up at Benny. "Nice choice. What's he do?"

Eddie took his hand back and scratched the back of his neck. "I am going to school for finance. I know... it's super boring."

Mira shrugged. "Someone has to make the money, your boy toy is a barista. Bet he goes for an art degree."

Benny frowned, taking offense. "I'm actually quite good at drawing. I got a full ride and start in the fall. At Eddie's school of course." He made heart eyes at the older boy and Mira wondered if they were even aware of how sickeningly in love they were.

Mira crossed her arms before she looked over at Eddie. "He actually any good?"

Eddie nodded enthusiastically. "Yes, ma'am, he's brilliant."

Mira pouted at them. "Aw. Of course he would say that." She reached into her bag and pulled out a business card, handing it to Benny. "Here. Send me your portfolio and we can talk about an internship if it's good."

Benny's mouth dropped open. "Oh my god! You're not only gay but an artist *too*?" He took the card and was practically bouncing up and down. "I will definitely hit you up." His eyes drifted to the card, and he turned it over, and then over again. "Uh, Mira, you didn't provide your socials on here."

Her face scrunched. "Why would I need socials?"

Benny gasped. "You don't have... Mira, how do you find work?"

She rolled her eyes. "I have a very good network from previous jobs, and people talk."

The barista shook his head. "As your intern, I vow to fix this right away. You have to have socials, we need to showcase your work, grow your brand..."

Mira raised a hand. "Slow down."

Eddie smirked. "He gets like this whenever he has a new idea, you'll triple your followers in a week. He's about to go full social plan on you..."

Benny turned and unlocked his phone, typing away. "I have to get started now if there's any hope. What is your last name? I need to start researching."

Mira groaned but relented. "Hansen." She watched as his eyes lit up as he must have located at least a dozen articles on her.

"Woah, you're like... super famous. We have to get moving on this."

What had she just gotten herself into? Sighing, Mira turned her attention to the menu. "Anything come with alcohol?"

Benny didn't look up. "You drove here. Can't drink and drive."

Mira snorted. "I'm a big girl, I can handle myself."

Barista Boy's eyes slowly raised. "I'm underage. We don't serve alcohol in the drinks anyway."

She rolled her eyes. "Tragic, I'm downrating this place on Yikes…"

"Yelp."

"That's what I said."

Benny rolled his eyes. "That's so not even a thing anymore. You just ask an influencer for ideas…"

Mira pointed at the board, hoping to shut him up. He was starting to give her a headache. "The bug one."

Benny's eyes widened. "The Ladybug Matcha?"

Mira shrugged uncomfortably. "Sure whatever, it… sounds good this morning, I don't know."

She pulled out her card, but Benny didn't take it.

"Oh, no, this one is on the house. I'll get it."

Mira waved her card. "Really, kid, I make enough. Just put it on my card."

Benny shook his head defiantly. "Absolutely not. You can pay next time. We are celebrating the launch of your new social media."

She watched as he took his own card and swiped it before bounding off to the little machines to make her drink.

Eddie turned to her with a kind smile. "He looks up to you. His whole family's straight. Hell, so is mine. It's... nice to find someone in the community for him to look up to."

Mira put her card away and grabbed some cash before slapping it to the boy's chest. "Take him out on a nice date, and if you tell him I gave that to you, I'll find you." She smirked and turned back toward Benny as he finished up and brought her drink in a to-go cup.

She saluted the boys before she turned to go.

"See you in the fall. I work remote, so you will too. There's some night and weekend work, but we can plan it out."

Mira had thought that Kahli would return by nightfall, perhaps with a dinner invitation or an offer for a moonlit walk before they would tumble back into bed. Unfortunately, Kahli hadn't shown up for any of that. But she had left another note.

For the first time in days, Mira spent her evening alone, drifting in and out of sleep. She tried putting a few shows on, but nothing kept her interest. Her phone died, and she neglected to plug it in. After a while, she decided that she had spent too many hours on the couch and took herself to the bedroom to try sleeping in a real bed.

# Chapter 20

Mira had drifted in and out for a while before she grabbed her tablet with the intention to draw. Occasionally, she twisted her little jade rock, which now sat prominently on her desk. She hadn't created anything for fun in ages. The last time had been when she and Amani were expecting Alex. Amani had wanted Timmy or Brayden, but Mira had argued that if she was the one carrying the baby, then she at the very least got to choose the child's first name.

Her eyes burned as she scrolled through the art she had started during her pregnancy for the child she and her wife had wanted desperately but were never able to have. Recurring dreams of the sea had filled her head and inspired her to create about a dozen images of waves, shells, and underwater castles. Pieces that she could blow up and frame for his wall. She had finished them just in time for her world to come crashing down.

She let her eyes glide over the tiled images before she opened a blank document and her stylus started to drift across the page. Her fingers zoomed in and out as she adjusted the line sizes. It took her a while to realize that she had been drawing Kahli. She erased the eyes, because while she had nailed her hair and face shape on the first try, she just couldn't get Kahli's eyes quite right.

Zooming in, she focused on the space where Kahli's eyes should go. Kahli's pupils were always decently large. She wondered if that had a simple explanation, like she had seen something she liked every time they were together. Mira smiled softly as she continued to draw. Opting to outline the rest of the image, she paused, wondering what Kahli was wearing in the drawing...

Mira rubbed her tired eyes and noticed that the night had worn on. Blinking rapidly, she looked back at the tablet and tapped it to check the time. It was nearing 1 a.m. She set the pad down and sat back in her chair. How had she not noticed the night passing away? That hadn't happened for days now. Maybe it was missing Kahli that drew her to need a distraction.

She leaned forward and looked out the window, half expecting to see Kahli bobbing along in the water. She didn't see Kahli, but she did see some sort of animal in the waves.

It was too far away to make out exactly what type of creature it was. Her tired eyes watched the thing pull itself onto land a little ways down the beach. It looked like a seal if the tail was anything to go by.

At least she had thought it was a seal… before she saw its tail split. Mira leaned closer to the window across her desk. The wood creaked under her weight. "What the…"

The animal moved to stand, as if its tail had turned into a set of legs. Mira's eyes grew wider as it approached her rental. When it was before the house it appeared… to be a woman. *Kahli.*

Mira knocked her tablet to the floor, jumping at the thud. She glanced toward the black square to make sure it wasn't broken before she looked back out her window to the beach. She watched as the other woman came under one of the porch lights, the glow illuminating her just enough to reveal Kahli's eyes were completely black.

Mira dropped to the floor. *What the fuck?* Her heart was hammering in her chest. She shook her head—she had to be asleep.

This had to be a hallucination. Kahli always went for a night swim. The woman was just doing her usual nightly routine and checking up on Mira since she had been gone. Mira was tired or lucid dreaming... that was all this was.

So why did she feel the very real urge to grab a weapon?

Mira crawled over to her bedroom door and engaged the lock, her ears picking up the eerie tune Kahli hadn't hummed for her in days. She felt the pull to open the door, to go down the stairs and greet her, but at the same time, she felt like she was standing on a cliff's edge, suddenly remembering she was afraid of heights and didn't want to fall.

Hearing, rather than feeling, her nails scratch as they dug at the dark wood flooring, it took her a few breaths to realize she was attempting to anchor herself. Then she heard Kahli call out to her from below.

"Mira? You home?"

The patio door creaked open. She stood shakily and wandered over to the window, peeking out in time to see Kahli enter the house. Mira scanned the beach, and right where she had seen the animal, there was a large drag line... as if something with a large tail had hauled itself up the beach.

Her mind flashed with Kahli's black eyes, instead of the honey they had normally been in the daylight. She shook her head as she remembered the beach the other night, how she had to drag Kahli away from drinking the sea water. How she hadn't been able to see her eyes well at the time, but now, as if waking from a vivid dream, she remembered them. Black and soulless.

In the memory, Kahli's lips parted to say her name.

"*You would follow me in? Just like that?*"

It was as if she were right back in that moment, stuck in a nightmare. She wanted it to stop.

"Where are we?"

Kahli took a step backward into the ocean. "Come with me."

Mira stood still, at the water's edge, ankle-deep. She didn't remember this part playing out the other night. It was as if her mind was twisting her memories. "No. It's... it's too cold. I don't want..."

Kahli's face shifted, angry. She had never seen Kahli look like that in real life. "I said, *come with me.*"

Mira tried to take a step back up the beach, but it was as if her ankles were being held down by the water. As if held down by heavy chains.

"What the fuck?" She panicked. She squatted and pulled at whatever might be holding her feet, but the water slipped through her fingers. "Kahli, let me go!"

She watched in horror as Kahli advanced, grabbing her roughly, just like Amani used to when they fought. Kahli pulled her further into the ocean, and Mira was helpless to stop her. She started pleading.

"Kahli, don't do this. Please! I don't want to go with you…"

Kahli's shoulders tensed as she turned and stared blankly, straight into her soul. "Why? You were planning on leaving anyway."

Mira screamed as Kahli smiled and…

She startled awake.

Mira's hands pressed against the wooden floor. How had she ended up on the floor? Had she fallen out of bed? Her eyes took in the shadow that passed under her doorway, hearing a knock at her bedroom door looming above her.

"Mira?" Kahli's voice sounded concerned. "Can I come in?"

Mira panicked. Kahli was already in her home, up her stairs. Mira was disoriented and unsure what was real or a part of her dream.

"No!" she roared. Looking around frantically, she saw her tablet laying on the table, not on the floor where she thought she dropped it. She must have fallen asleep... getting in bed to rest when she grew tired of drawing, and had rolled off the bed to the floor when she heard the knocking. It was the only logical explanation. So why did her body not hurt from the fall, but her throat did?

"Don't come in!" Her voice was hoarse. She could see Kahli's shadow just under the door as she heard her release the handle.

There was a creak in the floorboards, sounding as though it was in the room with her. She almost turned to look behind her to see what caused the noise, but was distracted by Kahli's shadow retreating from the door. The creaking repeated from the hall right in front of her. She must have misheard where the first sound came from. Old houses were known for their weird acoustics.

She felt a chill run up her spine and turned around quickly to survey the room, feeling as if something was right behind her. Though when she did, nothing appeared amiss, until she glanced into the mirror.

Mira stumbled back against her bed.

In her mind's eye, she had thought she saw the man from town. There was no way she had seen Theo in her mirror.

She shook her head quickly, trying to clear the image from her mind. She wasn't sure where all of this was coming from. She wasn't even self-medicating.

When she was brave enough to gaze into the mirror again, all she saw was her own reflection.

Kahli's voice came from the door. "Are... are you alright? Your back door was unlocked and you started screaming. I was worried when I heard a thud..."

Mira ran her hand through her hair. She was really making a mess of things tonight. "I just need you to go. I'm fine. Just... please go..."

She watched as Kahli's shadow lingered. "I'm... I'm sorry. I didn't come by sooner because...." Her sentence trailed off as her voice grew quiet. "Are you sure you want me to go?" She sounded so small and broken.

Mira tried to take a breath, but it was too shallow, and spots prickled her vision. "Come back tomorrow, in the morning."

"Mira... please, can we talk? I..."

Mira took one hand and pinched herself. The way it stung and her skin bloomed red in anger could only mean that she was definitely awake now. "Shit... just go. Leave! I was... asleep." She growled and hoped it would land.

"I'm... sorry. I didn't mean to wake you."

She watched as Kahli didn't leave right away, clearly worried something was wrong, but after a few moments, she retreated. Mira even heard her lock up, slamming the back door a little harder than she had probably meant to, if the muffled "sorry" outside on the porch was anything to go by.

Mira rolled onto her back and looked out the window. Little rain droplets started to splatter, a roll of thunder in the background letting her know a storm was approaching off the water. She should not have sent Kahli away. She hoped she didn't live *that* far, and maybe if she ran home she would be alright.

# Chapter 21

Unable to sleep, Mira ventured into town to the one bar that was still open. She ordered one shot and then another, trying to shake the dream from her mind. Things with Kahli had been going well, so why was her subconscious trying to sabotage her? It didn't make sense. She ordered another shot, but the bartender placed a large mixed drink before her. Mira's brow furrowed.

"I didn't order that."

The bartender nodded. "I know, it seems you have an admirer." He indicated someone in the back corner of the establishment through the dimly lit room. It didn't take Mira long to clock the man who had knocked on her door. The same man she thought she saw in her mirror. "Great…"

The guy behind the bar cleared his throat. "I mixed the drink myself. There's nothing wrong with it but if you don't want it…"

Mira waved him off as she took a sip, grimacing at how bitter it tasted. "It's fine, might as well not waste it." She took another sip before she wondered if potentially vomiting from a hangover would be worth it or not.

Her eyes stared into the glass as her mother's voice slithered through her head, coiling around her as it tended to do when there were drinks involved. Calling her a godless whore after Mira had timidly announced her engagement to Amani and that she was never seeing her again. She had meant it that time. Amani had insisted that she try and mend her relationship with her mother. If Wendy had found out, she would have killed her fiancé on the spot for even suggesting Mira contact that old hag.

She was pulled out of her head when someone slid in next to her.

"Hey neighbor, how's the drink? They make those custom around here."

Rolling her eyes, she noted that it tasted terrible because it had so much alcohol. "It's a bit much."

She recognized Theo instantly as he turned toward her, leaning his elbow on the counter. "The wife not home tonight?"

Mira felt her hackles go up. There was nothing more terrifying than being a woman who was perceived to live alone. "She's resting. I couldn't sleep."

She let her finger trace around the rim and it made a deep ringing sound. Her thoughts drifted to Kahli. This man must know her if they had both lived in the area a while.

"You've lived here for a long time, right?"

"That's right." He nodded enthusiastically, seeming to think she was going to ask him more about himself. Fat chance.

Mira tilted her head at his lack of drink. Interesting choice. Or was that on purpose? Who goes to a bar and doesn't get a drink?

"So, Kahli Delmar... what do you know about her?"

Theo frowned, going still at the abrupt turn in conversation. "Who?" His voice rose at the end as if he had never heard the name before.

That couldn't be right. Kahli was a beautiful woman. There was no way anyone with eyes wouldn't have noticed her. Mira tried again. "The woman with black hair, currently to her shoulders? Young, obsessed with swimming, always in the ocean?"

The man looked up in the air as if trying to rack his brain. "I've never seen a woman with black hair who's constantly swimming in the area... you sure she's not a tourist? No one matching that description lives in our neighborhood."

Mira's heart sank. What was he talking about? Kahli was ever present on that beach and in the waves. She started to feel the hair on her arms raise. Her nightmare clawed its way forward, showing her the dark figure pulling itself from the sea only to grow legs and march straight for her back door.

She downed more of her drink. She didn't want to think about her dreams.

Theo turned his attention back to her, smiling as if she had made a joke. "You sure you haven't made friends with a ghost? Maybe one of the sea creatures the old fishermen weave tales about?" He wiggled his fingers at her.

Mira smiled now, the scoff she let out seemed to alter his mood. "There's no such thing as ghosts, or sea... creatures." She looked at him mockingly. "What are you, twelve?"

He bit his lip as if refraining from what he wanted to say. Mira took another sip of her drink before he scooted it away. "That's really strong, you should slow down. Matter of fact, I shouldn't have ordered you something like that. Your wife would kill me if something happened to you, right? How about we make a deal. You can finish your drink, if I can drive you home."

Mira shifted uncomfortably in her seat. "I'm fine—"

He raised his hand to cut her off. "Seriously, you shouldn't be driving after that. And if your wife is resting, I'm sure we don't want to wake her up to come get you. I'm heading out soon anyway, it's no problem."

Weighing her options, Mira figured as long as she was in contact with Wendy, things would be fine. It wasn't like Kahli knew where she was to go and get her.

≈ ≈ ≈

Mira stumbled into Theo's truck while he held her arm and opened the car door. "Slow and steady, there ya go." She climbed in and decided against the seat belt, in case she had to make a quick escape.

Theo hoisted himself into the vehicle and turned the key, cranking the truck to life. He leaned toward Mira as he pulled out of his parking space. "She was my dad's old reliable." He patted the dash. "Gotten me through."

Mira cast him a half smile as she watched the road, noting that they appeared to be going toward her house. Her fingers lifted her phone to text Wendy that she was getting a ride home and to check in with her a few times. Wendy was quick to ask why she was getting in the car with strangers. Mira rolled her eyes. Why couldn't Wendy just be happy that she was checking in, doing at least one smart thing?

Theo started to whistle his tune from the other day, and Mira turned to him, intrigued, as it sounded similar to one Kahli would sometimes hum. "Is that song a product of growing up in the area? I swear I've heard it a few times."

"Ah, an old sailor's tune. Used it to cast off the mermaids, nasty beasts. They say a hundred years ago they walked straight out of the sea and settled on land, in this very town, slaying the villagers. Needed symbols on the doorways to keep them out."

Mira's mind drifted to the markings Kahli had left beside her doors and windows. "You don't say? Were they effective?"

Theo checked the next lane before he moved over. "That depends on who you ask."

Mira rolled her eyes. "Come on. Do you actually believe in mermaids?" She had expected him to shrug and brush off the notion as simply a story.

Theo nodded gravely, casting a quick glance her way before his eyes refocused back on the road. "One took my father, pulled him right into the sea when I was little. Never saw him again. It was terrifying. I also... lost someone I loved once to the sea. An evil sea witch dragged him in and he..." He attempted to clear his throat as emotion choked him up. "His body washed up on shore days later. I'll never forget the demon's soulless eyes, her dark hair, and deep green tail. I stay away from the ocean now... like to spend my time making sure they don't escape the water and take others. I'm always watching the coast." His hands gripped his steering wheel tighter as if renewing his commitment to his mission.

Mira had never seen Theo down on the beach and wondered if the weird man just sat at his back window whenever he was home, obsessively keeping watch on the water. Sharks were a thing, and more likely what he saw take his father; a traumatic event could do damage to the psyche, and she felt a little bad for him that he had turned out this way. Who would he have been if he wasn't so obsessed with the sea?

She needed to get out of this car, soon.

Mira checked her phone, taking note that it was at least another five minutes to get back. She didn't want to talk about Amani, but thought maybe someone hopelessly in love would be more of an annoyance and spur him on to their destination.

"So my wife and I have been together over fifteen years now. We're trying for a baby. And if you want to know the truth, I'm just waiting to tell her it worked so... well, I'll have to stop the drinking, but, I think if we come back here next year, it sounds like I'll have to keep an eye out for my child near the sea... make sure he doesn't get snatched up."

Maybe feeding into his delusion would help a bit. Maybe if he thought she were taking his warning seriously then he would back off.

Theo hummed his acknowledgment as his mouth shifted into a smile. "Oh, congratulations! And that's a good idea. I hear all kinds of tales in town, about all kinds of creatures around here. Best to be careful, especially with the little ones..."

Mira was glad he had at least stopped hitting on her, and even more relieved that they had arrived on her street. "Well, I really appreciate the ride. I'll tell Amani to thank you next time we see you for getting me home safe." She released her seat belt and grabbed the door handle, ready to be free from Theo when, out of the corner of her eye, she swore she saw him smirk. Briefly, she wondered if he was going to speed right past her home and if she might have to jump from the car, but he slowed down and parked on the street. His eyes didn't leave the road, and that was somehow even more unnerving.

"I'll see you around, Mira. Have a good night."

She nodded before she escaped, looking back at him twice as she headed to the door, just in case he was following her. His eyes stayed glued to the road. She let herself in and quickly locked up, automatically checking the back door to make sure that it hadn't fallen open again. Thankfully, she found it double latched. She let out a sigh of relief. It was past three in the morning, and she was sure Kahli had long gone home by now, no longer out swimming up and down the coast.

Turning on a small light in the kitchen, she poured herself a glass of water and started to sip slowly. Her body still held remnants of the uncomfortable and creepy evening across her goosebumped skin. She hoped she would be able to think more clearly come morning, after she got some sleep. If that was even possible before the sun came up.

She was about to head up to bed when shattering glass and a guttural scream echoed throughout the beach house. For a moment she was frozen, standing in the middle of the kitchen. The silence that followed had her questioning herself. Perhaps she hadn't heard glass shatter at all. But then came the slow, heavy footsteps.

She automatically moved to the back door, unlocking it quietly.

"Mira... you know it's not a good idea to be out here all alone, don't you?" Theo's voice carried from the hall near the bathroom.

Mira tried to shut the back door quietly and winced as it clicked.

She held her breath.

Nothing.

Sighing with relief, she crouched and eased her way to the stairs, avoiding the spot she knew would creak without mercy. Once she was at the bottom, she bolted down the beach toward wherever Kahli lived. It didn't matter if she found her, she just needed to get away. After she put some distance between her and the rental, she checked her phone, only to find that the service bars were gone. She bit her cheek. *At a time like this?* She always had service on this beach.

There was a bang in the distance, which must have been her door getting flung open. Theo called out into the night, "Oh, Mir-a. Where did you go, love?"

Her veins turned to ice. She really hoped his night vision sucked. The beach was long, and somehow, she had drifted toward the water, unsure where she could go. Should she start sprinting back toward the road for assistance? Would anyone even be driving through at this time of night? Or was she better off going down the beach?

Suddenly, one of her legs caught on a log and she stumbled, landing hard. She gasped as a sharpness burned up her leg and into her back. She inched backward as she saw Theo's shadow coming down the beach. Her leg was screaming with each movement. She contemplated the water. Would that be safer? She looked up and something bobbed at the surface. Her eyes tried to make out what was coming closer.

"Mira?"

That was Kahli's voice.

Mira frantically looked down the beach the way she came. She was about to get them both killed.

Her voice was unsteady as she whispered, "You have to go... That guy... He's chasing me. I can't... I can't walk. I think I broke something..."

Kahli's eyes hardened. When she came within reach, Mira watched as her whole body tightened. "We gotta go. *Now*."

Mira shook her head, tears collecting in her eyes. "Didn't you hear me? I think I broke something."

Gently, Kahli leaned down and lifted her up as if she weighed nothing. "It'll all be fine. Just relax, don't struggle."

Mira's eyes went wide as Kahli walked them out into the surf. "What are you—Kahli!"

The first unforgiving splash of the water was freezing. Her arms clung to Kahli's shoulders, heart slamming against her rib cage.

Theo's voice was feral as he bellowed, "Kahli!"

So he *did* know her. *He had lied.* She felt her heart speed up, thundering as if it were going to give out. The frigid water did not distract her from her panic in the slightest. She watched as Theo drew closer and could almost make him out clearly when she felt Kahli reach deeper water. Mira's fingers clung to Kahli desperately, unsure of how they were going to get out of this, when she was yanked underwater.

# Chapter 22

Mira's head throbbed as she tried to open her eyes. Gentle fingers ran through her hair with ease, a voice soothing her. Her eyes scrunched as she fought her way to consciousness, not quite comfortable with the idea of who was so close to her.

"You're alright, it's just me."

*Kahli.* Was she still dreaming? Had *everything* that night been a nightmare? Mira tried to calm her breathing as her mind frantically searched through her memories, rationality taking over. She must still be in bed with Kahli. Looking for the other woman, she rolled onto her side, but the bed felt *hard.* Her eyes flew open, and when she discovered she was lying on a smooth gray rock, she scrambled to sit up. Where was she?

Her eyes darted around, frantically taking in her surroundings. Dark, jagged rocks surrounded her at every turn. She was in some sort of cavern with a large pool taking up half the ground. A bright blue light emanated from the water, the ripples casting patterns across the walls and ceiling, allowing her to see well enough. Her eyes drifted around to piles of items she didn't recognize. When her eyes landed on Kahli, she was leaning her elbows on the flat shelf of rock Mira sat on, the rest of her body submerged in the water.

Mira felt her whole body slowly drain of any sensation. Her heart skipped a beat, as if it wasn't sure if it wanted to make things easier and stop working all together. It unfortunately continued, and Mira felt her muscles tighten unnaturally, the twinge low in her back ever prominent and now with the addition of more pain. Her lungs spasmed as her breathing grew dysregulated. Her head started to spin from the lack of oxygen she was taking in.

Where was she?

How did she get here?

Why had Kahli brought her here?

Was Kahli going to kill her?

"Just... stay calm," Kahli spoke softly. A hand raised to placate Mira.

As Kahli lifted herself up to sit on the rock, Mira's eyes bugged out. From the hips down, she was covered in deep, shimmery, emerald scales.

Each one was a glass-like green ombre, shifting from dark to light.

Mira scurried back as far as she could from the water, even with her messed-up leg. Dark spots crept into the edges of her vision as she pressed herself against the wall, eyes desperately darting around looking for a way out. "What the *fuck*..."

She gasped for air. Her eyes opened wide, trying to take in every detail of the room, but her vision wasn't clear anymore. Everything was blurry. She blinked rapidly to try to regain some focus, briefly wondering if she would wake up again if she passed out.

Kahli's eyes were dark pools of black, and yet they softened as she spoke to Mira. "Close your eyes for a moment."

Losing the ability to speak, Mira quickly shook her head, energy draining from her body.

Kahli frowned. "The transformation isn't pretty. I don't want you to have to see that. Just... for a few moments, at least look away? I won't come any closer."

Mira's eyes darted away to look for something to grip on to. She heard Kahli quietly hiss and she couldn't help but look back.

She wished she hadn't.

All of the green scales had been shed as if they were ripped off, leaving hollowed out wounds. What was once a solid tail had split into what looked like the beginnings of legs. Legs that were nothing but slabs of meat held together by tendons. The muscles moved, continuing to re-form themselves, and the skin attempted to regenerate.

Yelping in fear, she turned, smashing her face into the jagged rock wall. Forgetting her surroundings, she didn't even feel the cuts nor blood trickling down her face as the adrenaline crashed through her system. She pressed further into the wall, as if she could escape through it.

She felt hands on her shoulders and tried to scream, but nothing came out.

"*Shit*, Mira. Come here. Let me see your face. It's over, you can look now." Soft hands cupped her face gently, causing a stinging to radiate across her wounds before her skin buzzed with a gentle warmth, relaxing the pain away.

Keeping her eyes closed, Mira weakly shook her head. She struggled to get the words to pass from her lips. "I don't... I don't want to look."

Kahli tried again. "Baby..."

Mira lashed out. "You—" Her mind struggled to find the words for what she had seen, and she wasn't sure if it was the concussion or her fear that made her feel so hazy. "Your legs were fucking filleted, Kahli! Like when you clean a fish!"

Kahli removed her hands from Mira's skin and her voice returned to its previous softness, as if afraid of spooking Mira further. It was almost a whisper. "I told you not to look."

Mira's eyes darted to the other woman for only a second, too scared to see the soulless eyes and mangled legs. As she made more attempts to look, she grew braver each time until she was staring Kahli in the face, but her hands still clutched the jagged wall in fear. As if it would be able to save her.

Mira whimpered. "Don't," she rasped. "Please."

"Just let me finish cleaning your face. I promise I'll be careful." She placed her hand on Mira's leg, deep purple nails shimmering in the glow of the room. "Please."

Mira shook as she took in the face she knew. Kahli's dark honey eyes were no longer black and soulless, but were full of tears. When Mira looked down at Kahli's legs, they appeared in order, no longer a scene of horror.

"You hurt your face pretty bad." Kahli leaned in, smearing her tears lightly across Mira's cheek. "There, it's closing now. It shouldn't even scar. What am I going to do with you?" She cupped her face, smiling and drawing Mira close as she continued trembling. Kahli held Mira in her gaze, as if commanding her. "You are going to be fine. Just breathe."

Mira gripped Kahli's wrists, pushing them away from her. "Where..."

Calmly, she explained. "This is one of my treasure troves, I'm... a collector."

Looking about, Mira saw a pile of clothing she recognized as Kahli's, as well as a lot of random items, including an intricate green dagger. Her stomach lurched. She really didn't want to know what *that* was for. "You collect... bodies?"

Kahli's brow furrowed. "No..."

Mira's eyes darted around Kahli's face for any signs of deceit, her own body so tight with tension it was a wonder it didn't snap. "You sure?"

The other woman leaned away from her and nodded. "Not anymore. It's been... a long time."

Attempting to move further away only had Mira wincing as her leg protested the movement. Kahli's hands quickly shifted to glow over the swollen injury. "Just stay still for me while I fix this."

There was an intense spike of pain that Mira had to breathe through, but after a few moments, it subsided. She carefully tested if she could pull her leg to herself and it bent to her will. Her eyes went so wide; she felt like an animal caged for the first time, trying to figure out where the real danger was coming from... and if there was an opening she could squeeze herself through.

"You... were hunting me? Right?"

Kahli licked her lips before speaking hesitantly, as if the words physically pained her. "Well. Not exactly..."

Mira snorted as she tried to take a deep breath but came up short. "So what, you were actually just trying to get me to come out for a friendly swim?" She let out a humorless laugh. "Liar."

Kahli shook her head. "No. I... was trying to ferry you across."

Why did that sound like a death sentence?

Mira waited for her to offer more, but she didn't. "To where?" Mira prompted. The idea of being taken anywhere was not settling her fear.

Shrugging, Kahli sighed. "Wherever your final resting place is. I don't like watching anyone suffer." She looked around them. "Your aura is dark... it drew me to you. If it makes you feel better, when I met you, I gathered you weren't ready to go yet, but if you had been, you weren't going to feel a thing. I... I help end suffering when I can."

Mira scoffed. "Sure." She glanced at Kahli's fingers wearily, wondering if they might grow into claws.

As if she could hear her thoughts, Kahli chimed in. "They can... but I don't prefer my nails that way. I don't think you would either." Kahli's eyes looked back into the water before she glanced back at Mira apologetically. "You'll be safe in here, I promise, and I won't be gone long. I added my own protective measures to this place. I will tell you anything you want to know when I return. I have to deal with him." She turned and Mira grabbed her arm.

"You can't leave me here!" Her voice was shrill as she looked for an escape. The only thing worse than being trapped with Kahli in this cave was being trapped in this cave *alone*.

Kahli cupped Mira's cheek. "I have to go deal with him." Her eyes tried to convey the weight of the situation. "He's hunting in my territory. He could smell my scent on you and still he chose to try and take you. We... have a history." Kahli tried to compose herself. "He never quite understood that my desires didn't include *him*. A long time ago, I fell in love with a human woman and... he killed her." She cut herself off sharply at the end before she cleared her throat and continued. "He left her for me to find. I thought... that this time... with the wards and my... warnings, that he would stop. But he's been lurking and waiting for—" She closed her eyes a moment and her voice grew soft. "I should have sent you home. I'm sorry..."

Mira shivered. So Kahli had done this before. Fallen for a human, and failed to keep them alive. "Don't. Don't go. Please, I'll, I'll listen. D-Do whatever you say." She licked her lips as she inched her hand forward to touch Kahli, flinching when she made contact as if Kahli's flesh would incinerate her. "If something happens to you and you don't come back, I'll... I'll die in here." Her voice rose with panic at the realization. "I don't want to die in here!"

Kahli tilted her head like the idea had never occurred to her. "Mira, I'm coming back."

"What if he kills you and I suffocate in here!" Mira's hand pressed to her stomach as a sharp wave of nausea shot through her. She couldn't be left alone. There was no way out, she would starve or her oxygen would run out...

Kahli's eyes widened as she saw Mira's eyes dart to the blade, catching her hand as she went for it. Her head shook only once. "No, Mira."

Desperately, Mira tried to overpower her. "You have to give me a way out!"

The action only succeeded in bringing tears to Kahli's eyes. "No... not that," she gulped, "way."

Kahli was much stronger than Mira had anticipated, wrapping her arms around her easily and ceasing her struggle.

Mira began to sob. "Please... please don't leave me here, take me somewhere... anywhere else... I won't run. I'll stay there, somewhere where I can see the sky... please."

Kahli attempted to soothe her, but it wasn't working. "I've failed at this many times. I've tried to save people. From him, from... others. Once they were marked, it wasn't safe until I dealt with the hunter." Kahli cleared her throat as her words trailed off. "I'm coming back for you. You just have to trust me. You won't starve, you won't run out of oxygen. Just rest..." She lifted her hand to Mira's hairline, but Mira flinched away. Kahli's face fell at the broken trust, but she didn't change course.

Slowly, Kahli cupped her face, waiting for the initial twitch to subside as she stroked her thumb over Mira's cheek, humming softly until she relaxed before kissing her slowly. The tension bled out of Mira's body. "Kahli?"

She kissed Mira again. "I'll be back, baby. Don't go into the water, you'll never figure out the caves.

I don't... want to find you like that when I return. Please. I promise, I'll get you home. You'll be back with Wendy before you know it, like..." Her breath hitched and she seemed to have to gather herself to continue. "Like none of this ever happened."

When Mira blinked, Kahli was gone. Her hand covered her mouth as she knew that, even if she screamed, no one would hear her.

# Chapter 23

Mira passed out a few times from hyperventilating. Her body gave up on panicking after that as she lay on the cavern floor for what seemed like hours. Not trusting what might appear from the water, she attempted to move, wincing as her back tightened. She should have asked Kahli to fix that. Dragging herself over to the pile of clothing, she recognized things she had seen Kahli wear on more than one occasion. She grabbed a shirt and wound it in her hands, letting her voice make sounds that no human should ever make.

What hurt was that Amani wouldn't miss her, wouldn't even try to find her body if she went missing. Not the way Mira had sunk money into a private investigator when the police refused to help her find her wife, telling her it wasn't their fault that she had chosen to leave. That maybe if she had married a man this wouldn't have happened.

Her eyes watched the water as it rippled gently. As if the pool itself were breathing. She shuddered as she moved to the pile of items, trying to keep her mind occupied from her potential demise. Who knew how far Kahli had taken her?

Mira started to sort the items shakily, slowly steadying as she focused on her task. Her hands glided over countless crystals and jewels as they glittered in the light. There was even a stuffed animal, a bunny whose hair had matted down from its journey across the ocean.

She busied herself fixing its fur. Maybe she would get a pet if she ever got out of here. Wendy had kept offering to get her one, and she had been such an ungrateful asshole about it. She bit her lip, overcome with the sinking feeling that she was never going to see Wendy again. Clutching the bunny to her chest, she tried to find something else to look at.

There were different instruments, and some things she had no idea what they were for. Her hands shifted through the items when her eyes caught a glint of the dagger. So Kahli hadn't taken it with her.

Mira reached for it, clutching the heavy hilt in her hand. The blade was slightly curved and looked pristine, as if it had never been used.

Would she need to use it on herself? Her eyes traced the inlaid silver and green-webbed pattern that wound around the hilt before setting it to the side, just within reach.

She had no idea how much time had passed.

Eventually, she lay down facing the water, falling into a fitful sleep. Her hands clutched desperately at the bunny as she twitched.

When her eyes fluttered open again, the cave greeted her. She pressed her face deep into the bunny and sobbed. Kahli wasn't coming back. She was probably immortal—time must pass differently for her.

Her mind wandered back to her youth, to her mother's shouted words about everything that was wrong with her. How she had disappointed her. Her hand briefly lifted to her head as she felt the phantom pains of her mother tugging her by the hair when she had simply turned the wrong direction as they walked into town. She whimpered.

"Stop."

She saw Amani's eyes looking at her with nothing but hatred as the doctors said Mira would never carry a baby to term, *either*. That their fertility journey would be different than Amani had planned for. She remembered reaching for her wife's hands as she lay in a hospital bed and how they were ripped away. Her eyes stung and filled with tears as her mouth found a way to form the words she desperately needed. To beg Amani to not leave her. But she had.

She recalled the sadness in Wendy's gaze when she had arrived at Mira's door, telling her to come home. Mira had insisted she would be fine. But as she sat alone in her home, she had become increasingly worried about her own safety if she stayed isolated. Reaching back out to Wendy and finally accepting support from her and her partner had saved Mira's life.

As the cave came back into focus, Mira's body went numb. It was all over. She sniffed and took the knife, lifting it to her wrist. But... that was a slow way to go. She looked over the edge of the pool at her reflection. Her neck. That way would be faster.

She pushed her hair behind her ear as she took the knife to the ground and started to carve words into the stone. It wasn't until she was done that she noticed what she made: a tomb stone.

*Here Lies Mira Hansen.*

With shaky hands, she added her birth date and the date she assumed it was. She struggled to come up with anything else to write. What had she even accomplished with her time on Earth? Art designs for some of the biggest brands? What would that matter in the end? Her life was meaningless.

At first, she grew frustrated and tried to correct her numbers, to make them more legible, before she realized that no one was ever going to even find it. Or her body. Besides Kahli. If she ever made it back. Maybe she would mourn her a little. She hoped she would. Someone needed to.

Sitting on her knees, Mira started to rock, digging her nails into her thighs, using the pain to ground herself. She had wanted to be done for a while now, but as she sat at the end of her life line, she wasn't so sure she wanted to find out what was on the other side. Or what *wasn't* on the other side.

Mira lifted the knife to her throat, which bobbed with the emotion and fear she felt. She lowered and raised it a few times before she grew more certain that she would rather not starve to death waiting for a rescue that surely wasn't coming. Her stomach was already begging for something to eat.

She sucked in a breath, pressing the blade against her throat.

A sick pop sounded. Blood ran hot from the wound and dripped down her fingertips.

She gasped, digging deeper, crying out in pain when she heard a splash.

"Mira!"

She turned and took in Kahli. The other woman was covered in gashes that trickled with dark blue blood. Her skin was pale, her eyes gray instead of gold. But her hand was somehow quick as she latched on to Mira's arm, which was still holding the weapon to her throat.

"Stop. It's done. I... I've got you." She tried to ease the dagger out of Mira's grasp. "Just let me have that."

Mira gripped the knife tighter. This was her only option. Kahli didn't care for her. She wasn't here to help her. "You're not taking me home..."

Kahli tightened her hold. "I am. Mira, stop. Stop!" She pulled harder at the knife, but Mira doubled down as she shook her head. If she lost, there wouldn't only be death but *pain*. That spurred her on.

"You're going to kill me..."

Kahli's patience ran out. Her voice boomed. "For fuck's sake, Mira, I'm not going to kill you. I almost died for you! *You're* the only one trying to kill you!"

Mira cowered and loosened her grip just enough. Kahli took the knife, throwing it into the water. Mira lurched after it with a feral scream. "No!"

Before she could fall in, Kahli grabbed her and pulled her close. "What the hell!"

Slumping against her in defeat, Mira felt Kahli's tail twitch anxiously against her. She was hesitant as she spoke, and tried hard not to take in Kahli's features. "Will... will it hurt when you take me across? To wherever I go after this? I... I won't struggle if you promise it won't hurt in the end." She touched the wetness at her throat. "Please... don't make it hurt." Her eyes bored into Kahli's when she leaned back, pleading.

The pain disappeared when Kahli leaned forward and pressed her lips to Mira's neck. "I'm not taking you, not yet. You have a long, long life ahead of you." She smiled sadly when she pulled back. "Just stay away from the ocean from now on, okay? It's not safe for you. You draw way too much attention to yourself."

Mira hugged herself, her voice now barely above a whisper. "I want to go home."

She wanted that more than anything in the world, even if it meant Wendy yelling at her for putting herself in danger. Sure, Wendy would probably think her stories were medication induced and insist on rehab or Mira moving back in permanently, but she would gladly go along with whatever her best friend wanted as long as she was *home*.

"I can... do that. I can take you back." Kahli took a shaky breath. "While I have the strength. We should get going."

Mira grabbed the stuffed toy that lay beside her. "Can I?"

The mermaid nodded as she eased back into the water, floating. "Come on, we should leave."

Mira inched closer to the edge, hesitating before lowering her legs into the water. "I don't know... It... looks dark down there." Her eyes took in how the bright blue darkened as the tunnel plummeted into the depths, so deep that it turned black. She felt her back tense. She had zero desire to go down there. She didn't want to drown. Her mind started to conjure unhelpful images of Kahli pinning her to the ocean floor in the dark as she struggled.

Kahli lifted herself out of the pool, drawing Mira's gaze as she sat beside her. Mira's intrusive thoughts quieted as Kahli hummed softly, just for her. "It's okay, I'll make everything okay."

"I'm not ready..." She attempted to scoot back, but Kahli held her with one arm and stroked her cheek with the other, keeping her in place.

Kahli shushed her softly. "Take a breath… we can wait a moment." She leaned in to kiss her.

The warmth and safety Mira always felt around Kahli spread through her. Despite all of the opportunities to hurt her, Kahli never had. Maybe everything would work out in the end.

"Don't be afraid, I won't let anything happen to you." She kissed Mira until she responded.

Then Kahli pulled her down into the water before she had a chance to fight back.

# Chapter 24

Mira coughed as water entered her mouth. The sound of seagulls squawking alerted her to the fact that she was somewhere on land. She pressed her hands to the ground as she felt the shifting sand underneath her. Her throat continued to expel the water that had tried to drown her. Focusing beneath her, she saw the wave that had washed over her recede. She looked around, the light stinging her eyes, slowly recognizing the beach by her rental. Her eyes doubled back when they caught on a dark mop of hair, a pale body, and a shimmering tail, unmoving in the sand nearby. She quickly crawled toward her. "Kahli!"

She turned her over and saw her eyes were closed, her mouth slightly open. She hauled her up a bit out of the surf and pulled her upper body into her lap. Shaking Kahli's shoulders had no effect on her state. Mira's fingers trembled as she tried to locate Kahli's pulse at her neck, fearful that it would be gone. She let out a shaky sigh of relief when there was at least something there.

She looked about and knew there would be no one to call for help. Her eyes searched on instinct anyway.

Kahli's eyes fought to open as she gasped before she grunted in pain. "Mira?"

Mira smoothed Kahli's tense face with her fingers. "Relax. I got you. I just... have to get you to the house..." She felt the other woman's body shift and looked down as the skin on her legs started to split. Mira screeched, turning away, remembering that the transformation was only momentary. Not wanting to accidentally experience the horror again, she kept her eyes averted for longer than she thought necessary, just in case.

Peeking through her fingers, she saw legs that, while fully formed, were injured. Deep, jagged cuts spread across Kahli's calf and thigh on one side as if she had been slashed by a large knife. Kahli turned and tried to wriggle away from Mira, who grabbed her shoulders before she could tip over to the ground. "What are you doing?"

Kahli's movements were jerky at best and her eyes struggled to stay open. She dug her hands into the sand. "I got you back?"

Mira bit her lip before she spoke. "You did, yeah." She ducked under Kahli's arm, hoisting her to her feet. "I know you can't help much, just try your best."

Taking slow steps towards her house, Mira tried not to panic as the blue blood ran down Kahli's body and dripped onto the sand, leaving behind a trail of dark spots. It was a struggle to keep Kahli in her arms, requiring all of her focus to keep them moving forward. When her feet caught on something, she went down hard. As she tipped forward, she turned her shoulder toward the ground, protecting Kahli's body from the impact. Her own body jolted when she crashed into the solid wet sand, breath punching out of her a second later when Kahli landed on her.

Dazed, she lifted her head, only to lock on to the faded eyes of Theo. *Dead.* His skin ashen, his mouth open as if frozen in a scream, displaying the fangs hanging down from his upper jaw. His fingers ended in long, sharp talons stained with the same dark blue fluid that was crusting on Kahli's leg. His tail was ripped to pieces, rendering it useless as a means to get away.

Mira screamed so hard no sounds came out. She fumbled her hold on Kahli, trying to yank her up to get away from the decaying body. She struggled with the sharp pains now shooting through her back, her hips, and down her legs as she dragged Kahli up. As she staggered away, the wind picked up, engulfing her with the rotten smell it carried.

It took all her willpower to get Kahli up the back steps and into the house. She wasn't sure how she did it, but she got them inside before the other woman fully collapsed. Kahli's body gave out, and the younger woman slipped back into unconsciousness.

Mira left her lying on the living room floor and scrambled over items that had been strewn about in a struggle. Cabinet doors were cracked off their hinges. Drawers were flung onto the ground. The couch was the only thing still relatively unharmed, though it had been knocked away from its previous position and splattered in blue blood.

Grabbing a blanket from where it had landed against a wall, Mira spotted her phone on the floor. Running for it, she frantically searched for information about mermaids. None of the links were helpful until she found herself on an active forum with a ton of people online. She fired off her questions.

*How do you heal an injured mermaid?*

*What do you feed them?*

She was ready to launch through her phone screen when the first response was some asshole, probably a young man who lived in his parents' basement.

*ServingSteve247: Omg you're such a loser, you actually believe in mermaids? I bet they eat this dick.*

Snarling, she yelled her response. *"You're literally on the same fucking page! Go cry to your mom about not having friends."*

Trying to stave off her panic, she locked her phone and started moving, feeling the clock ticking down. Wounds must all be the same. She grabbed a first-aid kit, hoping that the contents wouldn't poison the poor woman. Remembering Kahli's instinct to drink sea water, she ran outside with a large bucket she found in the closet to get some.

She struggled back inside and let the door slam behind her, trying to ignore the blue streaks that covered the whole place when she went back to the kitchen to collect a cup. The walls, the counters... the couch were all stained blue. A strong metallic scent mixed with sea water invaded her nose. Trying to ignore the stench, she knelt beside Kahli and shifted the blanket to start cleaning her wounds. Blue dripped from the younger woman's lips. Mira's hands were quick as she pressed down on the larger gashes before wrapping them tight, hoping to encourage the wounds to close. She poured more water over her and watched as some of the superficial cuts began to knit together. She worked as fast as she could, hoping she would get them all. The last major laceration was on Kahli's abdomen, as if she had been stabbed. Mira hoped it had missed anything vital—she definitely didn't know how to do any kind of internal patchwork.

"Come on, pretty girl, just wake up and drink for me… please," she begged, before propping Kahli up enough to trickle some salt water into her mouth.

It took a moment, but Kahli started to cough it up, her eyes flying open, alarmed.

"You're fine, I need you to drink this."

Kahli grabbed Mira's arm, ignoring her instructions, and pressing her other hand to her stomach where Mira had just bandaged her up. "Is it bad?" she croaked.

Avoiding the question, Mira kept pushing the cup against her lips until she finally drank. Mira refilled the cup and repeated the action until Kahli raised her hand for her to stop.

"I'm good." She closed her eyes as she let Mira take on her weight. "Thanks."

Mira breathed a sigh of relief. "Is there anything else you need that would help?"

Kahli shook her head. "I mostly just need to regenerate. I just need time… I'm made of healing shit." She smirked, laughing at her own joke.

When Mira raised a brow, Kahli amended. "My touch, tears, blood… it's all regenerative." She wiggled her fingers at Mira. "Like magic."

Mira swallowed down the bile that tried to make its way up her throat. "Is he… dead?" He sure had looked dead.

Meeting her eyes, Kahli inclined her head. "Yes. I… once you're dead, you can't heal." She lifted a shaky hand and patted Mira's face. "Don't worry. I told you I would take care of it…" She winced as she blew out a breath, lowering her arm. "Shit. Everything hurts."

Mira's hand covered her face. "That was fucking insane. You kidnapped me!"

"Sheltered you. I told you I would get you home, didn't I?" As if the technicality made up for everything.

Indignantly, Mira dropped her hand so she could glare at the other woman. "I almost drowned on the fucking beach!"

Kahli shrunk back into herself a bit, mumbling quietly. "It's not my fault I passed out from blood loss..."

Mira closed her eyes and tried to center herself. "Why the hell have you been following me?"

Several moments passed before Kahli finally broke her silence. "I liked you." She shrugged. "It's not my fault your stupid dark aura called out to me. It marks you, by the way. Yours wasn't fully dark up close, though. You still had a bit of a will to live, despite what you thought." She trailed her fingers over the thick gauze at her stomach. "Also... I don't... not live around here. I just... don't live in a house." She shrugged again. "I'm also... a fair bit older, but my people can live for a long time, so I wouldn't get too caught up on the age difference..."

Mira snorted, interrupting her rambling. "You think, after all of that... that I want to, what? Continue to see you?" She huffed. "You're insane."

Kahli's face instantly fell. "You... brought me here. I thought..."

Mira went to extract herself, but when it caused Kahli to whimper in pain, she reluctantly stayed where she was. "I don't want to see you anymore. If you try to eat me—"

"I don't *eat* people," Kahli interrupted, growling. "That's gross."

"Then what... what do your people do with... the bodies? Why kill at all?"

Kahli looked away, refusing to look back. "We start off as low empathy, and most of us never mature past that. It's... fun, I guess? To hunt. At least in the beginning. Later... it's more the rush of power from taking a life that's addicting. We... don't dispose of them well. There's a reason there are so many that wash up on the shores. If we get lucky some other sea life... eats them."

Mira felt her spine straighten at the realization. "You're all psychopaths."

Kahli sniffled and wiped her nose. "Sure. Whatever you want to call it." Her brow furrowed in hurt.

"Why are you different?" Mira's eyes narrowed in thought. Kahli seemed to be interested in her beyond just the physical. Did she keep coming back because of beauty alone, or was there something more? Did Kahli actually feel when she was sad, hurt, angry? She pressed her hand to her own chest as she recalled how Kahli had soothed her after the call with Amani. Surely she couldn't have done any of that if she felt nothing, right? Mira needed an answer, her sanity depended on it.

One that Kahli refused to give until Mira fisted her hair and yanked her head back firmly. Kahli's hand shot up to Mira's to ease the pressure. "I don't know. I just *am*," she gritted out. When Mira didn't let up, she dug her nails into Mira's hand.

Gasping, Mira immediately withdrew her grip, eyes watering at the sting.

Kahli's eyes started to cloud with tears as well. "I'm... sorry. I didn't need to do that." She lifted her hand for Mira's. "Let me see that."

Mira twitched away.

"I can heal it, remember? I fixed your face."

Mira contemplated whether or not she wanted help from the person who had metaphorically bit her. Then she flexed her hand and decided the pain wasn't worth her pride. Giving her injured hand over, she allowed Kahli to bring it up to her eyes and wipe her tears on the nail pricks.

"There. I guess..." Kahli sighed. "Damn, this is hard. I saw a lot of suffering in my victims. The auras radiated with darkness but also so much... sadness. It... made it tangible for me. At first, I just wanted it to stop. It made me uncomfortable, so I ended them. But as I grew in power, I seemed to be drawn to them, and I was curious what was causing the darkness to be so... deep. I started talking to them, my... victims, and... I don't know, maybe

I'm just fooling myself, but I started to think what I was doing might actually be helping people." She tried to lift her lips into a smile, but it fell flat. "I really don't like *you* suffering."

Mira snorted, trying to let it sink in that, since she arrived, she had been chasing death more efficiently than she previously thought. Her mind slipped into some humor to try and make light of the situation. "You fix everything but my back pain."

Kahli bit her lip. "I can help. That's a bit more complicated, given that it's not a simple injury. It will take time, but I can fix that before you go."

"It's the least you could do for trying to get me killed."

Rolling her eyes, Kahli relented. "You tried to get yourself killed, but okay. Once I recover." Her fingers played with the gauze. "Are you... going to dump me back on the beach now?"

Mira wished desperately that she had something to lean against. Her body was exhausted now that her adrenaline was dropping. The danger seemed to have passed. "No, I'm not throwing you out there, unless that's what you need to heal."

Kahli perked up slightly at that, especially when Mira's hand threaded into her hair without much thought. Kahli sighed at the contact. "I could probably figure out the human thing, you know. If... if you wanted to keep seeing me." She shrugged.

Mira hummed as she continued to play with her raven hair, soothing herself as much as the woman in her arms. What would things look like if, against her better judgment, she did want to continue to see her?

"What do you mean by figuring out the 'human thing?' How does that work?" Mira pondered if she really wanted to know too many details, if her false sense of security about the world around her was about to come crashing down.

Kahli's words were slow at first. "I... shapeshift." She looked to Mira to gauge her reaction. "You've seen me though, my real form. It mostly looks like this... just... a bit more... frightening." She ran her hands down to where her tail normally was. "Sometimes, we walk among you. There are some... who choose to leave the sea behind. Usually not for great reasons." She adjusted as if she couldn't quite get comfortable. "We can... choose to stay in a form too long, and it can start to become permanent." Her eyes traveled to the door. "That's why I've been going for swims." She shrugged. "I don't know what I would do in your world... but maybe there's a place for me if I... gave this up." She tapped at her thigh. "Legs look weird though…"

Mira laughed lightly. "What does it feel like? Your tail."

Kahli tilted her head in thought. "Smooth, like… scales isn't quite right. Somewhere between that and glass." She wiggled her feet. "I actually hate how toes look, they're just… little fingers."

Well, that was definitely a statement given that she had been constantly willing to bang Mira's brains out. "I'm sorry my form bothers you so much."

Kahli nuzzled her face into her hand. "I like *your* feet just fine. It's like they were meant to look like that. Mine just… I was meant to have a tail." Her fingers pressed on the skin at her thighs. "I could get used to it." Biting her lip, Kahli tilted her head back to find Mira's face. "Could… you help me find some food?"

Mira's hands stilled. If Kahli didn't eat humans… What did she eat? She struggled to remember what they had eaten on their date. They had sushi, but were there only certain things she could eat? "What would I be looking for? Do I have to go on a scavenger hunt on the coastline or…"

Kahli pursed her lips and shook her head. "I eat what you eat… just get dehydrated faster. Coffee isn't very good for me. The sushi was fine… similar to what I normally eat."

"I can run into town and pick something up while you rest. If…" Mira swallowed and paused, stroking Kahli's hair in thought before she reluctantly shifted out from under her. "You'll be alive when I get back, right?" she asked, her body going cold with worry. What would she even do with the body? Would she bury her? Push her out to sea? Would it be safe, or would she be dragged in by something else lurking beneath the surface?

Kahli nodded, tossing her thumb up in the air, causing Mira laugh lightly.

Appeased, Mira grabbed her bag and keys. It wasn't like there were any dangers left; Kahli would have warned her.

Her mind wasn't right as she dissociated on her drive to town. Preoccupied with thoughts about how she was harboring a dangerous predator, Mira's mind filled with every piece of seemingly useless information she had gathered about mermaids. Besides the child-friendly versions. She had see plenty of tales to the contrary.

Years of Wendy warning her about the supernatural fluttered into her mind. Many cultures had tales about the demons of the seas that sang people to a watery grave. Stories of beautiful women that, in the blink of an eye, turned into your darkest nightmares.

She shivered, shaking her head rapidly. Kahli *was* one of those things. Was she stupid for trying to help her? It wasn't like Kahli was innocent. Mira's mind drifted back to details, like how Kahli had admitted to killing before. Should she be fleeing and never turning back?

Mira bit her lip as she pondered Kahli's too-human expressions of sadness and felt her heart drop. It might have been stupid, but she wanted to give Kahli a chance to explain herself. And with her being injured, Mira was almost certain that she would be able to get away if Kahli tried anything.

# Chapter 25

Mira booked it back home. The red flags had scared the fuck out of her, and her skin was still tingling. She rubbed at it subconsciously as if that would erase the feeling. Was she doing the right thing or was she just walking back into a trap she should have escaped? Was something else coming?

Surging through the front door, she breathed a sigh of relief when dark honey eyes looked her way and smiled. The upbeat "Welcome home" she received was hopeful, as if Kahli had wondered if she would return at all. Her guilt surged as thoughts of running away and abandoning Kahli resurfaced.

She deposited the food on the floor—the table was cracked in half—before kneeling beside Kahli to check her bandages. The blue blood had dried. Mira's hands lightly skimmed over the fresh scabs.

Kahli sighed. "My head is killing me. Probably dehydrated." She looked up nervously, her teeth chewing at her lip. "Would you... maybe, be able to get me more sea water?"

Mira nodded before she scooped more water out of the bucket with Kahli's cup and set it on the floor beside the food. She returned to encourage Kahli's arms to wrap around her neck. "Let's get you to the couch." Kahli wasn't much help this time either, but at least she didn't pass out. Mira set her down as gently as she could and helped her lean against the two throw pillows. She grabbed her blanket, now stained blue, and covered Kahli, tucking her in. Somehow, the TV was untouched, and Mira handed Kahli the remote.

"Put on that garbage that you like, I'll get plates." Mira reached out and handed the salt water to Kahli, who sipped it slowly as Mira patted her leg. "Good girl." She watched as the mermaid blushed, threading her fingers through raven hair in an attempt to soothe. Kahli melted at the gentle touch.

"You know, I meant what I said about not having photos of myself. We learned that... photos steal the soul, and... I don't really show up in them anyway. I'm not sure how that works." She looked guilty. "I do... show up in mirrors. I think I scared you a few times. You don't remember though." Kahli's fingers twisted in the blanket before she took the remote and navigated to her favorite show. As it loaded, she casually added, "The mind control is helpful…"

Mira's fingers froze. "Mind control?"

Kahli's eyes met Mira's. "I mean… I only used it to keep you safe." She bit her lip, seeming to notice her mistake.

Mira's voice was shaky as she uttered her question. "How… How many times?"

With a grimace, Kahli confirmed, "A lot. The mirror, the night Theo searched your house when we were down on the beach and I sent you off. I… thought I had dealt with him that night. I thought… he would be too weak to return…"

Trying not to hyperventilate, Mira forced herself to ask, "Are you… controlling me now?" And if she was, was this some part of a sick game she played with her victims?

Kahli placed her hand on Mira's wrist, breath unsteady. "Mira, no…"

Mira shivered. Her mind drew up images of the cave. Would Kahli take her back there against her will? Would she even remember this conversation for long? "If… If I asked you to let me go… would you?" Her vision blurred.

Kahli nodded, her voice soft. "Yes. You... you could even leave right now, if you want? I won't stop you."

Standing on shaky legs, Mira tried to step away from Kahli. She blinked as she looked around her, wondering what Kahli had made her do. Had any of it been her choice? There was no way to know for sure. She turned, quickly bolting up the stairs and gathering her things. It would be better if she were ready to go. If her things were packed, placed in the car. Just in case... just in case she needed to run. Did Kahli sleep? She had thought she had seen her sleeping... maybe she could leave if Kahli was distracted...

Mira grabbed her clothes, her electronics, her chargers, and shoved everything in her bags. She grabbed her pillows before she took the stairs, faster than she would have normally, and set her items down by the front door. Before going outside, she cast a glance at Kahli, who lay where she had left her, still as a corpse, hand hovering over the remote.

She cleared her throat. "I'm just going to... pack up my car... so it's ready..." She watched Kahli continue to look away, but as she nodded, Mira noted the tear that slipped down her cheek. Refusing to ponder that or how it made her feel, she escaped out the door with her keys, taking all her things in one trip. She unlocked the car and chucked everything in the back seat. No one was around; she didn't have to worry about her car being broken into.

Closing her car and returning to the front door, she lifted her hand, but stopped right before she grabbed the handle. She should go... she should get out while she still could. She looked over her shoulder at her car, then sighed as she let her hand fall. Of course the person who made her feel alive again was some supernatural being she should absolutely *not* be falling for.

Mira looked through the frosted window but couldn't see the object of her frustration. She wished she had grabbed the things from their art fair excursion. The little jade horse that Kahli had picked out for her would have been a nice way to remember their time together. She knew where it sat on the windowsill currently, looking out at the beach, and tried to come up with a way to get it back without having to see the other woman.

Deciding that it would be too risky to go back in, she backed away. Once inside her car, she planted her hands on the steering wheel. She reminded herself that the relationship wasn't going to go anywhere. It had all been a trick. She felt her stomach sour.

Mira struggled to make sense of Kahli holding her close, the way Kahli's eyes always lingered softly on her as if she were a work of art… Surely that couldn't all be fake.

She was in too deep already. Trying to get her herself together, she shook her head, as if that would get rid of the conflicting thoughts. She couldn't think with her heart, that would get her killed. And after everything she had been through, Kahli had been right, *she wasn't ready to die.*

Not quite committed to leaving, she inserted the key in the ignition. Somewhere in her mind she assumed it wouldn't start, and as she turned the key, preparing herself to reverse to the street, all she got was a click.

A cold sensation slid up her spine. Maybe Kahli wasn't as different from Amani as she thought. She threw the car door open and stormed back into the house, ready to shout at Kahli. The younger woman's face was painted in shock, as if she thought Mira would be gone by now. Why would she be surprised that Mira was still there if she had messed with her car?

"You have five seconds…" She quickly moved to the kitchen and took out the largest knife she could find. Watching as Kahli's eyes grew wide.

"Mira…" She lifted her hands in surrender, struggling to sit up more.

"No, you… you told me I could *leave*, but my… my car won't start now!" She pointed the knife at Kahli. "I want to leave! Let me go!"

Kahli nodded, her eyes looking around discreetly. Mira expected her face to shift into one of pleasure, that maybe this had been a long game all along just to mess with her before she ended her. Instead, Kahli's eyes widened in fear.

"I brought you back too soon…" She tried to stand and screamed with her full chest at Mira. "Get down!"

Mira dropped, not sure if it was her own decision or not. Her hands covered the back of her head as her forehead pressed to the floor. The door slammed back open and she heard the sound of two bodies colliding, as well as Kahli's scream.

She bolted upright. Knife still clutched in hand. A man she didn't recognize, with dark black skin, pinned Kahli to the wall, his *claws* digging through Kahli's stomach. Blue blood spluttered from her mouth.

The man's voice was unnaturally deep as he addressed Kahli. "You disposed of him as if he were a rotting *fish*?"

Kahli laughed even though it was distorted by the blood bubbling up her throat. She spit at him. "He... was hunting on *my* turf. You know the rules, Varl. He should have let her go."

She struck, her own hands growing sharp black talons as she shoved them into his face. His hand retracted from her body, dropping her to the floor.

The Black superhuman hissed before the sound turned into a manic laugh. "Theo could have killed her, you know? He sang her out to the water and she was *more* than willing."

Mira shook her head and Kahli's eyes marred with tears. "That's a l-lie." She spit out more blood as the man leaned over her.

Varl licked his teeth. "Did you know Theo was in her room? Before you reinforced the wards? She wandered around like his little *puppet* while you stammered in the hall. 'Mira, are you okay? Let me help you.' Pathetic." He spat. "He could have torn her to shreds or... suggested she find a knife and... get creative enough to leave a work of *art* for you to find." He laughed.

Kahli snarled.

A memory flashed through Mira's mind. Kahli's shadow on the other side of her door. Her head whipping around at the sound of a creak in the floor, only to stumble back as she came face to face with the tall, white man from town. She had reached for her own neck and started to choke herself as Theo placed a single finger to his lips and shook his head. His lips stretched the length of his face, delighted. She gasped but no sound came out, heart starting to hurt with the lack of oxygen while Kahli's voice rambled on in the hall. Her eyes were wide as she watched Theo stoop down and pick up her drawing pad, setting it back on the table before her vision cut out.

Varl's hand went for Kahli's throat.

Instinctively, Mira threw herself at his back before he could attack again, lodging the knife in as deep as it would go. The man shrieked in pain, making a sound she had never heard before, the sharp intensity of the pitch causing her to fall away from him and cover her ears.

His eyes turned on her as she scrambled back. This was not her fight. She needed to get out. She was ready to bolt for the garage when she saw Kahli struggling to catch her breath and instead ran for the kitchen, dropping behind the counter just as the knife she previously stabbed into Varl was thrown at her, hitting the fridge and sticking into it. Mira reached up and yanked at it before it finally released from its resting place. Whipping around, she stared at the man whose dark, braided hair shifted as he shook with rage.

"You should have just died like all the other vermin that trespass on the ocean! *He* should still be here. You're nothing but game to be hunted!"

He approached, and Kahli lunged at him, transforming into something frightening. A form Mira did not remember seeing before. Her eyes went black. Her face stretched longer, mouth ripping open to take up the width of her face. Her tail reformed then elongated to wrap around the man, squeezing like a snake.

They dropped to the ground, her hand clawing at his face as she dove in. Kahli's gaping maw, filled with pointed shark teeth, closed around his throat. Mira heard a crunching sound. Then the sounds of Kahli continuing to sink her teeth into him. The man thrashed wildly as Kahli's mouth tore out his trachea. There was so much thick blue blood spraying out that Mira felt like she might faint.

"Kahli... stop," she whispered into the air, on the verge of passing out. She wanted it to be over. She wanted Kahli to stop.

Mira needed a way out. Either the scent of blood would get Kahli to stop, or Mira would make it all go away. She placed the knife to her wrist, closing her eyes, and sliced herself open, crying out in pain.

When she opened her eyes, she saw the man's last movements as Kahli turned to face Mira, blood dripping from her lips. Mira could tell from the two shades that some was definitely Kahli's.

Mira had brief, conflicting, waves of terror and concern. On one hand, she should be going for the bucket, getting sea water to Kahli to help speed her healing. But on the other, she should be running for her fucking life if she were capable of it.

She didn't get to decide.

The edges of her vision grew black, and she saw her world crumble.

# Chapter 26

"Mira? Mira, can you hear me?"

The voice sounded far away and Mira tried to climb toward it

"Honey, you were in an accident."

Mira tried to open her eyes, and at first she wasn't successful, but she kept trying, kept pushing, and after a few failed attempts, a blurry image of Wendy came into view. Wendy's warm brown hand was waving over her face.

"Mira? There you are. Can you see me?"

Groaning, Mira turned to the side and heaved, her stomach rolling. "What... what happened?" She went to massage her pounding head but found her hand wrapped up tightly. Her eyes tried to focus on it.

Wendy leaned forward and placed her forehead to Mira's hip, choking on her emotions. Mira's eyes lifted to see Allie sitting beside her. Wendy's *girlfriend*. A woman who had grown up between the U.S. and China, and had happened to share a cubical with Wendy at her first job.

Allie's wavy, black, purple-tipped hair was still drying as if she had been mid shower when they got the call. She was rubbing Wendy's back, dark brown eyes soft as she took in her partner. "Baby, it's okay. She's okay. Come on, it's Mira freaking Hansen." She looked over and noticed Mira staring. Allie's face softened.

"You gave Wendy and me quite the scare."

Wendy's head popped back up as she looked at Mira angrily. "You promised me you would be safe and careful. Really? A jet ski accident? How the hell do you hit someone in the ocean! The only other person out there!"

Mira's mind scrambled, *she had hurt someone?* Her lips quivered as she tried to talk. "I... I hurt..." She closed her eyes. "Are they... alright?"

Wendy pointed a finger at Mira. "I swear, that's it. You're moving back in. You're a menace."

Mira was about to argue when Wendy tackled her flat to the bed, knocking the wind out of her.

"You're such an idiot."

Mira's hands came up instinctively to clutch at Wendy. Wendy, who always came back for her. Wendy, who may not be the love of her life, but was the chosen family that Mira never thought she deserved, yet clung to with all her might. "I'm sorry. I don't... remember..."

Wendy leaned back and wiped the tears from her eyes. "You... are... so grounded."

Mira smiled, her face stretching and she winced at the pain.

Glancing around the room, Mira's eyes landed on a woman with dark hair sitting in a corner in a blue plastic chair. Her face was pale, scratched up, and her hand pressed to a large bandage around her middle. *Was that the person she hit?*

Mira's eyes stayed locked on her, taking in her features and hoping to draw her attention. *Fuck.* She was *stunning*. The most beautiful woman Mira had ever seen. And she had to run *her* over? Honey eyes lifted to hers and she opened her mouth to speak, when Wendy demanded her attention.

"You are old enough to not be getting yourself into situations like this..."

Mira's chin dipped in shame at the fact that she had inconvenienced Wendy yet again. Before she could spiral, a soft touch to her face drew her attention. She was immediately drawn into the honey eyes illuminated by the bright fluorescent lighting, making them golden.

The raven-haired woman sighed. "I'm sorry, Mira."

Speechless, Mira grabbed the arm, afraid the other woman would disappear. She shook her head.

Wendy dropped into a chair on the opposite side of her bed. "Kahli, I swear I am going to kill you for letting her go out there on the rogue waves."

Kahli snorted. "As if I could stop her?" They shared a smile and Mira huffed, feeling confused and left out.

"Who is this?" She waved toward Kahli while glaring at Wendy. "Is she... the person I hit? Is she suing me?" She now eyed Kahli warily as Wendy's eyes narrowed.

"Yeah, you rammed your *girlfriend* with a jet ski. I can't imagine why she's here with you now and not dumping your ass. Maybe because you were hurt too."

Mira's mouth ran dry. *Girlfriend?*

"I... I don't have a girlfriend..."

Wendy pressed her fingers to her forehead. "Yeah, that'll be the partial amnesia. Luckily it's not that deep. You just don't remember the last couple weeks." She leveled her gaze. "You rented a beach house?"

Mira's mind was cloudy but it started to pull up fragmented images. A fire, a... cave. A painting, splattered in blue ink. The dark-haired woman's flushed face as she looked up at her from between her thighs. Mira's head pressure started to spike.

Her face flushed as the last image remained front and center. She didn't know what much of the imagery meant, but gathered enough about the last image to at least get the gist of her relationship with the woman before her.

"I... remember some things."

Kahli's eyes flashed with what appeared to be panic. "You... do?"

Feeling very hot, Mira decided her blanket was the most interesting thing in the room and nodded at it. She tried not to notice as Wendy's eyes swept between them.

"Well, at first I wasn't a fan of Kahli... but she really knows how to handle an emergency. She got you to the hospital right away and called me from your phone. She stayed even when we got here; she's pretty banged up and needs to rest."

Kahli smiled and gently shook her head. "I'm fine, I'm just sore. Mira... she took the brunt of it. I've never seen anyone bail a jet ski that bad before." She smirked. "She's worth it though."

Wendy rolled her eyes. "You two are gross. No more beach house for you. You're done. Kahli can go to your place."

Mira finally looked up and stared at the woman who felt familiar. "I... can go home?"

Kahli ran her fingers through Mira's hair. "I can come stay with you for a bit. Someone needs to check up on you."

Still on edge, Mira kept looking around for something before she finally realized what she was looking for. *Her wife.* Had it been a dream that Amani had reappeared? She heard her voice in the deep recess of her mind and it became louder, shouting. Something about the embryos, how she wanted them.

"Has... anyone heard from Amani?"

Wendy spoke slowly, carefully easing Mira into it. "She thinks this was a stunt... to get her back. I'm sorry, Mira... she didn't come."

Mira's eyes burned. It crushed her that Amani could think so little of her. Then Wendy's voice perked up, pointing at Kahli. "But you tried to kill this one and she's here."

Mira looked up at Wendy and glared. "Stop reminding her, she might leave."

As she looked back at this Kahli person, she somehow knew she never would. They shared a smile.

# Epilogue – Kahli
## Seven Years Later

Kahli Delmar sat at the side of her and her wife's pool as she watched their son cannonball into the deep end.

Mira yelped as the water sprayed her face. "Alex!" She laughed freely as if she actually enjoyed the chaos. The little boy whipped around as he giggled, his dark brown hair swinging into his honey eyes, identical to how Kahli's would when she shook the water out of her hair after a swim. Though his DNA was all Mira, they had gotten lucky in finding a donor who looked so much like Kahli. But what Kahli loved the most was how he looked like Mira when he smiled.

When Alex was little, Mira had wanted to make sure there were no drowning accidents and insisted on swimming lessons as early as possible. Kahli hadn't understood the need at first—they had a good alarm system on the doors outside—but she eventually relented. Luckily, Mira's worries turned out to be unfounded; he had been part fish since he started to swim as a baby.

Kahli held on tightly to the pile of towels that she had brought out. Alex always made sure that she brought an extra just in case she finally got in the pool. She always refused, but would have if there was an emergency.

Mira had been confused that she went from loving to swim multiple times a day to avoiding it at all costs. It had been Mira's idea to find a house with a pool for Kahli; she had insisted on it. Kahli didn't have the heart to tell her the truth. That she was afraid it would make her realize she missed the ocean too much and abandon her life on land.

There were stories among her people that all humans had descended from them. That humans were simply the first merpeople to walk on land and decide to partake in adventures in the air. And as they wandered further and further from the sea they forgot about its beauty and power and settled in, forming very different and fragile lives. One day that would be her, reduced to a simple human, no longer able to change back because she stayed in this form for too long.

Not that Mira would understand, as the walls Kahli had constructed in her mind weren't temporary. Kahli wished Mira remembered, every single day. But she knew that the way she killed Varl in front of Mira had broken her. It was clear in the way Mira refused to come back to her while Kahli pleaded with her on the living room floor of the beach house.

When she was sure he was dead, she had turned to Mira, who was completely unresponsive, no matter what Kahli did or said. It was easier to control her, to build walls in her mind that would last, rather than continue to fail to bring her back. Kahli had even contemplated leaving her alone and never seeing her again. But with the way Mira had experienced abandonment, even if she wouldn't remember, Kahli couldn't bring herself to return to the sea.

And because she planned to remain in Mira's life as long as she would have her, she had to fabricate an accident. It killed her to see Mira's eyes staring back at her, watching as she crushed her hand and used her sharp nails to rake cuts across her arms, legs, and face.

"I'm sorry... I'm so sorry," she had sobbed as she created the injuries and was surprised when a somewhat conscious Mira ran her hands through her hair, attempting to soothe her without knowing why she was falling apart.

Wendy had been kind when they met again, grabbing her and holding her tight. Kahli found that she really needed that.

"Thank you for getting her to the hospital," Wendy had gasped into her shoulder. Kahli was unable to do anything but nod, choking on her guilt.

When Wendy leaned back, she grabbed Kahli's face with both hands. "I was wrong about you. You're... Really good for her."

That only made Kahli's tears fall harder.

She had stayed with Mira at the hospital, sleeping on a cot, refusing her own medical attention because she knew what they would find. Something they couldn't explain.

Kahli's eyes took in how Mira smiled with Alex. She had done that. She had interfered and kept Mira from death, so that she could experience so much more *life*.

She had been hesitant when Mira first brought up the idea of children again, wondering if she would be happier with a partner who could participate more in the experience. Someone who could either carry the child or offer up their own DNA so everything wasn't solely on Mira. Fortunately, Mira hadn't been concerned about that at all when they discussed the process further. She was kind and patient and didn't push. She always told Kahli they could stop. That they could adopt or not have children at all. But with the way Mira was now, she was glad she had caved. Mira deserved more people in her life who loved her.

The surrogate they were matched with, Kate Summers, was a bright, energetic woman in her early twenties. She had been more excited about their potential baby then they were, asking if she could babysit and come to recitals or sports games. They had been nervous about Kate being in school, but when they found out she was not only gay, but had a long-term girlfriend, a lot of their worries faded away.

Kahli turned back to the pool, caught daydreaming when Alex shouted to grab her attention.

"Momma! Watch my new dive!" Alex made sure she was watching before he did a very ungraceful swan dive, getting a mouth full of water and a huge splash for his efforts, but his eyes were shining when he resurfaced. "Ow. Did you see, did you see?" He flapped his little arms, once again splashing Mira, who grumbled that she was going to go lay out in the sun.

Shaking her head, Kahli watched her wife go under and swim toward her. When she reached the edge of the pool, Mira propped herself on the lip, leaning forward so her breasts were spilling out of her favorite purple swimsuit that always had Kahli's mind racing for the gutter. Unable to stop herself, Kahli's eyes dipped for a moment, and when they came up to meet Mira's again, her wife winked.

"Hey hot stuff. Coming in?"

Kahli blushed and shook her head. "You know I don't get in…"

Mira stood tall and raised her arms, making grabby hands at Kahli. Kahli rolled her eyes but she moved closer. When she was within reach, Mira stared up at her, her hands slick as they slid up and down Kahli's legs. "At least put your feet in?" She pouted, and Kahli knew she had lost.

Nodding, Kahli moved to sit, hanging her legs over the edge and into the pool. Mira hummed while admiring Kahli's legs. She couldn't help but wonder if some thoughts had slipped through and Mira was seeing her tail in her mind's eye.

"What?"

Ignoring her question, Mira's face remained neutral as she placed her hands between Kahli's thighs and spread them, stepping into the space she created. Her face split into a smile as she reached for Kahli's face and guided her lips down to her own.

"Moms, that's gross!" Alex shouted from the other end of the pool just before they heard another splash.

Kahli could barely hear over the rush of her own heart.

Mira didn't remember much, but she must have liked what she did remember enough to give Kahli a chance, allowing her to stay with her as she continued to recover after the hospital. Kahli was forced to do plenty of mind control to get her affairs in order to become a human, but Mira made all the effort worth it. She just wished... that Mira knew who she really was. She didn't like lying to her. Kahli thought it would get easier, but as the years wore on, it never did.

She felt as Mira leaned away to look at their son. "Alex, that is the last one. You need to shower before dinner."

The little boy made a face that Kahli knew meant trouble, but Mira squashed it quickly. "No video games tomorrow if you don't come in."

Alex sighed and his last jump was more lazy than enthusiastic. He swam toward them and got out. "Can we order pizza?"

Mira narrowed her gaze but smiled. "Yes."

Alex whooped as he grabbed a towel and wrapped himself up before heading into the air conditioning.

As Mira climbed out of the pool and grabbed her own towel, Kahli took quick steps to snatch it out of her hands and be the one to wrap it around her.

Mira beamed at the attention. "Oh, how sweet." She leaned forward and kissed Kahli's cheek before she patted herself dry and wrapped the towel around her waist.

Kahli found herself calling out as Mira turned to go. "Mira... wait."

She saw her wife's back tense, taking a moment before she turned. "Yes?"

Kahli caught up and bit her lip. "I... I want to talk to you about something." She watched as her wife's eyes instantly dulled, her face falling.

"Oh..." Mira began to turn away when Kahli caught her wrist.

"Stop."

Refusing to make eye contact, Mira spoke to the floor. "Is it... because I've been working too much? I... I can ask Lydia to reduce my hours... We're doing well between the two of us. I know I shouldn't work so much..." Kahli watched as the telltale signs of Mira's life before her reared their ugly heads. Amani hadn't wanted her to work.

She had wanted her to focus on the children they would have.

"It's not that." Kahli grabbed Mira's hips and gently massaged them. She had successfully fixed Mira's back, but she never tired of easing her tight muscles after a long day.

Mira took in a shallow breath. "If you are going to leave…" Her eyes lifted. "Just say it."

Kahli cupped her cheek, her own voice going quiet. "Sometimes… I wish you remembered." Her mind drifted to the image of her true self that Mira would never have. She had sneakily talked Mira into drawing her as a mermaid once or twice, and while it was absolutely breathtaking, it wasn't quite her.

"Baby… if you could remember, would you? Even if it wasn't all good?"

Mira's hand covered Kahli's. "I wish I remembered every moment with you. Did we… fight a lot in the beginning?"

"No… but as I've told you before, I don't know that you liked me at first."

Mira finally broke into a smile. "I'm sure that's not true. Didn't I tell you that you were beautiful but probably horrible to look at in the daytime? That it was just the moonlight playing tricks on me?"

Kahli scrunched her nose. "Maybe I shouldn't have told you some stories."

Mira grew contemplative as she always did when their past was brought up. "I'm really sorry about the accident. I don't know why I would have veered into you. I... still can't make sense of it."

The feelings of guilt were overwhelming as Kahli took a step back and moved to one of the pool loungers. Mira didn't deserve to live with the shame of the accident; it hadn't been her fault at all. "Come sit?"

Mira's brow furrowed as she followed, lying down beside her, and when Kahli didn't immediately speak, she took her hand and relaxed as they looked out on their backyard. The large grass patch behind the pool was just calling for a dog.

Kahli took a breath. This was selfish. Mira was *happy*. The memories only served one person—herself. Her powers were fading, and she knew that if she didn't remove the walls in Mira's mind now, she would never remember. She only wished she had done it sooner, when her powers would have been strong enough to raise them again if her wife panicked. What if she couldn't handle knowing and...

"Kahli."

A gentle kiss pressed to her cheek. She didn't deserve this kind of softness right now. Not when she was about to rip Mira's world open.

"You're spiraling."

Of course she was spiraling. What if this all went horribly wrong and she lost the woman she was madly in love with for the rest of her long existence? Kahli leaned her head back and closed her eyes. "I just don't want you to hate me."

Mira brought their lips together, whispering softly as they parted. "I never could. You've given me so much since we met."

Kahli's eyes opened and she grabbed Mira's face before she could talk herself out of it. She needed her partner to know her, the real her. "Close your eyes." She couldn't believe she was about to do this.

She let her mind dig in, like all the other times, grabbing the reins and steering Mira's thoughts, though this time Kahli was driving them headfirst into walls she was destroying. The first one was rough as she pressed her power into it, meeting so much resistance that she worried it wouldn't break. But then it cracked, and then the crack splintered, before completely shattering. She felt Mira gasp as the memories flooded back to her.

Mira gripped her wrist. "Kahli... what are you doing..."

Kahli gulped. "Just... let me finish." She hit the next wall with full force and it fell like sand. She kept going. She pushed and pushed, returning Mira's memories, one by one, in chronological order. Her energy waning, she decided that she wasn't going to bring the last wall down, she was going to fortify it. She felt the next wall collapse and knew that on the other side of it was the cave. She felt Mira tremble. Knowing this one would hurt her.

"Stop... Kahli, stop... please." Mira shook as she started to beg.

Kahli made it to the second to last wall, and waited. "Just one more... please, just this one?"

Mira's face pressed against her shoulder from the weight of the memories. "What... why this one?"

"It's... when you took care of me. I'm... sorry I couldn't just let you be happy I... I felt so alone." Her voice cracked. Maybe she should stop. Mira didn't need to remember, she loved her without it all... Or did she only love her because she didn't remember?

Mira wove her fingers into the base of her skull. "Do it."

As it fell, Kahli sobbed but kept going. She took off for the next wall and poured herself into it, forcing everything she had left into fortifying it so it would never break. She couldn't ever lose Mira to a psychotic break again. She wouldn't be able to shift after this, she would never be able to swim in the sea as she had before. She was giving it all up.

She felt her body collapse against the chair, her eyes blinking open, and she was unable to move as Mira's frightened eyes turned to her.

Seeing that look on Mira's face once more nearly broke her. Kahli cried out in despair, body heaving as she tried to breathe. Her mouth formed the words, but nothing came out. *I'msorryI'msorryI'msorry.*

Mira's eyes fell to her legs. "You... I don't understand." She looked up, concerned. "Don't you need the ocean? How have you..." She looked around as if noticing their landlocked living situation for the first time.

Kahli shook her head. "I'm... becoming mortal, human. I... fuck, I do miss it, but I would miss you and Alex more." She wrapped her arms around herself, trying to hold herself together. She was weak, but she didn't dare ask Mira for comfort, not right now. Not when she made her remember things she was probably better off forgetting.

Her cries turned audible and she felt her heart start to beat again when Mira pulled her in, cradling the back of her head and holding her tight. "I love you."

Kahli pressed herself into Mira as she quietly whispered. "Please mean that…"

Mira sighed. "What's behind the last wall?" Her voice was gentle as her fingers scraped across Kahli's scalp.

"When I killed Varl. Theo's brother-in-arms." She felt the tears come harder. "You were so terrified, you broke." She sniffled. "I never want to see you like that again."

Mira turned her head and kissed Kahli's cheek. "It's okay…"

Kahli let out a sob, the force of her guilt crushing her. "The accident… there was no accident."

Mira immediately leaned back. "What?" Her voice was tinged with hurt. "Kahli… I've torn myself up for years about hurting you…"

Kahli bit her bottom lip and she nodded. "I know… I…"

Mira removed her hand. "If there was no accident… Why was I in the hospital?"

"Because it needed to look like an accident… so I… so I could cover everything up. Your memories… I had to hide them."

"My injuries... you did that to me." She looked like she was buffering, trying to take in the new information, the gravity of the situation starting to weigh on her.

Kahli's voice dropped to a whisper. "Mira... I'm sorry."

Mira scoffed. "That's what's behind the last wall." She glared, her face devastated. "What, did I beg you to stop? Did I? Did I promise you anything if you would just stop *hurting me*? What, Kahli?" Her voice grew louder and Kahli lifted her hands.

"No... no. You didn't *feel* anything..."

Mira placed her hand over her mouth as she stifled a sob before she screamed at Kahli. "How do I fucking know that?"

Kahli grabbed her hands and Mira tried to pull away.

"Are you going to do that again? Because you let me remember? Are you going to erase it now that you know how I'll respond? Put me back in the hospital and make sure I'm just grateful to be with you..."

Kahli whimpered. "No... I wouldn't."

Mira covered her face as she wailed into her hands. Kahli wrapped her arms around her and was surprised when, instead of throwing her off, Mira leaned on her.

"You watched me kill him... you couldn't handle it. I had to erase the memories to bring you back. It took removing them all for you to speak again." She took a breath. "I blocked the fight from your memory, made you forget, but it wasn't enough. I had to go further, drill deeper into your mind to remove the way you responded to me after what you had seen. It was like you locked down in self-defense to block me out." She held Mira tighter. "I made sure you wouldn't feel a thing. I blocked your sensory perception though you wouldn't have remembered anyway." She gulped. "You watched me break your hand, you watched as I cut your skin... you... wiped my tears as I lost it having to do that to you." She gasped. "Baby, I'm sorry..."

Mira shivered. "Would you hurt me again? If you needed to, to keep your secret. Would you... hurt Alex?"

Kahli shook her head. "I couldn't... I told you... I'm becoming human, the magic is depleted, especially after what I just did." She touched her fingertips to Mira's temple and felt how she flinched.

"There are ways to hurt people without magic, Kahli." Mira's eyes were wide and pleading, as if she wanted Kahli to fix this and make everything okay again.

The sliding door opened and Kahli felt Mira jump. Alex looked on in concern. "Moms?" He must have heard Mira yelling.

Without turning, Mira raised a hand to stop him. "We'll be inside in a minute."

Mira's eyes held Kahli's.

"Please... tell me you don't still control me..." She chewed on her lip and Kahli shook her head.

"I'm not."

Mira sucked in a breath. "You... wouldn't hurt Alex... right?" Her breathing grew erratic. "This is all I ever wanted... you... him..."

Kahli cupped both sides of her face to ensure that Mira wouldn't look away. "I would *never* hurt Alex." She paused, letting her statement settle before continuing. "And I will never hurt you again."

Mira's hands covered hers as she continued to cry. "What if I want to forget?" Her voice lifted, bordering on desperation.

This is what she was afraid of. Kahli sighed, her face falling. "Oh, Mira..."

Mira bit her lip so hard it started to bloom with red. "Please... I think I want to forget."

"Fuck." Kahli covered her face with her hands. She had been too rash. Mira couldn't—no—*didn't want to* remember.

Mira pulled on Kahli's arm. "When Alex goes to bed… maybe… you could…"

"I don't have that much power left."

Kahli's fingers lifted to Mira's bleeding lip, using what little she had left to heal the wound. "I can do this much." She smiled sadly, shifting her hand to swipe Mira's tears off her cheek.

Mira took a breath and then another. "M-Maybe… if we take you back to the sea… you could… recharge and…"

"If I start over… it'll take years to get back to where I'm at now and… I don't know that I can walk away from the water if we go there." She held Mira's hands in hers. "I'm sorry I let you worry that you hurt me for years. I didn't know what to do. I just… wanted to be with you and make sure you were okay, that you never reached such a dark place again. I didn't want you to beg for a crossing… and I thought I could keep you safe."

Mira's eyes fell. "I need… you to sleep on the couch tonight." She looked off toward Alex and tried to smile but it fell flat. "I need time."

Kahli nodded, biting her lip as she wondered if she was about to lose the love of her life. "I can live with that. I could… even go, if that's what you want."

Mira clamped down on Kahli's wrists at the mention of her leaving. Anchoring her there so she couldn't disappear from sight. "Don't you dare."

"Okay. Whatever you want, Mira."

"I'm mad at you," Mira huffed, her mouth opening and closing a few times, as if there was so much more to say, but she couldn't find the words.

Kahli sucked in a breath of air as she tried to stabilize herself. "Okay. I understand."

Mira's hand lifted to rub her chest over her heart, and Kahli wished she hadn't been the cause of this. She knew that Mira got anxious about her leaving. They had talked about her fears at length. It used to happen a lot in the beginning but had decreased in the years after Alex had come into being, as there were now more reasons for Kahli to stay.

Kahli wished Mira would trust that *she* was enough reason to stay.

"How... how long do you live for if you... become human?" Mira shifted her weight from one foot to the other uncomfortably. Her eyes spoke of her uncertainties, as if knowing too much about paranormal beings would cause her to run.

Unsure where the question had come from, Kahli tilted her head. "As long as you..." She let the words trail off. She had finally found her other half, and she didn't want to go on living for a few hundred years without her.

Mira wiped at her eyes, her breaths evening out. Her voice was flat as she spoke. "This is why you don't swim..."

Kahli paused, trying to explain how she felt with human concepts. "It's like... an addiction. I am sure once I am human I can... join you guys."

They sat in silence for a few moments, before Mira lifted her gaze. "If... you're staying, I want another child." Her eyes narrowed. "I've been asking and after all of this... you owe me one."

If that was all it would take for Mira to forgive her, she would cave. Kahli let her lips lift up into a hesitant smile. "Anything you want."

Mira sighed. Her eyes drifted to Alex as he still hovered in the doorway, thinking he was well hidden. Mira's voice lowered to a whisper. "He's upset."

Kahli cleared her throat as she inched closer and took Mira's face in her hands. "So are you."

"I'll live." She looked Kahli up and down, lifting her hands to hold her in place. "I've gotten this far, haven't I?"

Kahli smirked, knowing that Mira had a knack for surviving. "You're pretty good at escaping death. It's a talent for a mortal, considering the things you've gotten yourself caught up with."

Mira tilted her head. "Are there things besides mermaids out there?"

Kahli's breath caught for a moment and she kept her eyes steady as she lied once more. After this, she really would stop.

"Of course not, Mira, that's silly." She watched as the tension left her wife's face.

"Good. I think I need to curl up on the couch and watch a movie..." Mira stood, unsteady on her feet. "You coming?"

Kahli joined her, linking their hands.

"If I have nightmares from the memories, you're dealing with that..." Mira's words trailed off as her hands played with Kahli's.

When she didn't elaborate, Kahli indicated for Mira to continue.

Hesitantly, Mira asked, "When will you become human?"

"Soon. One morning I'll wake up and the humming, the magic in my skin, will be gone."

"I want to know the moment it's gone." Suddenly, Mira's hand shot to her chest and she gasped. Her eyes fluttered as she massaged the area.

Kahli took her arm, unsure what was going on. "You okay?"

Mira sighed as she gripped back. "I've been dizzy lately. I must need to eat more or something." Her chest moved unsteadily for a moment before it seemed to find her rhythm again. "I'll have a snack before dinner."

Kahli was unsure of her excuses, but decided to leave it for now. She gently guided them to the door, where Alex looked up at them nervously.

"Are you two getting a divorce? That happened with Tara's parents." He frowned.

Mira knelt before him. "No, baby... Momma did something dumb, but she is going to make it better. I'm just sad."

Alex pulled Mira into a hug. Kahli started to feel like she might be sick when her wife reached a hand behind her, offering to include her. Her eyes welled up as she took the opportunity and joined in.

Mira was going to let her stay. And if she was good, maybe that would continue on for at least a lifetime.

And when it was all over, she would make sure Mira got the crossing she deserved.

# Thank You

First and foremost I have to thank my wife, Shelley, for absolutely everything she does to support my writing career. The hours of listening to my stories as I plot them out loud, the amount of breakdowns I have over… well everything, but especially my cover for this book. The fact that it took over 100+ hours is insane, never let me do that again (remind me to check how it looks on my computer and phone), and for all your own hours and hours of editing to make sure it's the best it can be when it gets out there into the world. There is really no one that has the eye for editing that you do and I wish I could afford you full time. One day. I am proud of what we can accomplish together (when I'm not upset by my very specific wordings that I swear are a thing), here's to more book children and I am so sorry you married a writer. I didn't know when we met I swear! I would not be alive without you, and I continue to do my best to stay that way. Thank you for making me a priority. Also thank you for having such a cute butt, that also helps a lot :)

Thank you to my art buddy Gelli who also let me cry and moan about my book cover design struggles. I don't have the capacity to handle that stress, thank you for telling me I couldn't yeet it.

Thank you to the assistance team. Butts, Tiny, Lena Margie—you guys are sometimes all that stands between moms and a breakdown.

To my Nana, Grammy, and Papa who helped guide me in art, nature, and love. Papa, I feel sorry for whoever you have found to read my books to you—I hope they at least enjoyed them.

Thank you to my friends and family who read my first book. Your support means so much.

Thank you to my sister Jesse for the creative writing eye right before the proof. I love that we have always been able to set time aside to hang out and yap about the stories in our heads.

Thank you to my bookish and content friends. Kate, Juls, Leighelle. Thank you for pushing me to continue to talk about and make content for this book as it got ready, and thank you all for being my safe author space online.

Thank you to my ARC readers who wanted to read this book, and thank you so much to those of you who stayed after my debut to read the next one. And thank you to my street team friends who hang out with me online everyday yapping about books! Thank you all for supporting my stuff so hard!

Thank you to the queer, sapphic, neurodivergent, and spoonie communities for giving me a place I would never feel alone.

To past sick me who thought maybe it was all over quite a few times. To the person lying in that bed in the ER during COVID and feeling grateful that at least Nana wasn't alone when she went from sepsis, while I was going through mine. Thank you for fighting for us—this one's for you. You inspire me more than you'll ever know and you're the reason we have this work and all the rest. Thank you for pushing and never giving up. Look how far we've come.

And thank you to my Nana, Grammy, Will, my spirit guides, and Lilith for helping me continue to survive and make art. And thank you to our intermittent house ghost who has on more than one occasion stopped us from severe food poisoning. Also thank you to whoever told me, "the lights are about to go out get your phone," when I was in the shower that one time—you are right, I am not a fan of the dark.

# *About the Author*

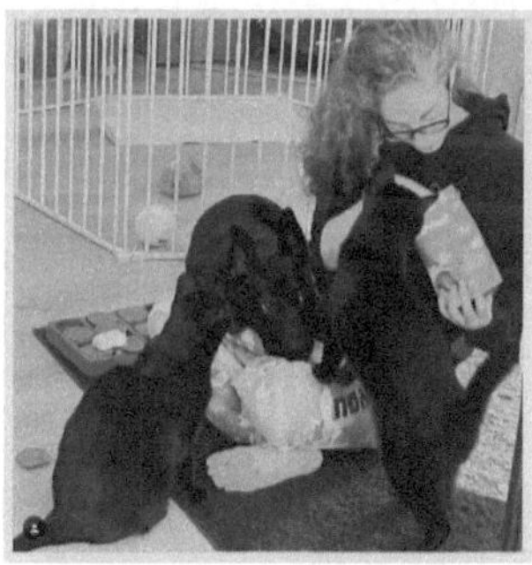

Kelly Preston is a neurodivergent, disabled, Midwestern, queer person who has determined that since Chronic Pain led them to write, then they are here gay-ing up your life. They write books with the core value of *empathy building* and challenge their readers to think on a deeper level about a character's experience.

Originally from St. Louis, MO, Kelly now finds themselves in the Bay Area after living in places like: Los Angeles, California; Denver, Colorado; and Auckland, New Zealand. They live with their wife, ESA cat babies Lunabutts and Princess Tiny Buttholes, and service dog Lena Margie.

Kelly is a fandom nerd and has many special interests. Don't mention New Zealand unless you are ready for nonstop yapping.

Kelly can be found online at:

Website: https://storiesbykelp.wordpress.com/

All Links: https://kelpywashere.carrd.co/ (All Links)

Don't forget to follow their socials and sign up on their website for their newsletter and ARC list for information on all future projects and special giveaways.

If you loved this tale in empathy please consider leaving a review on Goodreads, Amazon, Story-Graph, or your favorite review site! The author appreciates hearing how much you loved their work and it "really helps out the page."

*Coming Soon*

Look out for Kelly Preston's future novels:

**Thirst Trap**

**Artificial Dreams**

**If I Could Drag You Under: Book 2**

www.ingramcontent.com/pod-product-compliance
Lightning Source LLC
Chambersburg PA
CBHW051258130726
47987CB00004B/1573